ILLUSION

Book 1

An Eomix Galaxy novel

CHRISTA YELICH-KOTH

This book is a work of fiction. All characters and events portrayed in this book are either products of the author's imagination or are used fictitiously.

ILLUSION (An Eomix Galaxy novel)
Second Edition: October 2018

Published by CYK Publishing
Oregon, USA

ISBN: 978-0-9883470-5-2

Cover art: Creative Alchemy Inc, Conrad Teves, and CYK Publishing

For my Mom

THANK YOU'S

A huge thanks to you, the reader,
for bringing my story into your life.

Special Thanks **to Claire Kirchhoff:** For your tireless desire to help me from day 1. You were my rock.

Julie Horbinski: For listening every day at work when I'd tell you the next segment I'd written—and then for asking me when I was going to publish it. I had never thought about publishing until that point!

Tom Koth: For your continued support and willingness to read this book, even in its original un-edited SUPER LONG version.

Jessica Therrien, Holly Kammier, and Shelley Stinchcomb: For inviting me to your small and extremely talented group and helping ILLUSION grow.

The SCWC: For helping me turn my story into the best written version I could make it.

Jean Jenkins: For your incredible editing skills and encouragement during your Best Foot Forward program.

Reggie Hansome, Benjamin More, Conrad Teves: For your interest in reading and giving me necessary feedback. And to Conrad for the original cover art.

Creative Alchemy Inc.: For your help to create a new beautiful cover.

Stu Tighe: Words cannot express your importance to this book.

Darkness

Powerful.

Pathetic.

Jacin snorted a laugh. The sickly-looking man in the reflector unit snorted at the same time. He surveyed his own face and despised the bloodshot eyes staring back.

So much pain. So much work. All for nothing.

And no one would know. Everything he'd done, he'd done for them. All his power, his energy, his hope to establish a better existence, would be lost.

Jacin turned from his own haunted stare, shuffled out of the refresher unit, and into his quarters—the space reeked of mold, rotten food, soiled clothes. All around him, in the multitude of rooms aboard his command ship, the Enforcer, *individuals hustled about their lives, happy and focused. They felt part of something good, something unique.*

What a cruel joke.

Jacin descended onto his couch, the cushions already crusted into the shape of his worn-out body. Though only 43 standard years old, his slow movements and rickety joints easily added decades. Papery-thin skinned hands joined together on his lap as he thought about how no one would ever understand all he'd gone through, all he'd sacrificed.

A burnt ember glowed for a moment in his tired mind. There was one man who might still listen. Trey Xiven, the captain of his ship, had followed Jacin through all his struggles and believed in everything he did. But Xiven could easily head down the same destructive path. If there was a way to tell him, show *him what he needed to know...*

Jacin concentrated on the memories of his life, the good and the bad. He focused his energy, almost depleted now, and sent those memories to his second-in-command. Jacin felt the images lodge in the Captain's mind, a permanent fixture, never to be removed.

Xiven would realize soon what he'd been given—and there would be only one reason Jacin would have sent his memories. In response, he'd come to Jacin's quarters and try to stop him from what had to be done.

To save the Eomix galaxy.

To protect his daughters.

To free himself.

Jacin Jaxx, the most powerful being in the universe, a man who could change an individual's thoughts, who had ended dozens of wars, who was as close to a god as one could come, gave up.

Concentrating the flow of heat inside him, Jacin directed his body's energy away from himself and out into his surroundings. His skin glowed bluish-white, like cold flame. Electronic systems around him fizzled and popped. Plunged into interior darkness, his life bled away, trickling into the void. The stars outside his spaceship ex-

panded for a moment like miniature flaring suns. They fed off his essence, ingesting his energy as their own.

Jacin's eyesight faded to black.

His lungs deflated. His heart stopped.

The universe grieved.

Chapter 1

DAITH TOCC ROLLED her eyes. "Can't we take a break until we get to the Lax Shack?"

"You're the one who wanted to study, how did you put it, 'every possible waking moment before exams.'"

Daith lifted her long, dark hair off her sweaty neck. She glanced up at the large, spherical timereader suspended above the library they'd left. Showing both their planet's time and standard time, the orb was set against the biometric rhythms of the Tunlac sun—the center of the Eomix galaxy. "Did I say that?" she joked.

Her friend grinned, his teeth white against his caramel-colored skin. "You're a mere twenty-four standard years of age. Don't tell me you're losing your memory."

She pushed him playfully. "Fine, Torrak," she said. "You win. Where were we?"

"I asked what year, both standard and local, did Puffair join the Eomix United Front?"

Daith wiped her moist forehead while she thought. Another ridiculously hot day at Fior Accelerated Academy, which was why she and Torrak had abandoned the overcrowded, stuffy rooms at the library. Being at an academy for gifted students sounded great, but all it meant was working harder, faster, and better than everyone else.

If she'd known how intense exam sectionals would be, Daith may have reconsidered applying.

No, there wasn't anywhere else I could go.

A shadow blotted out the sun, interrupting her thoughts. She glanced up. A small, silver spaceship hovered above her, the whirr of its engine buzzing inside her skull.

"Torrak? What under the stars—"

The ship dropped, fast. Torrak grabbed Daith's arm and pulled her out of the way. Hot air and dirt blasted them in the face, knocking them off their feet. The ship bounced a sloppy landing. The moment the silvery beast settled the hatch opened.

"You okay?" Torrak yelled over the engine roar.

She nodded as he helped her from the ground. Dirty sweat stung her vision. She stumbled in Torrak's grip, clenching his hand tight. Coughing, Daith watched through clouds of dust as two men in blue jumpsuits exited the vehicle.

"It's her!" one of them shouted.

Torrak pulled Daith behind him, protecting her. The two men closed the distance.

"No!" Torrak shoved at the first man, but he was solid like a wall. He grabbed Torrak and yanked him away, but Torrak's grip held. Sharp pain shot through Daith's shoulder, now dislocated. The first man wrestled with Torrak. She lost his hand. Fingers dug into her hair from behind by the second man and he heaved her toward the ship. Pain seared her scalp like electricity.

"Torrak!" she screamed. Her hands found her attacker's. She

tugged at them. Her shoulder seared in agony. His grip did not give way. Dust irritated her teary eyes. "Torrak! Help!" A sharp sting flared in her tricep. She could see a hand emptying red liquid from a syringe into the back of her arm. The redness swirled beneath her pale skin like ink dribbled into a glass of water.

The ground below gave way to the metallic incline of the ship. A new terror overtook her at the thought of being dragged onboard.

"Let me go!" Daith reached back, higher up the man's arm, and yanked. Her hands slid down his hairy skin. He heaved harder and her head snapped back, pulling her closer to him. His stench reached her—a combination of body odor and mechanical lubricant.

You will be trapped once they get you inside. Do something! A heat rose inside her, licking at her insides, straining to be released.

NO! she screamed inside her head.

The heat subsided, but her panic remained. Scrambling, she got her feet beneath her and pushed backwards off the ramp, closing the distance between the two of them. Her assailant loosened his grip on her hair. She spun and brought her knee into his gut.

The man doubled over, releasing her.

Daith whipped around to flee, but pain overwhelmed her as fingers squeezed her injured shoulder. The second assailant had returned. His free fist came through the swirling dirt and struck her in the jaw. She spun, teetered for a moment at the top of the ramp, and fell face-first into the doorway of the ship. Her jaw shattered against the metal floor. In a swirl of pain and grit, blackness overtook her.

* * *

Commander Trey Xiven ran his fingertips over the smooth, rounded helmet of the Memory Machine. A relic from Eomix galaxy history. Instrumental now to what needed to be done.

He sometimes wished he could use the machine on himself to erase the memories of his past, his family, and Jacin Jaxx.

But his past fueled him forward, giving him drive.

The memories of his family kept him independent and strong.

And the knowledge of the last moments before Jacin's suicide?

What an ironic joke. Eight standard years earlier, Trey had been standing on the bridge of the *Enforcer,* second-in-command of an army that had spent years reshaping and remolding governments on dozens of allied planets when Jacin had implanted the memory of his final moments before death in Trey's mind.

And for what? The sequence carried no insight. No wisdom. Jacin hadn't given Trey any of his abilities. No. He merely got to watch, like a broadcast on a viewscreen, unable to do anything but observe a powerful man give up on everyone he'd promised to help.

That memory couldn't be erased. Embedded in Trey's mind, the thought clung deep inside where only a full mind-wipe would clear it. Jacin staring into the mirror, settling onto his disgusting couch, sitting in despair—which was always the moment Trey would awake in a cold sweat.

Trey relived the memory over again, night after night. For eight years he watched the same dream.

Better than the old nightmare about his mother's death. Substitute one terror for another.

Dr. Ludd had provided him a solution—pills to suppress the portion of the brain which allowed someone to remember their dreams. Though every once in a while, the dream found a way through the haze....

Trey pulled himself out of his thoughts. Now was the time to move into the future, not think about the past. He'd been informed Daith had been located and his soldiers were on their way back to his ship, the *Horizon.* They would dock within three hours.

Trey's hands trembled in anticipation. His plan was finally happening. After all the hardships, he could now take the vital step to once again reestablish peace in the Eomix galaxy.

"Doctor Ludd," Trey said, his words accented and clipped. "Is everything prepared?"

A pink, bulbous figure floated through the doorway, hovering on a mechanical device above the floor. "Yes, Commander Xiven." The normally verbose doctor had been restrictive with his words all day. Trey didn't mind. He could use a break from the usual incessant babbling.

"Good. Because of the injuries she sustained, you'll have to do some regenerative work—replacing her lost hair, fixing her dislocated shoulder, resetting her shattered jaw. But even so, the whole process shouldn't take more than four standard days. And no mistakes, Doctor.

"No more mistakes."

Chapter 2

THE YOUNG WOMAN'S eyes snapped open. A shrill scream erupted from her mouth.

She bolted into a sitting position, caught for a moment in an unfamiliar gray blanket. Flinging the cover aside, she scrambled off the bed, panting as she crouched on the carpeted floor.

Images of the nightmare flashed through her mind while she shook off the last vestiges of sleep: a small silver ship, tornadoes of dust, hands dragging her by the hair.

Tentatively she felt her head, convinced she would feel clumps of hair missing from her scalp, but everything felt smooth and intact. Still the dream had felt so real. She tried to remember if those moments had happened to her.

She tried to remember why she couldn't remember.

She couldn't remember anything.

Panic hit, squeezing her chest. She had no idea where or who she was. Her breath quickened as she took in foreign surroundings: metallic bed frame with a gray pad and blanket, metal desk, clear of clutter, with a single chair, smooth, gray walls, and a deep red carpet, worn and flattened around the edges of each door, one across from her, the other at the head of her bed. The lights overhead, nestled inside the ceiling, let off a fluorescent, factory-like glow, and provided the only light source in the windowless room.

Shifting her focus, she ran her hands along the long, white garment draped on her body. The gown smelled sterile and clung to her like satiny paper.

None of this helped her remember anything.

She breathed deep and focused her thoughts to recall something about herself or how she'd gotten to this place. The harder she pushed, the harder it was to concentrate, and her thoughts became more shrouded, like layers of a thick black veil falling across her mind.

"Hello?" she said.

No one answered.

"Hello?" she screeched, her throat straining with the effort.

Silence.

Goosebumps prickled the young woman's skin. She pushed herself to her feet, her legs wobbly underneath her. Once they steadied, she moved toward the door next to the head of the bed. With a rusty squeal she peered through the opening, which revealed a small, enclosed washroom. The room gleamed as if recently scrubbed.

She entered and gazed into the polished reflector unit.

Dark green eyes, long bronze hair, full lips, slender figure.

The image told her nothing about herself.

Tears blurred her vision. *Who are you?*

The young woman brushed the wetness away, the reflection doing the same. Examining a face she didn't know wouldn't help. Figuring things out would need more clues.

She made her way toward the other door. Completely sleek—no door handle to push or pull. A corroded control panel attached to the wall on her right. The unlit buttons did nothing when she pushed them. She pulled off its covering and stared with ignorance at the mass of wires.

A chirp made her jump. An access panel on the wall between the two doors glowed before a set of small sliding doors opened to reveal a dining tray, dropped from a tube above. She retrieved the tray and stuck her head into the tube, which reeked of melted plastic.

"Is anyone there?" she called. "I'm locked in this room. Can anyone hear me?"

The only response was her echo.

She stared at the platter covered in a gooey green substance. The odor tickled her nose and her stomach rumbled. She assumed the goo was edible, but she had no idea what it was. A favorite meal of hers? Had she ever had it before?

Her mind remained blank as she grasped for some semblance of a memory.

Frustrated by her lack of knowledge and control, she flung the tray across the room, the contents slapping against the back wall. The gesture provided no relief. Her hands went to her face—she rubbed her fingers across her forehead, willing herself to remember something. Anything.

Blackness.

Just focus on getting out of here.

She returned to the solid-looking door. Grabbing the edge of the desk, she slammed the furniture into the door.

Nothing. Not even a dent.

She rammed the door repeatedly.

Not a scratch.

Her skin prickled with perspiration. Tightness pulled at her chest. Her urge to get out of the room grew. She turned her concentration to the control panel. She stripped a few of the wires with her nails and pinched them together, hoping the door would short-circuit and open.

A jolt of electricity hit her, throwing her across the room.

The young woman woke, her skin sizzling in pain. The scent of burnt hair filled her nostrils.

She opened her eyes, her head pounding in protest. She could barely lift her arms to feel what was wrong with her head. Then she remembered her attempts to get through the door.

Must be why I'm sore.

The thought jerked her upright. The throbbing in her head doubled, but she didn't care. She *remembered* being in the room. She remembered trying to get out and fiddling with the wires. Then...

Then I electrocuted myself. Good work.

She chuckled at her own stupidity, the noise foreign to her.

A screech from the door opening refocused her attention. She clawed her way to standing, leaning heavily on the bed, to face the new arrival.

A tall figure loomed in the doorway, its head centimeters away from the ceiling. It glared at her with intensely dark eyes before its gaze lowered to a datapad. Short brown fur covered the face and rounded paws. Glistening claws curved from each digit. Its nose was wide and flat. Double rows of sharp pointed teeth protruded from thin lips.

"Daith Tocc," the creature said in a deep, rough voice.

There was a pause. "Are you talking to me?"

The creature snorted. "Of course."

"Then I guess I'm Daith Tocc." The name was unfamiliar, but relief washed over her at having a name.

"You are scheduled to meet with Commander Xiven."

Silence stretched between them for a standard minute before Daith realized the creature wasn't going to say anything else.

"All right," she said, "and you are...?"

The creature raised an eyebrow. "I am Lieutenant Koye."

"Right." Daith clucked her tongue against the roof of her mouth. "And Commander Xiven is...?"

"Commander Xiven is the Commander."

"I should've guessed." Daith's cheeks warmed with annoyance. "Want to tell me what's going on? Who am I? *Where* am I? Why can't I remember anything?"

Koye's paws contracted for a moment around the datapad. "I will return to escort you to meet Commander Xiven." Lieutenant Koye clicked his teeth together as he placed a set of clothes on the bed. The motion terrified her, like an animal snapping at prey. "Change," he ordered.

After he left, Daith tried the door. Locked again. Though still angry, some of her tension ebbed as she registered she wasn't alone.

Daith inspected the new clothing—a faded green one-piece jumpsuit. After she slipped it on, she folded the wispy gown she'd been wearing and placed the garment on the edge of her bed. She plucked the papery slippers off her feet and slid on the black, cloth shoes. The clothing fit her quite well. Either the jumpsuit had once been hers or they'd made it specifically for her.

She felt her body shape, hands sliding over the coarse material. Her body was unknown, like her surroundings. Fear once again threatened her.

"My name is Daith," she muttered. "Daith Tocc. And I *am* someone. I will find out who that is." Her shoulder muscles unknotted and she let out a deep breath.

While she waited, Daith wondered if she should try to escape when Lieutenant Koye returned. But because she didn't know where she was, she might find there was nowhere to go. For all she knew she was on a deserted world or on some desolate ice-covered island. Until she knew more, she would have to bide her time.

Feeling less panicked, but still impatient, she tapped her feet against the carpet. Her door chimes rang. To her surprise, the door didn't open. The chimes sounded again.

"Come in?"

The door opened to reveal Lieutenant Koye.

"This way," he demanded.

She let out a deep breath, squared her shoulders, and followed

Chapter 3

A PAIR OF dark blue eyes lit up like methane storms.

Useless. All of it useless.

Commander Trey Xiven growled. How was he expected to run his ship, keep control of his crew, successfully complete his mission, and oversee operations when presented with ideas like these?

Commanding officer aboard the *Horizon,* Trey knew his ship front to back. He'd memorized every bolt from the cargo rooms to the prison cells, knew how every weapon worked, the intensity and coverage of the shields, and how the silari engines powered the massive bulk on which he currently stood. If he could, he would run this ship by himself.

Impossible. So instead he must rely on others. Though times like these, while he scrutinized the massive mess of garbage scribbled in front of him....

He whipped around to face the man responsible for his anger. Raqz, the *Horizon's* chief engineer, stood at the end of a large oval table in the center of the meeting room. The space was comically empty—the table able to seat 40—with only the two of them at one end. Cheap, harsh, white lights reflected off the table's slicked, metallic surface and Raqz's balding head.

"You call these ideas good?" Trey sneered and gestured toward the stack of datapads on the table. His dark hair, broad shoulders, and chiseled face created an attractive, but imposing figure. He used this to his advantage and towered over the other man, stooped with old age.

"I can see a dozen flaws, from your so-called security upgrade to your increased shield output. Not to mention you need personnel to help with the installations. Where would you find a dozen extra hands from our skeletal crew?" Trey grit his teeth as pain mounted in his head—another side-effect from the dream-deflector pills he took. "I kept you on this crew when I took command because you were the previous chief engineer. I believed I could count on your knowledge and expertise. But perhaps I made a mistake."

"You didn't really have a choice."

Trey's eyebrows rose, surprised at the tone of defiance. "What?"

The old man cleared his throat. His voice, thick and gravelly, matched his pitted skin and protruding gut. "I have been a part of this army for a long time. Longer than you. Even when I joined, I weren't young. But I'm a part of this because you need me here. You can't afford to lose no one else. I know we gots a skeleton crew. When are you going to accept things ain't the same as before? You're going to have to learn to deal with what you got." He shoved his thumbs into his chest. "And that means dealing with me."

Trey studied the short, balding man, his shirt untucked on one side, a smear of grease across his left cheek. His uncleanliness made the commander's skin crawl, like the shrieks of flying itsu birds at night from his home planet, Sintaur. Trey was tired of laziness, dirtiness, and excuses.

"You're right, Raqz. We may not be able to lose anyone else, but extra baggage is worse. It's taken us eight years to come back from the losses we suffered and you know how important this mission is. I can't jeopardize our plans, not for anyone." He nodded to the guards.

Raqz's eyes widened to the size of his fists. "No, please! You need me here. No one else can do what I can do."

Trey's voice held no warmth. "Everyone is expendable."

"Commander, you don't have to kill me!"

"I can't have a bitter ex-employee telling our secrets."

Droplets of gray sweat glistened off Raqz's bald scalp.

"I won't tell anyone. You know I won't! Please, have mercy—"

Trey raised his hand and the guards waited. "I wish I could afford to grant mercy, but our cause is to reestablish peace. And sometimes casualties come with peace. Even if you swore you wouldn't say anything, we both know there are ways to make someone talk. There is no other option. I can't let you live." Trey flicked his fingers and the guards moved on while Raqz continued to plead for his life.

One of the guards shook his head as he turned the corner. Trey understood why some of his crew didn't agree with the way things ran now, but there was no other option. If news of their plan leaked, the results could be disastrous, and more innocents would be killed.

Raqz had solid ideas, but he hadn't physically seen the devastation six years ago when the Aleet Army had been betrayed, its remnants slaughtered at their main base. Trey had returned from an unsuccessful mission—attempting to reinstitute a peace only Jacin Jaxx, while alive, could maintain—and stood shocked at the scene. Buildings reduced to mounds of rubble. Bodies strewn in bloodied heaps throughout the base. Ash had stung his skin and lungs while he choked on debris from the detonated explosions inside the city.

Raqz had been away. And the newer soldiers couldn't comprehend the utter destruction of not only a place, but the last planetary symbol of what Jacin and the Aleet Army stood for.

Trey wouldn't, *couldn't,* let betrayal happen again. Especially because of their new cargo.

If that meant sacrificing one to save the many, so be it.

"Commander Xiven."

Trey paused in picking up the datapads from the table. "Yes, Lieutenant Koye, what is it?"

"I have brought Miss Tocc."

Trey turned. Next to Koye was a slender brunette. Trey assessed her, trying to figure out the best way to start the conversation. One misstep could cost him her trust.

Daith came in, the gray, old carpet flattening under her feet.

"Commander Xiven, is it? I have some questions for you," she said. Her voice remained calm, although Trey could see a flicker of emotion in her dark green eyes. He could tell she wanted to maintain the appearance of control.

Trey snapped out of his reverie. "Of course," he said in the sweetest tone he could muster. He took a seat and gestured for her to do the same. "I'm sorry for all the secrecy, but we needed to be cautious to secure your safety."

Questions slipped from her mouth. "Secure my safety from whom? And why would you need to? And where exactly am I in the first place? And—?"

Trey held a hand up to silence her. When she quieted, he felt a trickle of satisfaction purr inside of him. "Please, let me speak. I am Commander Trey Xiven. My second in command is Lieutenant Koye."

Daith's gaze flickered toward Koye. "Charmed."

Trey could nearly see the sarcasm drip off the word. His jaw clenched for a moment before he widened his smile.

"I'll get straight to the point. My crew and I were hired to rescue you to keep you from being assassinated. We kept you confined to your quarters until we could confirm the threat was gone.

"I'm sorry to have caused you any anxiety, but you are safe now. I'm doing what I can to speed up this process so we can get you back to your life." Trey gestured to Koye. "Lieutenant Koye will escort you back to your room."

Before Koye could reach her, Daith stood from her chair and backed away, her lip curled in disgust. "That's it? I'm supposed to be satisfied with those answers?"

Trey's patience wavered, though he kept his voice low and gentle. He motioned for her to sit back down. "I understand your frustration. You have been cleared to leave your quarters, but there are still security risks revolving around the attempt on your life. The fewer who know your whereabouts, the better. I will try to help in any way I can."

"Why can't I remember anything?"

Trey mustered his best look of sincerity. "So your memory hasn't come back? We did all we could. I had hoped...." He leaned forward.

"There was an accident," he said in a hushed tone.

"What kind of accident?"

He had to move lightly now, get her to trust him.

"When we went to transfer you to a more secure location, a ship landed next to us. It carried the assassins. There was a huge explosion and shots were fired. One of them grazed the side of your head and you were knocked unconscious. We got you on board and took off, leaving many of my men behind.

"You suffered severe head trauma and we weren't sure if you'd pull through. Our medical technicians healed your physical wounds, but when you woke, you had total memory loss. We hoped the affliction was temporary."

Trey studied her reaction. Confusion, pain, disbelief—all these emotions danced in her eyes, showed in the way she twisted her fingers. "How long have I been here?"

"Four days."

Daith shook her head, her forehead creased. "I don't remember anything before today."

"There's more." Trey paused for dramatic effect. "I sent a search team to go back to your home after we knew the enemy had gone. Nothing remained. Your family, your house, all information about you had been destroyed."

"What?" she whispered. "They're all gone?"

Trey took her hand. "I'm sorry, Daith. I will tell you everything I can, but I'm afraid what I say won't be of much help. Your family hired us, yes, but they didn't divulge much about your life. Only your danger."

Daith's hand tightened.

"I'm sure your family loved you very much—"

"I'd like to go back to my room now," she said abruptly, standing. "I can't... I need some time to deal with this."

"Of course. It is rather late so we can meet again tomorrow. Your communications panel is now turned on and you can contact me for whatever you need."

Daith followed Koye out of the room; her face a reflection of her churning thoughts.

When the door closed, Trey chuckled. Things with Daith were going well, better than expected. As long as she believed his list of lies, he knew she wouldn't be any sort of problem.

* * *

Emotions flooded her during her trip back to her quarters. Anger at Commander Xiven for the secrecy, grief-stricken over the loss of a family she would never know, and hateful at those who attacked her and caused her memory loss. She hadn't been prepared to find out her whole family was dead, even if she didn't remember them.

Daith entered her room in such a daze she didn't realize the space had been cleaned. The food she'd thrown was gone from the wall and carpet, her bed was made, and the wiring on the door had been reconstituted.

Questions wrestled each other in her mind, each fighting for more importance, struggling to be the first answered, but she had no answers to give. The constant flow of thoughts caused a throbbing pain in her head.

Rubbing her temples, she realized something else bothered her. Something hadn't felt right about Commander Xiven. She didn't know why, but she'd felt he'd been lying to her. There was nothing to indicate he was nor any reason for her not to believe him, but she could *sense* his dishonesty, like how anxiety knotted a stomach.

Sitting on the bed, Daith dismissed the feeling. A yawn escaped her mouth. Sleep beckoned her to ignore her thoughts for now. *I'll sleep for a few standard hours then I'll search this place and get some answers.*

Daith peeled off her jumpsuit, stepped out of her shoes, and slid under the gray cover. She yawned again.

"Computer, lights off."

Within moments, slumber took her.

Chapter 4

SPACEPORT C27. A rusty metallic orb hanging in space surrounded by blackness pinpricked with points of starlight. Built ten standard years ago by the Aleet Army during its prime, the spaceport's location was known only to captains of vessels who had served the Army. When the remnants of the group were betrayed by one of their own, most individuals who knew the spaceport's coordinates died with that knowledge. Since then, the contraption had fallen into disarray, its oxygenized insides rusted, its outer clamps frozen from non-use.

One captain, now Commander of the *Horizon*, still knew the spaceport's position. Docked there now, the last time he ever would be. Yet he felt no nostalgia for the place that had been a safe haven to so many of his fallen leader's followers.

On the final occasion of its use, Spaceport C27 would allow the Commander to convene with the one man who could tell him if he had indeed found his prize.

* * *

A small, curvy ship, the *Reminiscence,* pulled up to the *Horizon's* docking port. The *Horizon,* secured by Spaceport C27's brackets, loomed over the smaller ship, extended its docking clamps, and fastened to the *Reminiscence.* The metallic claws screeched. The smaller ship latched onto the metal frames of the larger ship to create an airtight seal. The passage hatch of the *Reminiscence* hissed open and a man around twenty-nine standard years old stepped into the conjoining corridor of the *Horizon.*

He stretched his arms above him after the long flight and tossed his dark brown hair off his face. Catching a glimpse of himself on a shiny section of the ship's wall, he hoped the dark circles under his gray eyes only existed because of the long trip. He rubbed his hands over his pointed nose, thin lips, and up his strong jaw-line in an attempt to wipe away some of his weariness.

It was late. The *Horizon's* inner lights cast a dim, eerie glow through the corridor. Years had passed since he'd been on this ship, and he noticed the lack of care and maintenance. Her corridors were dull and scratched, the gray carpet worn, and burnt-out lights dotted the ceiling. Stale air entered his nostrils, not old, but recirculated for too long without a filter change. The ship should have been quiet, but he could hear the creaks and moans of a stressed hull, overworked engine, and rusted frame.

Regardless of the changes, and even with the alteration of the ship's original name, the *Enforcer,* to the gentler-sounding name *Horizon,* he still recognized her. This had been the ship of a hero with a vision—the sole piece of machinery which had brought hope and peace to warring planets throughout the galaxy. Of course, many others viewed this ship as the most infamous transport of its time, conveying a tyrant to the planets he helped destroy.

The pilot stood outside a large, lackluster metallic door and pushed the chime button. He waited for a response, his hands clammy.

What am I even doing here?

The door slid open, revealing a semi-circular room. If he hadn't just made his way through the shabby corridors of the rest of the ship, he would never have thought this area belonged to the same craft. He noticed the worn carpet and dulled walls, but the rest of the room was spotless. The metal desk in front of him shone, recently polished. Stacks of datapads and folders lay piled neatly on one side of a vidlink screen while the rest of the table was completely cleared of clutter. Nothing else existed in the room. No other furniture, no pictures hanging from the walls, no dirt, no trash.

Nothing except the Commander who sat behind the desk—his image a perfect reflection of the immaculate, sterile room.

"Trey," the young pilot said. "I can't believe this ship still flies." The accented and clipped inflection of his words remained, even though he'd been away from home for years.

Trey laughed, brusque and forced.

"She's still got some spirit left, Dru," Trey said, motioning for the pilot to sit. "I know the *Horizon* appears to be in rough shape, but her condition really isn't too bad. Besides, how could I give her up? With all the fond memories I have, she's like my second home."

Dru swallowed hard. There were definitely memories. Although he wouldn't call the last one they shared here fond.

The conversation lagged and Dru felt the tension in the room spike. He struggled to keep his face neutral while doubts raced inside his head.

What a stupid idea. How could I think we could work together? How could he ever get over what happened?

"I called you here for a special reason," Trey said, breaking the silence. "I need your help."

"What kind of help?"

"First, I have something to show you."

Dru eyed him, suspicious. *It's a trap. This meeting has to be a trap.* He shook the thought away, angry his first notion was one of mistrust.

Trey pulled up a file on his vidlink and a yellow-lined, three-dimensional image appeared. Dru strained to adjust to the grainy picture. The display showed the inside of a room, small, with a bed and a door to a washroom. A figure lay on the bed, a woman, her breathing the slow and steady rhythm of someone asleep.

"You brought me here because of a woman?" Dru asked.

"Not any woman," Trey said with a tight-lipped smile. "We believe she is Jacin Jaxx's youngest daughter, Daith."

Dru leaned closer, his suspicion replaced by excitement. "Really? How did you find her?"

"We used a patterning buffer to track movement in the past four years of two women around the ages of Jaxx's daughters. The search took close to a year, but after some surveillance, this girl seemed to be the most likely candidate. That's why I need your help, to determine if she really is who we think."

"How do you expect me to do find out?" Dru asked.

"By determining if she has her father's abilities."

Dru chose his next words carefully, not wanting to incite an argument. "I'm not sure why you asked me to help you with this. We can't pretend our last encounter wasn't...strained."

Trey leaned back in his chair and laced his hands behind his head. "Simply put, you're the most qualified. I did my research. Not only do you have an extensive background working with empaths and telepaths, but there are only two individuals who have ever worked with Jacin and his abilities. One of them is dead." Trey stopped short at the word, a shadow passing over his face. The change only lasted a moment, but a chill ran through Dru all the same. "The other is you."

"I take it there's a catch."

"The catch is she has no memory. She doesn't know who she is and she has no idea she might possess any of these abilities. I know you have worked extensively with memory-loss patients, so this shouldn't be difficult for you.

"I'm not asking for a favor," Trey continued. "I don't want you to do this out of some sense of obligation or because you're my younger brother and we're family. I want to hire you. You'd be a paid employee and that's all. No strings attached."

Dru stared at the image of the girl. The offer tempted him, but he had to know more. Working with a descendant of Jacin Jaxx wasn't something to do without careful consideration. "I'd need to meet her first. Then I can give you an answer."

Trey nodded sharply. He opened up a map of the ship and showed Dru where he could work. "You're more than welcome to stay on your own ship, of course, but we converted one of the conference rooms on the third floor for you if you'd prefer. Plus they are on the same level as the simulation rooms."

Dru thought of his cramped little ship and welcomed the open space. "Thanks."

"Good," Trey said as he stood. "I'll see you with Daith in the first meeting room on the other side of your floor tomorrow at 0700. We'll go from there." Trey awkwardly patted him on the back. "It is," he paused, "it is good to see you, Brother."

Dru left Trey's office and made his way to the quarters provided for him. The first part of the suite boasted a shiny metallic desk, a vidlink system, three chairs, and a sofa. Moving through, Dru went into the smaller room, which had a hefty-sized bed, a shelving unit for extra storage, and a smaller table. A washroom was located off to the right.

After he'd undressed and used the facilities to wash away some of the day's travel, Dru slipped into bed. He couldn't believe he might get to work with Jacin Jaxx's daughter. If she had even half the power and abilities of her late father, who knew what she could accomplish. And he would be the first to work with her to help her relearn her abilities. His influence would ensure her gifts didn't get out of control the way her father's had.

But what to do about his brother? Did Trey really believe the two of them could work together after what had happened? That personal feelings wouldn't get in the way?

Dru's eyelids closed and listened to the silence around him. His stomach roiled with nervous excitement. He tried to think of questions for the next morning, but what do you ask someone who might be related to *the* Jacin Jaxx? Even though his brain wanted to stay awake and think, the weariness from the long day's travel washed over him and sleep pulled him under.

Chapter 5

TREY'S EYELIDS DROOPED. His head jerked back, kinking his neck as he started.

I need to finish this report. His fingertips massaged the ache. *Then I need to talk to Cadet Mip. I can sleep after.* He noticed the hair on his neck felt a bit too long and added a mental note to get a trim when he had time.

Time. Right, he thought sarcastically.

Trey's hand became a prop underneath his chin to hold up his head as he reviewed the datapad report on his desk. His objective seemed tantalizingly close. If he could hang on a little longer...

Trey knew he was dreaming, but the knowledge changed nothing. The memory would continue, unless something from the outside woke him. The last moments before Jacin's death would play for him, like a vivid viewscreen presentation.

But something was different. This memory wasn't the same.

Jacin appeared young, before he had even considered creating the Aleet Army....

Jacin Jaxx stood in front of his history class. Rain popped angrily outside against the windowpanes. His students scrambled to put finishing touches on their presentations, to be shown shortly.

Jacin gazed out into the dark, stormy day and his thoughts drifted toward his own family—his wife, Elor, and their two daughters. He wondered what they were doing right now. He'd recently gone back to teaching and missed staying home to take care of them. But Elor's grant money had dried up and bills needed to be paid.

Someone screamed.

Jacin yanked himself from his thoughts. One of his students had collapsed, hand clutching her chest. Sending another student to get help, Jacin rushed over to hold the paled, shaking girl. She trembled in his grasp, eye rolled back into its socket, teeth chattering under blued lips.

Before his own panic could take over, Jacin felt a warmth fill him. Heat spread through his body, attempting to make its way to the point where his hands touched the girl.

The sensation was intense, like a fever. Perspiration coated Jacin's face and nausea threatened to overwhelm him. But the girl needed him.

What can I do? How can I find out what's wrong with her?

A strange pressure settled over him. He could see the back of his eyelids—dark, but not completely black—as sparks jumped around in front of him. Jacin's eyes flipped open. He no longer saw the rain-streaked windows of the classroom. Instead, electrical discharges shot through tubes in front of his him. Pink, globular shapes filled his view while the bolts streaked from one section to another.

He could see inside the girl's brain. Nerve impulses flashed through translucent tubes of tissue, issuing orders from her mind to the rest of her body.

This is crazy! How can I be in *her brain? What's happening to me? What's happening to her?*

Jacin's mind hurled into one of the tubes. In less time than it took him to think the thought, the ride was over, and he could see the girl's 5-chambered, magenta heart. It beat, but erratically. Jacin felt a sudden pull toward its left side. There. He could see the problem. A sizable tear in one of the chambers.

The warmth inside of him increased, swirling into chaotic patterns of flame. Jacin half-imagined, half-viewed the heart in front of him. Waves of fiery energy flowed from him.

He knew what to do. He could heal her.

Jacin directed the heat toward her heart. He could see the muscle fibers wind together, repair themselves, and close the hole. After the heart healed, Jacin jolted back into himself. The last thing he remembered before blackness took him was the girl, pale but calm, opening her eye....

"Commander?"

Trey's eyes snapped open at the tentative voice. Confusion buffeted him for a moment.

"Yes?" he said, automatically. His mind cleared. A young man, about a head shorter than himself, stood upright with his hands behind his back.

"Cadet Mip reporting, Commander."

Trey rubbed the bottom of his face—disgusted to find a trace amount of saliva—and motioned the cadet to sit. Mip sat, posture rigid, dark yellowish-green eyes quivering in their sockets.

"Cadet Mip," Trey said. He shook away the dream and focused

on the task at hand. He'd forgotten he'd asked Cadet Mip to report to him. This was *not* a conversation he wanted to have half-asleep.

"You and Cadet Roilster were the two members of the team who went to retrieve Miss Tocc from Fior, correct?" Trey asked.

"Correct, Commander."

Trey pulled up a file on his datapad and read a segment out loud.

"'Roilster and I retrieved the subject at the predetermined destination. We injected the subject with a sedative to insure safe passage. A witness was discovered. Witness was injected with targeting memory blockers, but escaped custody before entire mixture was delivered. Witness fled into a non-designated area. Allotted amount of time for capture of subject expired. Roilster and I boarded with subject and departed.' This is your report?"

"Yes, Commander."

"Your responsibility included witnesses, correct?"

"Yes, Commander."

Trey's jaw clenched. "Tell me, Cadet, why did you think letting a witness go without a full injection of memory blockers was acceptable?"

Cadet Mip swallowed. "We ran out of time, Commander, and didn't want to risk exposure, but—but I'm sure I injected the witness with enough serum to prevent any memories from resurfacing."

"Did you follow up on the witness?"

Cadet Mip appeared confused. "No, Commander. I didn't know his identity."

"Did you capture his facial image for further identification? Did you use a genetic sample from the tip of the syringe to determine his profile?" Trey's fingertips whitened from pressing them on the table.

"N-n-nuh-no, Commander."

“Of course not,” Trey snapped. “Know why? Because I’m surrounded by a bunch of young, untrained, *children* who have no idea what they are doing. Do you have any idea how much damage you may have done if this witness *does* remember anything?”

“Commander, I—”

“You are dismissed from my service.”

Cadet Mip didn’t move for a moment. Then his body sagged. “No, Commander, *please*. You can’t do this. I didn’t know.”

“It’s already done.”

Cadet Mip arched in his chair. The yellow of his eyes intensified before a whitish liquid oozed from their sockets. He twitched once, then again, before he fell onto the arm of the chair, his gaze vacant, and his mouth open in an unheard scream.

Trey removed his hand from a small button under his desk and the two prongs in the back of the cadet’s chair retracted into the plush cushion. The nerve toxin injected into the cadet’s body was no longer a threat for Trey’s next visitor.

Trey skirted around his desk to Cadet Mip’s body, reached under the armpits, and pulled forward, heaving the dead weight out of the chair, and toward the door. He pushed the call button for Doctor Ludd. The doctor answered with his usual peppy tone and Trey interrupted him before he could say more than a few words.

“I have one for you, Doctor. Nerve toxin. Dispose of the body.”

Doctor Ludd murmured an acknowledgement and Trey cut the line. A medical orderly came to Trey’s office moments later and removed the corpse.

Trey pinched the bridge of his nose. He knew he couldn’t take care of everything himself, but this situation made him wish he had been there for Daith’s pick-up. He couldn’t believe a witness had been left behind. And a witness meant a possibility of others knowing about Daith’s disappearance.

Trey had hoped he wouldn't need to erase the sister's memories, that Daith would simply be another unsolved missing citizens report, but if the witness alerted her that Daith had been kidnapped, the investigation could continue.

He did not have time for this.

Trey called for Cadet Roilster to come to his office. Roilster showed up a few standard minutes later, his face flushed.

"You sent for me, Commander?"

"Cadet, I have a three-part assignment for you. I need you to return to Fior. Our plan has been compromised due to the witness who remained after your retrieval of Miss Tocc. I need you to contact the authorities and find out if a report has been filed of Miss Tocc's disappearance. If so, you are to delete the report and erase the memories of the individual heading the investigation.

"Your second task is to locate Miss Tocc's sister, Valendra Tocc. Pertinent information will be in your shuttle's database. Her memories pertaining to Daith must be eradicated.

"And third, you are then to find the witness, erase his memories, and report back to me. You are not allowed to vacate Fior until all tasks have been completed. This is confidential and any communication on this subject with any other crewmember will result in your immediate dismissal. Understood?"

After Roilster agreed and left the office, a wave of despair washed over Trey. *What was I thinking? Why did I think I could ever pull this off?* Trey's body shook with fear. Fear of failure, of making the wrong move.

Trey willed himself to stop shaking and forced his fists to unclench. *No, I'm doing fine. Set-backs are to be expected. This operation is too big not to think there would be mistakes. I have to focus. Keep going. Focus. keep going focus goingfocus....*

The words blurred together in a twisted mantra as Trey read

the next task, his brief dream of Jacin's memory about saving the girl gone like a wisp of smoke.

* * *

Daith's feet moved beneath her.

Where am I?

The sun beat down from above. A layer of sweat coated her body.

She took in her surroundings, the motion slow.

Happiness filled her. This was a good moment. A moment with a friend.

The scene shifted. A gust of wind struck her face. She staggered backwards, the shadow next to hers pulled in the opposite direction.

She fell. Dry, tasteless dirt filled her mouth. Pressure on her arm. She turned toward the pain. Red liquid swirl underneath her skin.

Am I bleeding?

Her gaze flickered upward and her throat tightened. A large silver mass hung suspended in the air above her.

A ship?

Her face pressed further into the dirt. She struggled to breathe, but she could do nothing except feel the heat from the sun and a fire inside her—

Daith awoke with a start, gasping. A chill reached her bones though a film of sweat covered her shuddering body. She wiped her forehead with a clammy arm and inhaled deeply to calm down. The vague flashes of her dream slipped away.

"Just a dream." she muttered. But the images had been so powerful, so real. She couldn't remember much, except the intense heat and something hanging above her. A shiny and silver shape, but she couldn't place it. *A machine? A piece of metal?*

After cracking her neck, she lay back down. Her stomach clenched with a feeling of dread she couldn't shake. "It doesn't matter. It was a dream." She said the words, but sleep came uneasily.

Chapter 6

DRU XIVEN PACED under the cheap lights of the meeting room, his shadow following him back and forth across the gleaming table. His sleep hadn't exactly been restful—punctuated with moments of revelation or anticipation jolting him awake—but this morning he jittered with pure adrenaline.

Jacin Jaxx's daughter. I can't believe it might be her.

He forced himself to calm down, taking in and letting out deep breaths. He didn't want to get too excited until he actually met her, but he understood the body didn't always respond to logic.

Daith might have her father's abilities. And if guided in the proper way, she could succeed where he'd failed. Dru could be a part of that.

He grinned to himself. *I wish Riel were here.*

The thought caught him off guard and he stopped mid-step. Under the circumstances, Riel would probably not have wanted to be here.

A pang of guilt hit him, tightening his chest. He hadn't thought about her all morning. This was the first time he could remember since her death when she wasn't the first thought he had when he awoke.

Dru's feelings dissipated as the door slid open. He slapped a nervous grin on his face, wanting to seem comforting to the girl. The smile faded as Trey entered, alone.

"Morning."

"Morning."

Silence fell over the two brothers.

"So where is she?" Dru asked, taking a seat.

"She's on her way." Trey remained upright, his hand resting on the back of the chair across from his brother.

Tension mounted in the room.

"Trey," Dru said, "how have things been?" The question sounded stupid and vague. Dru wiped his sweaty palms on his pants.

"Things couldn't be better," Trey said, his face a complete blank. "Before Daith arrives, I thought you should know I haven't given her any foreknowledge about these abilities she might have."

Dru raised an eyebrow. "Why not?"

"Think of the situation like a blind test. If she isn't Jaxx's daughter, I don't want to confuse her by telling her untruths. I also don't want her to know we've searched for Jaxx's heir so she can't tell anyone if we let her go."

"Then what will she think I'm here for?"

Trey fluttered his fingers through the air. "Tell her you are here to work on restoring her memory."

Dru peered at him, puzzled. He opened his mouth to ask another question when the door slid open and Daith strode in, dwarfed by her escort, Lieutenant Koye.

Dru studied the slim brunette carefully. He gauged her stance, mood, body language. How her eyes hungrily ate up every detail in the room, how she immediately faced Trey, acknowledging a presence she knew. She seemed quite calm and collected—not the twisted, scared mess he'd often seen in memory-loss patients.

Then he opened up his body and mind to *sense* her. His ability to feel another's emotions wasn't as strong as those he had studied, but he had always been able to receive an impression of others around him. His empathy wasn't too specific, usually a presence in a room or an intense feeling when someone passed by, but it had helped him with his clients more times than he could count.

But this woman—he didn't even have to try. Waves of energy poured from her. Her physical stance appeared relaxed, but her entire being screamed at him to back away.

If this indicated what sort of untapped potential she might have—

Dru felt his pulse quicken at the thought of it.

And then, she smiled.

And his pulse missed a beat.

She addressed Dru's brother. "Good morning, Commander Xiven."

Trey motioned for her to take a seat. "Good morning, Daith. I hope you slept well."

"I slept fine, Commander." Her smile widened, but her eyes looked red and tired. Dru wondered what had kept her awake. Pain? Nightmares? Flashes of memories?

Daith sat straight, legs crossed, arms folded across her chest.

A guarded body position. *That's to be expected.*

"Who is this?" Daith asked about Dru. "Another crew member as welcoming as your Lieutenant here?" Koye shifted his stance at the insult.

A smile played on the corner of Trey's mouth. "This is Dru. He is a memory specialist. I have asked him aboard to help restore your memories, but only if you are interested."

"A memory specialist?"

Dru jumped in. "I specialize in memory retrieval using relaxation, hypnosis, and therapeutic tactics."

"I know not having your memories must be hard," Trey told her, "and I want to do what I can to help. Dru is here, if you want to work with him."

Daith's gaze finally shifted toward Dru. Her dark green eyes were cold, calculating. But underneath, they quivered with desperation.

I'll do anything.

Dru blinked. He could've sworn she'd spoken the words and yet she hadn't opened her mouth.

"I'm willing to try. It's not like I have anything to lose," Daith said out loud.

"All right then," Trey said, pulling back his chair to sit. "Where do we start?"

Dru cleared his throat. "I'm actually going to have to ask you and Lieutenant Koye to leave." Dru's heart pounded. He squeezed his legs together under the table.

Silence.

Daith's gaze danced between the two men, one stopped halfway to sitting, the other trying to hold his ground.

"Doctor-patient confidentiality," Dru added quickly.

There was a moment where Dru thought Trey would argue, but then a smile bloomed across the commander's face.

"Of course," he said, pushing the chair back toward the table. "I understand."

Dru nodded. He felt his shoulder muscles relax.

Trey pulled at the edges of his immaculate uniform and addressed Daith.

"If you'd like, we could meet later and go over any questions or concerns you may have. I want you to feel comfortable here."

"Thank you, Commander."

Trey smiled. A glint reached his brother's eyes, a light Dru couldn't quite interpret.

"Well then, I'll leave you in the good doctor's hands." Trey left, signaling Lieutenant Koye to follow. The door slid closed, leaving the two alone.

"For a second I thought he was going to insist on staying," Daith said.

"You and me both." He pushed his hair off his face. "He's protective of you and wants to make sure you're all right."

"He must trust you a lot then."

Dru forced his face to stay neutral at her statement. "We've been through a lot together."

Daith uncrossed her arms, a signal to Dru that she felt ready to open up. "Where do we start?"

"I want to get to know you first."

Daith raised her eyebrows. "In case you've forgotten, I don't know who I am."

"You'd be surprised what someone can tell about you without knowing a thing. The way you came in the room for example, how you spoke to Commander Xiven, and your immediate decision to work with me gives an outline of who you are."

"So what does that list tell you?"

"It tells me you are strong-willed, eager to move forward, and a natural-born leader."

Daith laughed, the sound melodic and full. "A leader? How could I lead anyone when I don't even know what's going on?"

Dru settled into his chair, the back squeaking. "I'm not saying you need to lead anyone right at this moment, but the potential is in you. You just don't remember."

Daith's face fell for a moment, her guise of control shaken. "What if I never remember?"

Dru scooted forward, closing the distance between them. "That is a bridge we don't have to cross yet."

Her eyes brightened, hopeful. "We?"

"I am in this with you, every step of the way. But I'll need your help."

Determination returned to her face. "What do you need from me?"

Dru picked up a datapad to take notes. "Fill me in on the things I don't know. How far back you can remember? What have you done since you woke up here? Dreams? Flashbacks? Whatever you can give me."

"You do understand how unnerving it is to tell a complete stranger a bunch of personal things you've been through, right?"

"I do. And I know this will be a lot harder for you than for me. But you aren't the first memory-loss patient I've worked with."

"Not with me, I hope, but I can't remember."

Dru smiled at the joke, but his eyes held sadness. "I have never met you, talked to you, or seen you before today." His mouth felt dry. His words weren't a lie, *technically.* "Whenever you're ready."

* * *

Trey ground the knuckles of his fist into his other palm. "Doctor-patient confidentiality," he sneered, mocking his brother's words. Dru wouldn't even be here if Trey hadn't arranged the meeting. And to be cast aside like a stranger to the situation? Daith should trust *him*, not his brother.

Trey took deep, calming breaths as he made his way through the ship's corridors to his office. Once there, he let the sterile smell fill his nose and clear his mind.

Daith had to connect with Dru first. Trey didn't have to like it, but the step was necessary.

Besides, in the end, it would be Trey who got the girl.

Chapter 7

DRU TILTED THE datapad of notes to adjust for the reflective glare from the meeting room's sharp lights.

Has had a couple of dreams. A good sign. Her memory might be trying to resurface. She seems to be missing a few days from when she arrived here. Possible damage to her short-term memory neurotransmitters. No way to know until we move forward.

"Doctor?" Daith asked, breaking his internal dialogue.

"Sorry," he said. "Wanted to make sure I've covered everything." He leaned onto the table with his elbows. "This is where I tell you whether or not I think I can help you. Based on what you've told me, what you remember, and the dreams you've had, I'd like to keep working with you. I think there is a good chance we can get your memories back, provided there isn't too much neural damage. There are a few tests to take if you want to continue."

Daith's forehead wrinkled. "What kinds of tests?"

"Nothing to be concerned about—motor skills, short-term and

long-term quizzes, sensory stimulation, things of that nature. The tests will check other areas of your brain to make sure there isn't any damage. For example, some of the memory tests deal with smells or sounds to trigger responses, so if there is an issue with those areas, we won't pursue them."

Dru tapped on his datapad. "Even if the test results are positive, you will still have to put in a lot of hard work. I don't know what memories you might uncover. Some could be painful. You could also experience headaches, poor sleep, and, lucky for me," he said, "irritability. And even if your brain functions are normal, I can't promise you'll get any memories back."

"I understand, but I'd rather take the chance then wait around and hope something happens on its own."

"Good. I'm going to put some things together and talk to Commander Xiven. We can meet tomorrow morning to begin the tests." Dru gathered his notes to leave.

"Wait."

Though only a verbal command, Dru felt a strange fluctuation in her energy—pulling on him to stay. His whole body tingled. He'd never felt such an instant connection with someone, although she didn't even seem aware she'd done anything.

"What is it?" he asked.

Her dark green eyes peered straight into his, determined. "I need some questions answered."

Dru paused, uncomfortable. "I'm not sure what kind of answers I can give."

"How am I supposed to learn about who I was if no one will tell me anything? I feel like this place is a vault." She folded her hands on the table. "And where am I? I mean, what planet are we on?"

"Planet?" Dru asked, settling back into his chair. "We're not on a planet. We're on a space ship called the *Horizon.* Both it and my ship, the *Reminiscence*, are docked at Spaceport C-Twenty-seven. If you decide to work with me, I'll stay on board the *Horizon* and travel with you."

"Where are we going?"

"Uh," Dru said, apologetic. "I don't actually know. I haven't accepted the position yet so I haven't been told. I guess you'll have to ask the Commander."

"So is this spaceport we're on close to other planets? Like my homeworld?"

"I don't think we're really near any populated areas, but...what's your home planet called?"

Daith bit her lip. "I thought—I thought Commander Xiven told me. He *must* have. But I can't remember an actual name. My home was whatever planet they rescued me from during the attack."

Attack? "I'm not sure what you mean."

"Commander Xiven told me I was attacked, which is the reason for my memory loss. He said a stray shot grazed my head."

"He didn't tell me anything about an attack."

Puzzlement crossed her face. "I figured he would have told you how the memory loss happened."

Me too. "I'm sure he'll fill me in, but maybe he decided to wait until I took the position."

"Oh, well tell me more about this space station. Are there other ships docked here besides your own? Can I search through it? How can I find out about what happened to my family after they were killed? Can I go visit my home once security isn't an issue anymore?"

Dru shook his head, not to refuse her questions, but to deny her the answers. "I can't tell you anything—at least, not yet. I understand the urge to want to see things and touch things which may trigger your memories, but we don't have access right now. What we *can* do is work on our tests until then. I'll find out what I can from

Commander Xiven about your circumstances and we can go from there."

Daith pursed her lips.

"I know this is aggravating," Dru said, "and I know it's a lot to ask, but please trust in me. I promise I know what I'm doing." He paused. "So we will meet tomorrow then? Same time in this room?"

"Do we have to wait so long?"

"Unfortunately, yes. I have several things I need to sort out first. Besides, working too hard too fast can actually stress the situation and make us backtrack. Progress may seem slow, especially at first, but I promise, this is the best route to take."

She let out a sigh. "All right."

"Thank you. And have a good evening, Daith."

* * *

Daith left, waving to Dru as he headed the opposite way down the corridor. Once out of sight, she changed direction and went back to the conference room. She peeked around, making sure no one witnessed her, and slipped back inside. The door slid closed behind her, the harsh lights flickered on, shining on emptiness. Daith ignored the chairs and made her way to the back of the room, to a console in the wall she'd noticed during her meeting with Dru. She didn't want to wait another moment, much less a whole day, without knowing who she was.

Her palms prickled with perspiration.

Technically no one had told her she couldn't use the ship's computer to search for information about herself, but she had a feeling if she asked, she'd be told it was 'classified' or 'off limits for security reasons.'

Timidly, she touched the screen several times, leaving moist fingerprints on the darkened surface, but the display remained off. She frowned and tapped harder.

"Come on," she muttered. She noticed a small, white button on the lower left-hand side of the console. With a tap, the screen hummed to life.

Eager, she prepared to search through the databases to find out about the ship she was on, its crew, and anything about her home planet.

To her disappointment, the only thing splayed across the screen was a blinking box, asking for a security code.

She cursed under her breath.

"Can I help you?"

Daith whirled around at the words. To her horror, Lieutenant Koye stood in the open doorway.

"N-no," she stammered. "I'm fine." She used her body to block the lit screen.

Koye glanced around the room, his dark eyes narrowed in suspicion. "Where is Commander Xiven?"

"Oh, him," she said, waving toward the door. "He and Dru left."

Koye glanced over his shoulder, taking the bait. Daith quickly hit the white button again and the console turned off.

"I don't see them."

Daith trotted away from the wall, giving what she hoped was an innocent grin. "Well, I mean, they left a couple of standard minutes ago. I needed to think about everything we talked about. Dru said I could stay in here for a bit until I wanted to return to my room, which," she said, squeezing past him through the doorway, "I think I'll do right now. Have a good evening!" Daith raced down the corridor, feeling Koye's glare follow her the entire way.

Back in the safety of her quarters she let out the breath she'd been holding. Finding out information alone wasn't going to work.

Somehow, she had to get someone's password.

* * *

After he'd waved goodbye to Daith, Dru headed down a floor to Trey's office. *I'll want to start with some sensory triggers—see if those prompt any memories. And perhaps emotional stimuli to instigate any of her suppressed abilities. I could have sworn she spoke to me with her thoughts before—but maybe she actually said them out loud....* Dru rang the chimes and the door to his brother's office opened.

Perhaps other emotional reactions would also stimulate her? Powerful ones—anger or pain? If only I could speak with Jacin Jaxx again! His knowledge would be invaluable. But with his death, all of his secrets died with him....

"... are you listening to me?"

Dru blinked away from his own thoughts. "Sorry?"

Trey's jaw tightened. "In your own head again? Some things never change." He gestured roughly to the chair across from him. "I asked how things went with Daith."

"Quite well," Dru said, taking a seat. He glanced at Trey's timereader, surprised three standard hours had passed. He was glad he'd chosen to wait until the following day to do more work. "I've decided to help her and she has agreed. I've started to plan out sessions to optimize both memory resurfacing and ability stimulation."

"Ah. About that. I need you to see if she has Jacin Jaxx's abilities without her memories resurfacing."

Dru blinked slowly. "Wait. You *don't* want her memories to return?"

"It is a delicate and physically demanding process to eliminate memories. I'd hate to have to subject her to the M.M. again."

Dru dug through his memories of history class. "You can't mean a Memory Machine. The ones the Chears used over three hundred years ago? They'd all been commissioned for destruction."

"I managed to acquire a broken one and fixed it." He scowled at his brother. "Wipe that disdain off your face. It will be destroyed when I'm done. I have no desire to deal with Central Authority."

"And you used it to erase her memories?"

"Erased is such a harsh word. Let's say we suppressed them, temporarily of course. The M.M. does have the ability to restore memories again."

"Why bother removing them in the first place?"

Trey's smile was tight. "Well if you were Jacin Jaxx's offspring and somebody came up to you and said 'Hello! I used to work for Jacin Jaxx and wondered if you were his daughter', you'd probably be a little reluctant to say 'Of course I am!' Especially with all of the anti-Aleet Army groups still out there. The army may have disbanded years ago, but there's no reason why someone wouldn't still search for a remnant of Jacin Jaxx's bloodline."

"Like you."

Trey scoffed at the harshness of his brother's insinuation. "Yes, but unlike those other groups, I want to preserve it. I want to protect this girl so she'll never have to worry about being hunted again. Helping her is the least I can do after what her father did for us."

"I can't believe anyone else is looking for her. Once Jacin died, I hadn't even thought about the rest of his family."

Trey looked at him with pity, like he'd found a lost pet. "You may not have thought about them, but I assure you, others have. Do you think the Controllers stopped their search when Jacin died? They knew about his daughters. I'd been monitoring their searches and I can guarantee I'm not the only one who still had an interest in

Jacin's offspring. Daith deserves the chance to live a normal life."

"Who says she wasn't doing fine?"

Trey showed his brother a datapad, its shiny surface catching the room's harsh light. "I tracked what she'd been doing and mostly, she'd been in hiding. She changed her last name and moved with her sister to a planet her father never influenced. You truly believe she could live a normal life, even after Jacin's death? How could she ever tell anyone who she really is? She would have to hide her gifts, always afraid they might come out, and someone would connect her to her father. No, I can't believe she would want that kind of life."

Dru hesitated, his stomach uneasy. "Shouldn't she choose?"

"She will," Trey reassured. "I told you, the memory effects are only temporary. I want her to see what life could be like, free to be herself, without judgment, without running, without fear. Then I'll restore her memories and she can decide what she wants to do."

"And if she happens to want to lead what's left of the Aleet Army, you wouldn't have any objections?" Dru asked, haughty.

"If she decides to pursue a cause like her father's, I would be honored to serve her. You know how much potential he had. We could give his daughter the chance he never had, a second chance for her to have her own life."

A second chance... Dru's thoughts churned, desperately searching for a way to rationalize the erasure of Daith's memories. His only defense stemmed from Trey showing him she'd been wasting her gifts. With others hunting her, she could never live up to her full potential.

"I'll need to know what story you've told her." He ignored the hard knot of unease in his stomach.

Trey grinned. "I knew I could count on you, Brother. You will receive a full report soon."

Chapter 8

DAITH WOKE THE next morning in darkness. She'd been dreaming again—the same dream at first. Swirling dust, an unbearable heat. Someone grabbing her. Only this time the images shifted. She'd stood in front of the computer console in the meeting room and had the password to gain access, but her fingers wouldn't push in the correct sequence. Alarms blared. She knew she could finally find out who she was if she could only get access to the computer....

Daith rubbed her eyes as the remnants of her unsatisfying sleep slid away. She blinked until she registered her surroundings.

A space ship docked at a space station.

Her pulse quickened, and a desperate need to see prickled across her in a chilled wave.

"Lights. Computer, lights."

The room's lights faded up, bathing her in harsh pools of bright white. She was still in the same room, in the same bed.

Metallic. Cold.

Foreign.

And yet somehow she felt comforted. The familiar room reassured her. Her fear revolved around finding herself somewhere she didn't know, lost once again.

Frustration rolled through her. Would she always feel this way? Would she wake every morning terrified until the lights came on, afraid she wouldn't know where she was or how she'd gotten there?

Daith sat up, thoughts pulsing through her mind. Her dream remained with her, reminding her she didn't know who she was, that she might never know. She stood and rubbed her hands against each other, on her thighs, across her arms. She felt uncomfortable in her own skin, stuck inside a foreign body, a foreign room. She was terrified, alone. Trapped with nothing but her own thoughts.

The room, though moments ago a refreshing sight, filled her with fear. How could she know what to do, how to act, what to think, when she couldn't even trust herself? The gray walls seemed to bend toward her, pushing at her from all sides, restricting, confining.

Daith hopped into her jumpsuit and bolted out the door, dashing down a set of nearby stairs.

She strode down the long, dim corridor with no destination. Her bare feet padded quietly, an unfitting contrast to the pounding of her heart. She felt as if she couldn't breathe, imagining the stale, recycled air around her. What if something went wrong? What if an air seal broke?

Full-blown panic threatened to engulf her. She needed to see someone else, to know she wasn't alone, but the hallways remained void of life.

Daith paused when she reached a T-intersection. Straight ahead appeared the same as behind, but her left opened into a widened hallway, with two huge, white doors on either side of each wall. She didn't know where she was. Would she be able to find her way back to her quarters? Where *was* everyone?

Daith approached the first of the doors, hoping someone might be inside. Hand poised to knock, a soft chime startled her. The noise came from an access panel set in the wall next to the door. A disembodied female voice spoke.

"Welcome to simulation room one."

Silence.

"Um—hello?" Daith said.

"Welcome to simulation room one," the voice repeated. "Please select a program."

"Program? Program for what?"

A moment of silence. "Welcome to simulation room one. Please select a program."

A simulation room? "What types of programs are there?" she asked.

The access panel next to her lit up.

"Academics, Exercise, Leisure, Sports, Training, Custom." Daith scrolled down and selected 'Exercise.' A new list emerged, longer than the first. "Aerobics, Acrobatics, Calisthenics..." Daith trailed off. She clicked on 'Aerobics' and a third list appeared. "Another list? Are you serious?"

The computer responded to her rhetorical question. "Program not recognized. Please restate program request."

Daith let out a sigh. Her body itched with anxious energy. She needed to expel her unease and calming down didn't seem to be an option. "How about jogging track?"

"Color scheme preference?"

Daith rubbed her face. "I don't care."

"Track length?"

"Doesn't matter."

"Location preference?"

Bitterness seeped into her response. "Listen, I don't know. I don't remember anywhere so how can I have a preference?"

"Program not recognized. Please restate—"

"Sorry. I get it," Daith interrupted. "No location preference."

"Stock parameters for color scheme, length, and location have been recorded. Program installation will take two point four standard minutes. Do you wish to proceed?"

"Yeah."

"Please enter when ready."

The large door opened and Daith stepped into a large, white, empty room. The sound of rushing air signaled the door closing and her breath caught in her throat.

The room melted.

The white walls oozed like liquid, wet and slick. Swatches of blue color ran down the sides of the walls, like the ship's blood. The walls filled with blue and Daith noticed the same thing happened to the floor, except the surface filled with gray, surrounded by a white track. Thick, lighter blue squares appeared in the center of the floor—stretching mats for warm-ups.

Daith stood in awe. "Computer?" she whispered.

The soft chimes rang.

"Please select a program."

Daith cleared her throat. "I would like to pick a color scheme preference."

Silence.

"Um, I would like red walls and a black track."

"New parameters have been set. Program installation will take one point two standard minutes."

The chimes rang again—the walls bled red and the floor swelled with pools of ink.

Daith still just stood there. "This is crazy. I must be dreaming." She took a seat on one of the mats in the center, soft, yet firm. She had no idea how this could be possible.

The room astounded her. She could wish herself anywhere. But where? She didn't know any place but here. As soon as she knew her home planet, she would come here to see it.

Chimes rang. Startled, she glanced around, but saw no one. Opening her mouth to ask the computer what the chimes meant, she snapped it closed when her surroundings changed.

The red walls crumpled and bunched into shapes like beige rocks. Shrubs and bushes pushed through the floor at her feet. The mats turned fluid and dissolved back into the floor while the black track changed into a long, dirt path—its smooth surface replaced by tiny granules of dirt and rock. The far wall pushed back to reveal the path's destination. Disorientation hit her as the room expanded.

The dirt path led through a small copse of trees straight to the edge of a cliff. Daith stood and cautiously advanced to the lip. She thought she'd hit the wall, but she never reached it. Before her lay a huge, green pasture. On her right, a large waterfall cascaded down the side of the cliff, beginning a long, sparkling river that cut straight through the field. Her left revealed thousands of flowers and trees, showing a mix of greens, pinks, and blues. Their sweet, airy scent filled her nose. Daith watched small rainbows appear through each drop of water from the raging waterfall. Everything seemed so real. She didn't understand it, but she felt like she'd been transported to an actual place.

Had the computer read her mind? Had it somehow created her home? Is this where she'd lived?

Lost in the moment, Daith didn't register anyone behind her until she felt a hand on her shoulder. Surprised, she turned and shrieked, instinctively striking the figure.

Daith put her hand to her mouth in horror. Commander Xiven stood there, hand on his nose, and peered at her through watery eyes.

"I'm so sorry!"

Xiven waved his free hand in dismissal. "It's my fault for barging in without notice. The system wasn't locked so I thought someone had left a program running."

"Are you okay?"

"I'll be fine. Remind me to show you how to lock off the system." Xiven wiggled his nose, wincing. "You've got some reflexes."

"I didn't know I had them." Daith paused, turning back toward the view. "Commander Xiven, what—"

"Call me Trey. Please."

"Okay, Trey." She turned her attention back to the scene. "What is this place?"

"This is my home world, Sintaur. It's one of the smaller planets in the Fracc system."

Daith watched jewel-toned flying creatures flit through the waterfall, their four sets of wings catching and tipping the droplets into the mouths of large, yellow, plants below. "It's beautiful."

"I created this program a few years ago to preserve my memory of it. Sintaur's landscape has changed considerably."

"What do you mean?"

He stepped out next to her. The trees hummed with a low vibration—their black and gold leaves quivering in the sunlight. "This was my planet before civil war destroyed it." Trey reached up and rubbed one of the golden leaves between his fingers. When he released it, the residual marks turned a shade of russet.

"It didn't happen all at once," he continued, his gaze overlooking the cliff. "First, soldiers patrolled the streets. A curfew for citizens went into effect. Then non-native species were forced from their homes. The Manach and Grassuwerian families, my mother, brother, and I lived with, were kicked out of our building."

While Trey spoke, Daith could envision the episode—doors of houses burst open, civilians pulled from their homes, the streets littered with bodies of those who wouldn't cooperate. Though she didn't know anything about Sintaur, she could picture the landscape in her head, as if there. Tears clouded her vision.

"Later in the year," Trey went on, "the government passed a law requiring civilians to open up their homes. Give supplies to any soldier. We offered what we could, but eventually we ran out." His face went blank.

"They dragged my mother outside to 'punish' her," he continued. "My punishment entailed listening. My father was dead and with my mother now—gone—my brother and I were taken and placed in separate family care. The actual combat started when I was sixteen. I was 'recruited' to fight."

Once again Daith could *see* what Trey spoke of—distant sounds of gunfire, a sickness released by the enemy that decimated the camps, leaving so many scar-marked bodies in the fields the soldiers were forced to abandon them. The images churned her stomach.

"I left the planet when the war ended four standard years later."

Daith released a slow breath.

Trey's head twitched at the sound and he snapped out of his memories. "I'm sorry. I don't know why I—" Trey peered into Daith's tear-rimmed eyes. "It just came out." Trey's face flushed. "I didn't mean to interrupt your use of the simulation room."

"It's okay," she said, brushing roughly at the wetness. She wanted to say she didn't mind the company, but he'd already turned his back to her.

As he left he told the computer to restore the image of the circular track. The beautiful scene vanished. He hadn't even shown her how to lock off the program.

What was that about? Daith couldn't find an answer. Here was a man who seemed in control of everything and he'd told her his life story.

I'm glad he's not lying to me anymore.

The thought came easily. When he'd spoken to her before about her situation, she'd felt uneasy, with a knotted stomach. But this time it felt different. Like a wave had come off of him and pulsed through her.

She brushed away the notion.

"I'm just imagining things."

* * *

Trey sat down behind his desk and smacked himself across the face. The noise echoed in the empty room.

"What is the matter with you?" he asked himself. "Telling your life story to some girl you don't even know? Quit being soft. Softness is weakness. Attachment is weakness." He slammed his fists on the table, bruising the sides of his wrists. "Each time you feel yourself losing control remind yourself of what happened to Jacin. He went soft, weak, and look where he ended up. You have too much riding on this plan for you to fail now. Suck it up!"

Trey kept his hands clenched into fists for a few more moments before unfurling them with a loud exhale. He reviewed the ship's engine modifications to see how soon they would be ready to leave. His head pounded as he read the specs, the harsh light in his office piercing into his eyes.

Trey's eyelids closed and he willed the pain to go away. He put his hands over his ears, resting his elbows on the desk, but the throbbing continued. Lowering his head, he crossed his arms and rested his forehead against the coolness of his skin. He didn't have time to rest, but if he could at least get the headache to leave...

Trey was in a haze. He'd fallen asleep. But the dream of the moments before Jacin's death didn't happen. Like the last time. Some other part of Jacin's life....

Jacin's heart raced while he waited for the vidlink call to go through. He'd recently gotten out of the hospital after healing the student's heart from his class. The episode had caused him to slip into unconsciousness and he'd awoken the following day under medical care. His wife had been there, worried sick, but Jacin hadn't told her the truth about what happened. How could he? Elor would think he'd lost his sanity.

No, he needed to figure out what had happened first before he told anyone else.

Even with the house empty—Elor had taken the girls shopping—Jacin had still crammed himself inside their washroom, vidlink monitor perched precariously on his lap, the heat from its energy source warming his legs through his thin trousers.

A pale green, heavyset creature appeared on the viewscreen. Its bulbous eyes blinked so rapidly Jacin dizzied.

"Are you—?" Jacin had barely gotten the words out of his mouth when an excruciatingly loud buzz filled his skull. Teeth rattling, Jacin's hands flew to his head. He screamed. As abruptly, the noise, and the pain, stopped.

"A thousand apologies!" the heavyset creature cried out. "It's been so long since I've been contacted by a non-connecter I'm afraid I forgot to connect vocally."

"It's all right," Jacin said, massaging his temples.

"I am delighted to receive your communications, Teacher Jacin Jaxx. Now, what can I do for you Teacher Jacin Jaxx?" the creature asked.

Jacin picked up on the repeated use of his name, which he knew held a lot of importance. "Well, Connected Counselor Imah of Tela," Jacin said, "During my research for a history class, I came across a study on a telepath. The study claimed the subject had healed another using telepathy. Since your planet is known for teaching telepaths, I wondered if you know of any record of this?"

"Oh, yes, Teacher Jacin Jaxx. We can connect and heal or soothe anyone in distress. Our minds can link to the thoughts of others, understand their process, and offer support and relief."

Jacin corrected himself. "I'm sorry Counselor, I meant physical healing."

Counselor Imah seemed to think about the concept before he spoke. "Physical healing through the connected use of the mind is not possible. The mind is not able to make the jump between energy wavelengths and physical change. I'm afraid the information you uncovered is false."

Jacin thanked the Counselor for his time and disconnected the call. His fingers trembled as he set the vidlink machine aside. Telepathy was uncommon in the Eomix galaxy, and most who possessed the talent originated from the planet Tela—or were sent there for training. Jacin thought for certain if anyone could answer his questions about how he'd been able to heal his student, it would be someone from Tela.

Except Counselor Imah said that type of energy transfer wasn't possible.

But Jacin knew the energy shift could happen. He'd done the process with the girl in the class, when he'd healed her heart....

Trey snapped awake, his arm sporting a large, circular red mark which he assumed matched one on his forehead. The dream had been vivid—like a memory—like the one where Jacin saved the girl. But why? He'd only ever seen the memory right before Jacin's death. Why was he seeing these earlier images now?

Trey thought back to when he'd had the first new dream. The change had occurred shortly after Daith's arrival on his ship. Had she somehow triggered the rest of Jacin's memories?

Why had Jacin given them to Trey in the first place? Unless the memories were for a purpose. Maybe to teach him about Jacin's gifts. If this ability to make the jump from mental energy to physical change was so rare, then Daith might be a bigger prize than Trey could ever have imagined.

Trey made the decision there and then to stop taking the dream-deflector pills. He needed to see the rest of these memories, to learn from them, and determine how to use what happened to Jacin to control Daith.

Chapter 9

TREY'S EYES STUNG at the harsh lights of the meeting room. He shook away the lingering grogginess. Having these dreams felt like he hadn't slept at all. Now wholly awake and trying to focus on the day, he questioned his decision to stop taking them. If they were messages from Jacin, he didn't want to miss them, but if they were simply memory echoes from Jacin's life with no meaning—Trey didn't have time to not be fully alert.

The decision would have to wait. Right now he had other things to concentrate on.

Daith sat patiently at the end of the oval table. Trey noticed how even the harsh lighting in the room brought out the highlights of her dark hair. She really was stunning, and if things had been different, if he had time, maybe....

He took a seat and shook the notion from his head. She couldn't be anything more than, than what? His protégé? His tool? His gift to the galaxy?

"Good afternoon, Daith."

"Hello," she said, eyebrow raised. Her gaze peered behind him. "I thought I was meeting Dru?"

"You are. I wanted to check in on you. I left you quite abruptly this morning in the simulation room."

"I'm fine." Daith chewed on her lower lip. "I'm really sorry again."

Trey smiled and touched his face gingerly. "I assure you, it's not bad."

"I really don't know what happened, Commander—"

"Trey," he insisted.

"Trey," Daith corrected.

"You have natural reflexes. It's not a bad thing. Besides, I felt awkward enough myself."

Silence hung in the air as they remembered his verbal purge of his past.

"Dru should be along in a minute," Trey told her to fill the space. He wasn't even sure why he'd shown up. His brother was only going to ask him to leave, and yet, he couldn't help but want to see Daith after what had happened. He wanted to explain he wasn't usually like that—he didn't normally blurt out his life story to a complete stranger. But he couldn't say anything. Embarrassment that the outburst had happened at all kept him quiet.

The two of them waited in silence—Daith absentmindedly picking at her fingernails—until Dru came into the room. He paused and registered Trey's presence. "Morning, Commander."

"Morning. I wanted to check in on Daith and wait with her until you arrived." The lie was flimsy even to Trey.

"Very thoughtful of you," Dru said slowly.

Careful to keep his face neutral, Trey let a slow anger fill his chest. Dru might be superior now, but things would be different soon enough. "All right then," Trey said, doing his best not to snarl the words. "Is there anything else I can help you with?"

"Not that I can think of."

"I think I'm fine," Daith added. She put her hand on Trey's arm. "I—"

"I'll leave you two alone then," Trey said, pulling away. "Call me if you need anything."

Trey paused outside the room after the door closed and let out a deep breath. He didn't know what Daith would say—probably another apology—but he couldn't stand her mentioning anything about what they'd discussed earlier.

Not in front of his brother.

* * *

Dru mentally sorted through what he'd read in Trey's report. The details included the assassination attempt and the reason for Daith's memory loss, but he hadn't found any indication why someone tried to kill her. The report ended with a note stating her home had been destroyed and her family murdered.

Dru had struggled all night with his decision to work with Daith. He didn't enjoy the idea of lying to her about how she lost her memories, since, as her doctor, he would need to establish a bond of trust, but maybe her recovery would be better this way. With a clean slate, she now had the chance to live whatever life she wanted without her father's actions hanging over her. And if she did possess his abilities, she would be able to learn about them in the company of those who wouldn't judge her for her father's mistakes.

Mistakes? More like catastrophic blunders.

He'd finally decided none of his thoughts mattered unless she had Jacin's abilities. But first he had to get her to open up.

"How are you feeling today?" Dru asked.

"Fine." Her tone was clipped and she laced her hands together on her lap.

"Did you sleep all right?"

"I guess. I woke up early this morning, though. Couldn't get back to sleep."

"How come?"

Daith shrugged.

Still guarded. "Dreams?"

Daith nodded.

"What did you dream about?" Dru pulled the datapad closer to take notes.

Daith pinched her eyebrows together, skeptical. "You really want to talk about my dreams? Don't you want to ask if I've remembered anything yet?"

"Have you remembered anything yet?"

Daith pursed her lips. "No."

Dru gave her a half-smile. "I didn't think so. What did you dream about?"

"You don't have to be smug about it."

The smile vanished. "I'm sorry. You're right. I guess my bedside manner is a little weak."

Daith hesitated before answering. "The dream is pretty hazy. I only remember intense heat and someone grabbing at me and—," she stuttered. "I don't know. Nothing else I guess."

Dru wondered at the break. Could she be holding something back? "Maybe you're trying to remember what happened right before you came here—a ship landing and Commander Xiven's crew taking you on board?"

"I thought you didn't know what happened to me?"

"Commander Xiven sent me a copy of the report last night."

"Oh."

"It seems like your mind is trying to reconstruct some events of your life. This could help narrow my choices for tests. Let's first try to access these memories, or dreams, for now."

A pause, filled only with the constant background noise of the air recycling system. Dru watched Daith's shoulders fall, her hands unclasp.

"So what's the next step?" she asked.

"There is a series of memory-retrieval techniques I've had high success with when dealing with dreams. I'd like to start you on those. They place you into a semi-conscious state where we maintain verbal communication. It's similar to dreaming, except we can talk to each other. What do you think?"

"Is it dangerous?"

"Not in the least. If at any time while we are working the outcome exceeds the safety parameters, the program ends."

Daith thought for a few moments. She inhaled deeply and let the breath out slowly. "Let's do it."

"Great. We'll use simulation room one."

"I'm familiar with it," she said with a small smile.

"Good. I will need a couple of days to set up the programming."

Daith's body tightened. "Two days?"

"I'm afraid the simulation program is a bit complicated, not to mention connecting the system's computers with my sensory-data collecting program. I know it seems like a long time, but—"

"It's fine," Daith said abruptly.

Dru sensed a prickling on the back of his neck. "All right then. Over the next two nights I'd like you to relax your whole body before you go to sleep. Give your muscles and mind the opportunity to slow down. The process should increase the chance of dreams, which could help us. Shall we say, two days from now at the same time in simulation room one?" Dru asked, rising from his chair.

Daith agreed.

"I'll see you then." Dru exited and headed toward Trey's office. Once inside, he was surprised at his brother's reaction.

"She's been having dreams?" Trey asked.

"Yes," Dru said, confused by his alarm. "But so far they are a bunch of garbled images."

Trey rose from his desk and paced. "Listen, we can't have her memories resurface through her dreams. Talk to Doctor Ludd and see if he can start her on some dream-deflector pills. I don't want to risk having to run her through the M.M. again."

"Dream-deflector pills? I've never had a patient use them."

"They are...experimental, but work incredibly well."

"Do they have any side effects I should be aware of?" Dru asked.

"No," Trey told him, and then paused. "Perhaps heightened anxiety or irritability."

"Those shouldn't pose a problem. I'll talk to Doctor Ludd later today about starting her on those pills."

"Good. And make sure when you give them to her, she doesn't know what they really are. Tell her...tell her they are needed for some medical purpose, to help with your program."

"Fine," Dru said. He left the room, his stomach queasy at the thought of more lies.

* * *

Dru headed toward the medical treatment room to speak with Dr. Ludd, his mind heavy with thoughts. This whole situation seemed wrong to him somehow, and yet everything Trey had told him made sense.

Dru rang the chimes for Dr. Ludd's office and the door slid

open.

Dr. Ludd's lipless mouth spread into a huge, floppy grin. "Ah, Doctor, how good it is to see you again." He hovered around his desk to greet Dru, his body wobbling on the gravlift.

"It's been a long time," Dru said.

Dr. Ludd slapped a flippered hand on Dru's shoulder. "It has. And what unusual, and if I may say so, horrifying circumstances, what with Jacin Jaxx's death and your visit with your brother and how you went your separate ways, but I assume things have progressed since you are here again working with him on such a highly sought-after project with Jacin's daughter, Daith, who seems like quite a lovely individual—"

"Yes, Doctor," Dru interrupted. He'd forgotten about how the doctor would continue to talk if not stopped. Dr. Ludd had explained the reason to him once—on his planet and in his native language, the spoken word was considered an art form. Individuals could go on for days describing something as simple as how they woke up in the morning. Dr. Ludd had told Dru when he'd learned Universal, the language which most of the planets in the Eomix galaxy learned for travel and commerce purposes, he'd found the mode of communication lacking. All the words seemed too short and didn't give enough detail for each situation. He'd said it explained why so many species argued—they never took the time to fully explore and give accurate details for each point of view.

"Commander Xiven sent me to pick up dream-deflector pills for Daith."

Dr. Ludd's pink, gelatinous face drooped. "Why?"

Surprised at the shortness of the question, Dru didn't answer right away. "Oh, um, he worries if she starts dreaming again, her memories will resurface. She'll be under the impression they are needed to help monitor her nervous system throughout my programs."

"Yes, of course, that makes sense and we don't want her memories to return, especially with everything we've done to ensure she doesn't have any memories of herself and her past, because that will make things easier for us—and her of course!—I didn't mean to say Commander Xiven doesn't know what he's doing, I mean after all he has done to reunite this cause and—" Dr. Ludd's mouth slapped closed.

Dru eyed him, suspicious. "Is something else going on Doctor?"

"What? No, of course not. I mean, even if there was, it's not my place to say anything. You should speak with the Commander if you want to know anything else and frankly I was merely letting my mouth run away with itself, not literally of course, but—"

"I understand," Dru said. "I can ask you this, however. Do you feel, as a physician, there is any way these pills will harm Daith?"

"Harm her? Not at all. She may be more susceptible to frustrating situations—quicker to irritability, less patience, things of that nature—but nothing to cause any physical or long-lasting damage." Dr. Ludd placed a bottle on the table. "She needs only to take one before bed each night."

Dru grasped the small bottle, lightweight in his hand. Somehow he'd expected the container to be heavy—like the thought of giving it to her.

Dr. Ludd gurgled to get Dru's attention.

"Doctor, Daith is a special woman."

"Yes, I know," Dru said.

"What I mean to say is, if you plan to take her down the road I believe she is to travel, no amount of dream-deflector pills will keep her memories from resurfacing."

Dru tucked the bottle into his pants pocket. "What do you mean?"

"As one of the only other individuals to work with Jacin Jaxx, I am aware of many of the abilities he had. Things you couldn't dream of, Doctor. And he had a way of knowing things he couldn't know."

"I know. It's called telepathy."

Dr. Ludd shook his head, his cheeks jiggling. "Beyond that. He knew things even if you weren't thinking about them. He knew things about others who weren't near him. And if Daith explores the same route, she *will* find out who she really is. And who we really are. Will Commander Xiven continue to run her through the Memory Machine each time? She will not stay ignorant forever."

Dru stood for a moment, unsure of how to respond. Dr. Ludd was right. Even if her own memories didn't return, she could become powerful enough to sense everyone's lies.

"It won't matter," Dru said. "Trey's only goal is to give her a chance to learn about her abilities without the stress of her past weighing in on her. Once she's established those skills, he plans to restore her memories and let her decide what she wants to do. She's never had that choice before."

Dr. Ludd's face returned to neutral. "I see. He told you he plans to return her memories. Well, then, my comments are unwarranted. Good luck with your sessions, Doctor. Please keep me updated on Daith's progress."

Not expecting such an abrupt dismissal, Dru waited for a bit before muttering a thank you and leaving the room. He headed toward Daith's quarters to give her the pills and wondered about the doctor's reaction. But perhaps Trey hadn't told Dr. Ludd his entire plan. He hadn't told Dru everything until he'd agreed to work with Daith. Trey had good reason not to trust everyone around him after the Aleet Army base's destruction. After such a betrayal, how could anyone blame Trey if he only sought out those who'd been with Jacin from the beginning, or who were young enough not to know much more than what the history vidlinks told them about Jacin Jaxx.

Dru rang the chimes to Daith's room. She answered, a tray of food propped precariously on the edge of her bed.

"Hey," she said, welcoming him in. "Did you forget something?"

"I did." He held up the small vial. "I picked these up from Doctor Ludd."

"What are they?"

"They contain a special dye that magnifies the nerve responses in your body," he said, feeding her the lie he'd concocted. "The equipment in my programs will monitor this to see how you are responding to the process. You'll need to take one before bed, but I need to build up an amount in your body, so I'd like you to start taking them tonight. Then, in about a week, you'll need to check in with Dr. Ludd."

Daith took the bottle. "Easy enough." At the comment the tray fell off the bed and splattered her meal on the floor.

"Oh, stars!" she swore.

Dru bent to help, but Daith brushed his attempt aside. "I'm okay," she said, her cheeks tinged with pink. Her beauty still held strong even through her embarrassment. "I can handle it. But thank you."

Dru straightened while she picked up the clumpy pieces from the carpet. "All right. See you in two days then. And good night."

"Night!"

Chapter 10

A DREAMLESS SLEEP left Daith feeling completely refreshed the following morning. Even though she knew her dreams could be memories trying to resurface, she enjoyed awakening without a film of sweat on her skin.

After washing quickly, Daith wondered what she should do with her day. She didn't have to meet Dru until the following morning and Trey hadn't given her any suggestions. What would she have normally done with her time? She had no clue. There were no inklings about hobbies or passions she enjoyed. Was she an artist? An athlete? Did she enjoy games or reading or…anything?

The dark cloud over her mind remained resolute. Daith had all this time on her hands with nothing but her own thoughts—which led her nowhere.

Her stomach gurgled unexpectedly.

Daith patted her belly, happy to have a distraction. "All right, you hungry monster. I'll order some food." She tapped the controls on the wall, but before she chose anything, she paused. Did everyone dine in their rooms? Or was there a place where everyone met to eat?

Daith called up the ships schematics on the panel. The vessel, which consisted of five floors, each spread out in cross-shaped patterns, indicated a mess hall located in the center of her floor.

Excited, Daith turned off the monitor and exited her quarters. She made her way to the center room. Several rows of tables stretched in front of her. A mix of spicy, fruity, and burnt smells filled her nostrils. The room wasn't packed with people, but quite a few small groups of crewmembers congregated in different sections. Perhaps the crew ate breakfast later? Or maybe they ate in shifts? Either way the design indicated the area could hold a lot more than this.

Following the worn trail of scuffed metal flooring, Daith made her way to what seemed to be an ordering counter. Green walls brought color into an otherwise gray-metallic room, but the harsh lighting gave everyone's skin a yellowish-green hue.

When she came up to the edge of the counter, a small creature, about a meter high, came over. The little being with three legs, was bright blue and covered with white bumps. Two long, flexible arms protruded from where the legs met. It had no apparent head; only a flattened top where all its legs met, like a three-legged stool. Many of these creatures flitted around in the background carrying large trays of food on their flattened heads.

It squeaked at her and handed her a datapad with a listing of food options, a larger variety than what she could order from her food chute in her quarters.

"I'll have the broiled kapari root soup, please."

The small being squeaked and rapped the datapad with its three stubby fingers.

"Oh, sorry." Daith tapped the soup she wanted and handed the datapad back. The creature chirped and scurried toward the kitchen.

Daith waited for a few standard minutes and the creature returned, the soup balanced comfortably on its head.

"Thanks." She took the soup and searched for a place to sit. One table sat four young men, who appeared to be about her age. They laughed while one of them told a story. The long, metal table could seat many more, so Daith approached with caution, nervous to ask to join them. A desperate feeling surged through her—loneliness. With no one to talk to and too much time on her own, Daith felt a need to reach out to someone.

And perhaps they'd be willing to help her gain access to the ship's computers.

She came up to the open end of the table and cleared her throat.

"Morning!" she said, her voice higher than usual.

The individual telling the story blinked his wide, blue eye in surprise. His large stinger swished behind him briefly before it settled back onto the floor. The other members of the group stared—one man briefly choked on his food, another paused mid-bite, juices from his sandwich dribbling down his chinless face.

"Mind if I join you?" she asked.

Each of them eyed the other, waiting for the other to take the lead.

"Of course, Miss Tocc," the storyteller finally said. "Although we were finishing up. Got to get back to work, you know."

"Yes," chimed in the one who'd choked, his voice wheezy. "I'm full."

The others nodded in agreement, standing quickly and clearing their dishes.

"Have a pleasant day," the storyteller said.

Daith remained standing, alone. She hadn't failed to notice most of their meals were only half-eaten.

A little put off, Daith wondered if perhaps they felt embarrassed by the story they were telling and didn't want her to join. Or maybe they really hadn't realized how much time had passed and didn't want to be late.

Still determined to meet someone, Daith set her sights on a young woman with bronze skin and short, reddish hair who sat eating alone, a datapad in her hand.

"Good morning," Daith said as she approached. The woman's amber eyes widened considerably when she noticed Daith.

"Miss Tocc," she stammered. She dropped her datapad into her vegetable mash, coating the back with purple clumps.

"I'm sorry. I didn't mean to startle you."

"No, no, it's fine." The woman picked up the datapad from her food and wiped the mess off with a cloth. "I didn't expect—I mean you're here—I mean it's fine you're here...."

"I wanted to ask if I could join you," Daith said, trying to salvage the situation. "Miss...?"

"Ikar. Cadet Ishia Ikar."

Daith put her soup down on the table. "Pleasure to meet you, Cadet Ikar."

Cadet Ikar's stared at the soup. "Oh, um, the thing is, Miss Tocc, I'm really busy with this report and, not to be rude, but I would rather eat alone."

Daith watched Cadet Ikar cringe at the end of her statement.

"No problem. I understand," Daith said, picking up her soup. She heard the cadet let out a breath. "Perhaps another time?"

Cadet Ikar swallowed hard and a hesitant grin touched her lips. "Of course," she said.

With quick steps, Daith moved away, troubled. That encounter also seemed unusual. But perhaps Cadet Ikar worried about offending her. And she had seemed busy.

Deciding not to push her bad luck a third time, Daith sat away from any other crewmembers and ate her soup alone. If her answers lay inside the ship's computer and she needed an access code to get to them, a connection with someone on board would be necessary. But even though everyone seemed to know her, no one would talk to her.

When she'd finished, she brought her bowl to the front and turned to leave. As she did, she spotted two other individuals congregated around Cadet Ikar, speaking softly. One of them glimpsed over at Daith and quickly averted her gaze.

A blush crept into her cheeks and Daith left the mess hall quickly and returned to her quarters. She felt herself wishing Dru was around. She didn't know him well, but he'd been the only one so far who hadn't treated her with…what, exactly? Fear?

Daith let out a sharp breath. What was everyone's problem? *She'd* been attacked, right? Why did everyone act like she was some sort of disease to avoid?

Anger swelled inside Daith's chest. A slow warmth, like a flaming ember, burned in the pit of her stomach. *I just want to find out who I am and get off this stupid space station and go home.* Why bother wishing? There wasn't even a home for her to go back to.

Daith left her quarters. She didn't want to be there, alone, again. But no one wanted to be around her. She wouldn't see Dru until the next morning and she knew Trey was extremely busy. Wandering brought her back to the simulation rooms. Simulation room 3 appeared empty. She took a seat on the white floor.

"Please select a program."

Daith thought for a moment before she answered the computer. "The planet Sintaur, please." She felt like sitting beside the huge waterfall Trey had shown her, letting the spray wash away some of her thoughts.

"Program will take three point four standard minutes to load."

Daith closed her eyes and breathed deeply, trying to regain some sense of calm. Frustration bubbled inside her. She wanted to remember something—anything—about her life, her home, her family.

"Program complete."

Daith opened her eyes and brought her hand to her mouth in horror.

"Computer?" she whispered. "Is this the planet Sintaur?"

"Correct. This is the most recent image capture of the capital city, Wolina."

Daith peered over the same cliff edge she'd been with Trey. The waterfall still lay to her right, water cascading into the valley beneath. But everything appeared horribly different.

The water itself, now brown and dingy, pooled below at half the volume of before. The golden-leafed trees at the base were gone, replaced by rotten stumps which stuck up from the ground. The remaining grass in the valley was charred, but most had been paved over with large slabs of gray concrete, creating a crude road. Birds didn't fly. Insects remained out of sight. The whole place was quiet, except for the sound of rushing water and loud bangs in the distance. Daith peered into the horizon. A multitude of buildings silhouetted, shrouded in a low, gray cloud of smog.

Daith lowered her hand from her face and pushed herself up. How terrible for Trey to know the change to his homeworld. No wonder he'd created the other program, holding on to the memory of what things were like before Sintaur's civil war.

"Computer, end program."

The scene vanished before her, enveloping her once again in whiteness and silence.

She left the simulation room, heading back to her quarters. Could this be why Trey had withheld information about Daith's own home? To prevent her from feeling the pain when she witnessed her house in ruins?

Along the way, another crewmember approached, this one again close to her age, but with dark skin and ripples of long, yellow twisted hair hanging behind his head. His three eyes widened at the sight of her, and he moved himself closer to the opposite wall, scuttling past on pincer-shaped legs.

Daith entered her room, scowling, and kicked the wall beneath the console. What was going on here? Everyone seemed terrified of her. How would she ever learn about herself if she couldn't find out on her own—or ask someone else for help?

She couldn't access the ship's computer without a password. She couldn't get a password out of anyone because no one would come near her.

Her pale arm streaked through the air as she pummeled the bed's pillow.

The only one she got any real information from was Dru. At least he didn't cringe at her mere presence.

Daith plopped on the bed, her legs tucked underneath her body, and wrapped the gray sheet around her slim shoulders. If she wanted to find anything, she needed to start with Dru.

Chapter 11

BREATHE. JUST BREATHE.

Dru repeated these words while he paced. He'd finished setting up the final parameters for his program a standard hour ago and had been waiting outside simulation room 1 for Daith to arrive. He didn't want to get too excited, but if she really was Jaxx's daughter...

Breathe. Just breathe. Breathe. Just—

Daith came around the corner and flashed him a smile. His nerves jolted and melted at the same time.

Dru motioned toward the door. "Shall we?" The two of them stepped into the empty white room.

"Computer," Dru said, "activate program X-Dru-one." The walls seemed to pull away from them and left black, empty space behind. Pinpoints of light poked through the blackness. Dru heard Daith gasp. The floor beneath them melted into the gaseous ring of a planet. Swirls of lavender and silver from the planet's surface flickered across their faces.

"Sometimes I forget how realistic these simulations can be. And how beautiful," Dru said. Daith's dark green eyes absorbed her surroundings, hand held lightly against her chest, the colors dancing across her skin.

A flush crept throughout his body and Dru cleared his throat, surprised by his strong reaction to her beauty. He hadn't felt such a physical response to someone since Riel. Physically they didn't resemble each other at all, although they both had strong energy. Dru pushed the thoughts of his recent loss away, knowing he had to stay professional, and that pain would only distract him. "Ready to begin?"

Daith wrung her hands. "I suppose so."

"This program is designed to interpret your brain-wave patterns. The computer will record those patterns through these," he said, holding up two, small white pads. He secured them to her temples, brushing her hair off her forehead so the pads' adhesive wouldn't catch any stray strands. His skin tingled at the contact—the energy from her already strong and at the surface.

"Once we start," Dru continued, "the computer will monitor and record your mental energy output. I will then ask you to do a series of five tasks. The simulation will change based on your responses."

"I'm going to pretend I know what that means," Daith said.

Dru patted her shoulder reassuringly. "Lie down and relax. If you ever feel uncomfortable, let me know and we'll stop."

Daith lay on the spongy surface. She let out a deep breath and stared up into the millions of simulated stars above her.

"I want you to clear your mind and focus on the stars. Let your thoughts float away into the blackness of space." He waited a few moments. "Now, find one star and concentrate on it. Focus all your attention on this single star and make all of the rest of the stars fade away."

Dru stared upward and watched the stars begin to vanish. As the program progressed, the computer would read more sensitive brain waves, calculating the strength of the individual. This would give Dru an idea of Daith's mental capabilities and would show if she had a strong enough energy level to have psionic abilities.

A single star shone above them. Daith passed stage one.

"Good. Now bring the star closer to you." He waited while the image of the star got larger and closer. She had passed stage two.

"Stop the star right there," Dru told her. The star stopped moving. "Now, I need you to take one particle of the star and bring it toward you." Dru's breath quickened. He'd never worked with a patient who had ever gotten past the third stage. This would be the first indication she might indeed be Jacin Jaxx's daughter.

* * *

Daith's head vibrated with tension. Her whole body felt warm, feverish, as she concentrated on keeping a single star above her. Now she needed to remove a single particle from a gaseous pulsating ball of light?

Daith stared at the star, conflicted about what to do next. Droplets of sweat trickled down the sides of her face, tempting her to break her concentration and wipe them away. But she ignored the sensation.

I don't know what a star is made of. Maybe if I could see it up close....

Daith's perception split as her mind's focus ripped in two. In one part she held onto the star, in the other, she felt detached, and a part of her consciousness pulled away from her toward the star. Startled by the ruptured reality, her mind clicked back together.

Curious, she tried again. This time she allowed the detached part of her to continue to float away. She felt her mind penetrate the star—tiny pinpoints of light suspended in empty space. Locking onto one of the particles, she pulled. The glowing spot floated toward her, slowly. She brought it back to her body.

"Pull the particle into your hand," Dru's voice told her.

Daith, barely able to hang on to the tiny piece, felt her mental concentration slip. The particle slid back toward the star, but she managed to reestablish her link. She concentrated her energy behind it to push, rather than pull. The particle came closer again. She focused and gave a huge push. It flew at her with incredible speed. She reached out and snatched at the air. The tiny dot glistened in her palm, like a grain of sand glinting in the sun. She sighed with relief. Sweat drenched her whole body. Pinprick goose bumps rose on her skin as the perspiration evaporated.

"For your final task," he continued, sounding far away, "you must throw the particle back at the star. This will cause the star to explode."

Daith studied the spot of light in her hand, small and powerless. It would never be able to destroy the star.

"No."

"What?"

"No. I can't do it."

"Very well. I see you're not strong enough to save us."

"What do you mean?" she asked.

"That star is on a collision path with us. If we don't destroy it, it will crash into our planet, killing millions. You were our last hope."

Moisture beaded her face once more. Her insides quivered. "I'm holding the star in place," she said, her voice trembling with uncertainty. "It won't crash."

"You can't hold it there forever. Eventually, you will weaken and the star will continue toward us. The only way to save us is to extinguish the threat."

Daith didn't know what to do. Her body vibrated with the effort. She didn't want to die, but throwing the particle at the star would resolve nothing. *There must be another solution.* Daith focused on her energy that held the star. *If I can hold the star, then maybe I can destroy it.* The energy grew. She felt warmth percolate inside her. Its heat overtook her, filling her insides, like her body was made of flame. Energy collected, growing stronger and hotter, searing her from within. The power burst forth from her. She propelled the built-up ball of energy into the star.

Her body arced into the air, contorted, all the energy rushing from her. Once drained, she slammed back onto the ground, and fell into darkness.

* * *

Dru ran to the motionless girl and felt for her pulse. A heartbeat, but faint. He rushed to the communications panel and called for a medical officer. He didn't understand what had happened. The program should have shut down if Daith over-exerted herself.

The medical officer arrived. Her diamond-shaped eyes blinked in awe at the complex program before she placed Daith on a gravity-controlled stretcher and transported her to the medical wing. Dru followed on the medical officer's heels, his face pale and sweaty, when the computer beeped to remind him his program still ran.

"Oh yes," he muttered to himself. "I'll be right there!" he called out to the officer. "Computer, end—" The star exploded.

His heart thumped loudly in his chest. Somehow, she had succeeded. But she'd still had the particle in her hand.

How could that be possible?

Dru let out a low whistle and flipped his hair from his face. His mind raced with the promise of what this could mean. Riel would have been amazed by these results. She would have known exactly what they meant, especially since she'd designed the program. But Dru needed the results compiled.

"Computer, end program and send data to my quarters," he finished. Consumed with the implications of what he'd witnessed and thoughts of Riel, Dru left the simulation room and hurried to his office.

* * *

Dr. Ludd glanced up as the medical officer rushed in with Daith in tow.

"Cadet Milastow? What happened?" he demanded. He searched for Dru. "Where is Doctor Xiven?"

"I don't know," Milastow said. She peered behind him through the doors. "I thought he was following me."

"No matter." Dr. Ludd swung his bulbous belly around his desk, taking a moment to adjust his gravlift. "We need to get her stabilized."

"She is stable, Doctor. Merely unconscious."

"What?" Dr. Ludd checked her vitals. Everything seemed normal, except a high body temperature and the fact that she wouldn't wake. "This doesn't make sense. What did Doctor Xiven tell you happened?"

"He didn't say. They were in the middle of a simulation. I don't really know what they were doing. I assumed he'd fill you in when we got here." Milastow's head twisted and turned, expecting Dru to come marching into the room.

"No matter. Right now she's in no immediate danger. I will contact Doctor Xiven and ask him what happened. I'm sure he's...busy."

After the officer left, Dr. Ludd shook his head in disapproval. He pulled a medical blanket up to the young woman's shoulders and placed one of his pink, flippered hands on her warm, sweaty forehead.

"What are they doing to you, my dear?"

Chapter 12

TREY'S COMMUNICATIONS PANEL lit up with a soft ping. He lowered the engine report he'd been reading at his desk.

"Yes?" he answered.

"Commander, this is the bridge. You have an incoming transmission from Cadet Roilster's ship."

"Patch it through." Trey rubbed his weary eyes.

"Commander Xiven?" A voice crackled over the com. Static hissed in the background.

"Yes."

"I request permission to board the *Horizon*."

Trey's shoulder muscles relaxed. "You were successful on all three parts of your mission then, Cadet?"

Cadet Roilster hesitated. "I successfully erased the memories of all individuals investigating Miss Tocc's disappearance and those of the sister, Valendra Tocc. However, I was unable to locate the witness to Miss Tocc's retrieval."

Trey's jaw tightened. "What happened?"

"Commander, when I followed up on the witness's whereabouts, I couldn't find anything. There hadn't been any other reports filed about missing persons other than the one from Valendra."

"Did you check the local hospitals?"

There was a pause. "Hospitals, Commander?"

Trey clenched his hands around the arms of his chair. "The witness was injured during the altercation, which means he or she was probably hospitalized."

"I-I didn't think to. It didn't occur to me to—"

"Enough."

The com fell silent. Trey spoke again, his words sharp as knives, while his fingers moved to a small circular panel on his left.

"I am disappointed, Cadet Roilster. You showed promise. I gave you this assignment so you could prove yourself to me. And prove something you did."

"Commander, I—"

"You proved you are worthless." Trey punched in a code and pressed the execute button. "Failure is not tolerated under my command. If I can't depend on you..."

"Commander! My instruments! They are malfunctioning! I...Commander! I—"

"...then you are no longer of use to me," Trey finished.

Static hissed into silence. The computer informed Trey his connection had been terminated.

Trey's intercom lit up again. "Yes?"

"Commander Xiven, this is the bridge. I've lost communication with Cadet Roilster's shuttle. Would you like me to reestablish a connection?"

"Not necessary. Cadet Roilster has been dismissed.

Communications out." Trey rubbed his temples as a headache grew. *I can't even rely on my own crew.*

Failure surrounded him. Ineptitude encircled him. Trey had hoped he could do everything himself, but not with such an inexperienced crew. He had to change tactics. And quickly. His partners wouldn't wait.

He needed a bounty hunter.

Kircla would be the best choice, but she wouldn't be easy to find—and she'd be expensive.

Trey's head throbbed. *It'll be worth it.*

He put out a communiqué to search for her and turned off his computer. Glancing at the reports on his desk, he pushed them aside, scowling. He couldn't read one more datapad. He glanced at his time-reader—Dru and Daith's first session should be over by now.

Trey straightened the few things on his desk and left his office to check on their progress.

* * *

Dru gasped. He had just read over the results from Daith's simulation test. The graph line representing Daith's power output spiked at 400.

He couldn't believe it. Through all his studies, the highest mental energy output rank from a student topped out at 143. His own test peaked at 110. Daith should have been dead at 250. And yet this proved she had surpassed this point and still lived. He ran the program through an error check and got the same results.

"This can't be."

"Talking to yourself?" a voice behind him asked.

Dru spun. Trey hesitated in the doorway before swaggering in, picking his way carefully through the messy office. "I guess some things never change."

Dru ignored his brother's jab. "These are the results from the energy tests I did today. Look at her chart. Her readings are off the scale."

Trey studied the graph carefully. "Where is she now?"

Dru scrunched up his face, anticipating Trey's anger. "In the medical wing."

A muscle in Trey's jaw twitched. "Is she all right?"

"I'm sure she's...actually..." Guilt hit Dru. He'd completely forgotten to check on her. How could he be so insensitive? He'd been so wrapped up in the success of her test and thinking about how happy Riel would have been.... "I don't know. She fell unconscious after completing stage five. But I'm sure they'd notify me if—" His communications panel lit up. Dru opened the channel.

"Hello, Doctor Xiven, this is Doctor Ludd. Miss Tocc is stable, but I'd like you to come to the medical wing when you have a moment."

"I'll be right there." Dru started to rise.

Trey pushed him back into his chair. "Actually, Doctor, I'll come and check on her." He closed the communications channel.

Dru's chest swelled. "She's my patient, brother. I have the right to visit her."

"You're the one who put her in the medical wing with your program," Trey snapped. "Until you figure out exactly what happened and how you can prevent any further complications, I don't think I'd care to call her your patient. Figure out what went wrong."

"You don't understand," Dru said. "Nothing went wrong. The safety protocols for the program shouldn't have allowed this. It's designed to shut down if there are any problems with the mental safety of my patients, which means Daith didn't reach her full mental energy output. She just physically couldn't handle it."

A hunger touched Trey's stormy eyes. "Does this mean she is who I thought?"

Dru shifted in his chair. "Daith has Jaxx's potential, but this one test doesn't prove she's related to him. Certainty would only come if we had a genetic sample for comparison or if she had her memories back."

Trey dismissed Dru's irritation with a wave of his hand. "She is his daughter. When we first brought her onboard we gave her a lie-inhibitor and she told us all about her kinship to Jacin Jaxx. Then we erased her memory."

"What? You told me you didn't know who she was."

"I didn't know if she was the real thing or not. She could have been a decoy. She could have been trained to tell us she was Jacin Jaxx's daughter. I needed confirmation and only proof of his abilities would suffice. These tests you put her through can't be faked."

"You could have told me—"

"I didn't want it to skew your data."

Dru clenched his jaw. Anger burned in his chest, even if his brother was right.

"Keep perusing through these charts," Trey continued, "and let me know if you find anything else of value. I assume it's safe to say you plan to continue your work with this girl?"

"Yes."

"Good. Then make sure you change your parameters so this doesn't happen again. I will check back with you later."

* * *

"Hello, Doctor. I am here to check on Daith."

Dr. Ludd glanced up. "Ah, Commander Xiven, please follow

me." He floated over the top of his desk, narrowly missing the stacks of datapads, jotted notes, and pictures of his family. Trey followed him into the patient ward.

Dr. Ludd glided toward a set of white curtains and opened them. Daith lay there, unconscious. Sweat coated her face. Her eyes raced beneath their lids. They matched the click of the monitors connected to her, following her pulse and respiration.

"She's been in this state since my assistant brought her in," Dr. Ludd said, "but she seems to be stable. The only discrepancy is her core body temperature is running a bit high. All her systems are functioning and her brainwave patterns are still active, but it's as if her brain and her body aren't connected—like her body is waiting while her mind figures out what it's going to do.

"Because of the unusual tests Doctor Xiven is performing," Dr. Ludd continued, his words rough with displeasure, "I can't give you any reasonable diagnosis on her condition except if you expect her to come out of this without serious damage, she's going to need constant medical surveillance and I don't see her leaving the medical wing for at least three months. I'd like to keep her—"

"Three months?" Trey interrupted, his face ashen. "No, no. I need her back on her feet in three weeks. Max."

Dr. Ludd gurgled. "Three weeks? You can't be serious. Her brain waves are extremely unstable. I could perhaps get her normalized in six or seven weeks if I used steroid stimulants, but I wouldn't want to risk it. Medically speaking, she needs to stay here and—"

"I'm telling you to have her well in three weeks. There is a timetable to be kept, Doctor."

Dr. Ludd's jaw flapped open. "Commander, with all due respect, your timetable doesn't matter. If I push her that quickly, it could produce many problems, including severely reduced physical capabilities, diminished mental capacity, and lack of emotional control. Or it could have the opposite effect, causing her brain to over-stimulate and produce an even larger energy release. Even worse—"

"A larger energy release? How large? What else would she be capable of?"

Dr. Ludd gawked at him. "Have you been listening to me?"

Trey flicked his fingers. "Yes, yes. But talk to me about this energy release. Would it be stronger than the first? And could I get her to perform more than once?"

Dr. Ludd motioned for Trey to follow him back to his desk. He turned on his medical log screen with his flippered hand. A blue-tinged three-dimensional graph appeared, rotating slowly in front of them.

"This is Daith's brain-wave pattern. Use of steroid stimulants will change the chemical balance in this part of her brain." He pointed. "Usually, this type of stimulation is used sparingly to help boost the patient's reflex response until they can match the wavelength themselves. If I do what you suggest, she would become totally dependent on these stimulants for simple everyday motions. Her natural recovery process would have no way of equalizing the chemical reaction so quickly—"

"But she will still be able to release these large amounts of energy, correct?" Trey asked, his gaze on the doctor, not on the graph.

"Technically," the doctor said slowly, "it could be done. But I cannot stress enough the danger of what you are asking me to do. I don't think—"

"Don't think, just do it," Trey said. "Unless you want to find a job somewhere else? I'm sure a different crew would be ecstatic to work with a former doctor of the Aleet Army."

Dr. Ludd lowered his gaze. If he couldn't practice medicine...

"She will be ready in three weeks."

"I know." Trey paused. "You will send me a report every eight standard hours on her condition and notify me immediately if there is a change. Don't forget to add in dream-deflector dosages so she doesn't dream while she's unconscious. We still don't want her memories to resurface, now do we?"

"No, Commander."

"And one last thing, Doctor," Trey said the title with a sneer. "If she dies, you die."

Chapter 13

TREY'S PULSE RACED, his fingers trembled, his breath came in ragged gulps. Daith's first exhibition of power and she had ended up in the medical wing. He must be insane to think he could pull this off. He had no idea what he was doing and at the rate things were going, he would damage beyond repair the only being in the entire galaxy who could help him.

Trey willed himself to calm down. There must have been something he'd missed. But what? He had Dr. Ludd—one of the best medical physicians caring for her, Dru—one of the only doctors to ever work with someone of Daith's caliber guiding her, and the only crew that wanted her safe protecting her. But these abilities of hers, no one could predict everything—her triggers, her limits, her feelings.

No one except her father. And he was dead.

Trey paused mid-thought. Jacin may be dead, but not his memories. Those were lodged inside his own subconscious.

For the first time in years, Trey purposely didn't take a dream-deflector pill and lay on his bed to sleep. Granted he didn't know what type of dream he'd have, but since Daith had come on board, they'd all been about Jacin. If Trey could figure out his secrets, who knew what he could learn.

Trey's head felt heavy on his pillow, the weight of the day pulling him into the sleep his body desperately desired. In moments he swam into the realm of dreams.

Trey stood in front of a tall building. Mugg General Hospital printed across the front in shiny letters. He remembered the place—but since the structure appeared intact, then this had to be before the riots—before Jacin Jaxx revealed his gifts to the galaxy....

Jacin stood in front of the brand-new hospital with a sense of purpose. He and his family had moved to the capital city, Mugglie, on the planet Mugg two weeks before. Determination to help others filled him now that he knew what he could do with his abilities.

He could be a healer.

Jacin marched through the doors, their gold-colored plaque glistening in the glare of the planet's hot sun. He met with the administrators and shared his thoughts on how he could help the hospital staff. Skeptical at first, they soon marveled at his gifts after several demonstrations.

After completing the paperwork with the administrative office, which included his own consulting office and sleeping quarters, Jacin threw himself into his work. Nothing else seemed to matter. Jacin's wife, Elor, expressed her displeasure at having her husband away so many nights, but her concerns seemed trivial compared to his accomplishments. The thrill of helping others, saving lives, dominated him.

For the first time, he felt as if he'd found his destiny.

Weeks slipped by. Jacin, so involved in his work, didn't realize he'd begun to make a name for himself. Word spread about a man who could heal the sick without surgery. Beings from other planets flocked to Mugglie to meet this man.

Jacin's focus extended only to the virus wreaking havoc in the patient's body in front of him.

After a few moments, Jacin opened his eyes, and let the flow of warmth inside him recede. "You should be fine, now," he said to a young woman, the disease now eradicated.

"Thank you," she gushed, turning to her weeping family.

Jacin excused himself and left the room. He stumbled into his own office, his head pounding. The twentieth patient of the day and he hadn't eaten a thing.

In fact, his workload had doubled in the past few days. His time in the hospital existed as a blur of mashed-up faces, strange body parts, grotesque insides, and gratitude.

The drumming in his head cinched it. He needed a few days off.

Jacin stepped through the automatic doors of the hospital and onto the street.

"There he is!"

Jacin stopped mid-step. The crowd turned at once, like a massive trembling wave, engulfing him. Several individuals tugged at his arms, begging for his help, offering rewards. One woman actually fell at his feet and kissed them, thanking him for healing her daughter.

Panic stricken, Jacin raced back inside, his clothes torn by the gripping hands. The doors closed behind him. Bodies pressed up against the glass while security tried to keep them at bay. Trapped, Jacin ran to the rear entrance of the hospital, but the crowd's thickness remained. A mass of writhing individuals surrounded the hospital, their wails and cries deafening, their body odor seeping through the cracks of the door, filling his nostrils, nauseating him.

Jacin felt desperate. He had to get out. The hospital staff called Central Authority, but their task force couldn't even get to the front door. Claustrophobia set in. Jacin's throat tightened and he couldn't breathe.

Plowing straight into the crowd, he pushed and shoved, clawing his way through the masses. Bodies somehow moved away from him, even if he didn't touch them. He kept pressing forward, determined to get home. With one last stumble, he broke free, into the fresh, sweet air. Jacin took off at a sprint. He ran faster than he'd ever run before. Through parks, past stores. Houses blurred until he burst through his own door.

Elor jumped out of her chair. "Jacin!"

"Pack your stuff. We're moving back home. Now." Jacin moved her toward the stairs.

"Why? What happened? You look terrible. Jacin, talk to me!"

"I'll tell you on the way. Where are the girls?"

"They're next door."

"I'll get them. You go upstairs and pack. Then, vidlink an Anywhere and You're There! vehicle and have it come here right away." After collecting his two daughters from the neighbors, Jacin found Elor waiting with three large bags.

"I couldn't take everything, but we can come back later," Elor said.

"No, we probably can't. But don't worry, whatever we leave behind we can replace," Jacin reassured her. As they waited for the vehicle to arrive, Jacin began to tell Elor what had happened at the hospital, when he glanced at their viewscreen, which was still on. A newscaster reported about the hospital.

"Creatures and beings, I can't believe what I'm seeing.

Hundreds have gathered around Mugg General Hospital, the one where Jacin Jaxx was reportedly last seen. Many are chanting and praying to Jaxx, waiting for him to heal them. They say...oh, my! Creatures and beings I can't believe what I'm seeing! A small group has rushed the security guards and broken into the hospital. Everyone is streaming inside to get to Jaxx. They're throwing rocks, breaking windows. The hospital's plaque above the door has been pried off the building—they're using it like a battering ram. I've never seen such mayhem. You there, may I have a word with you?" The newscaster approached one of the beings in the crowd, his silver skin shining in the bright sunlight. The being held a little girl in his arms—her skin a dark silvery-gray, her head lolling like a broken doll. "What is going on here?"

"I'll tell you what's going on. That 'healer' in there is an egotistical xenophobe! He won't save my child because I'm Carnillian and he only helps his own kind. I hope one day I can meet this Jaxx so I can give him a piece of my mind! He has no right to keep his gifts to himself. He has no right not to help other species. He has no right to be this selfish and stubborn and—"

The viewscreen exploded.

Trey woke with a start, his jaw snapping closed onto his tongue. Cursing, he stumbled to the washroom and rinsed his mouth, spitting a glob of pink liquid into the sink.

Jacin's anger had been so hot, so intense. He'd hated the Carnillian on the screen for accusing him of discrimination. And the power behind the energy he'd used to blow up the viewscreen....

Trey wondered while he ran his wounded tongue softly over his teeth. There had been so much more force, and the action had been so destructive. Could anger be a trigger?

Trey made a mental note to speak to his brother about changing his sessions—focusing more on emotional outbursts—when he remembered Daith, unconscious in the medical wing, unable to do anything.

If he lost her right when he might know how to control her....

A flash of panic hit him and he left his quarters.

I just want to make sure she's okay, he thought. Trey's heart rate slowed only when he arrived at medical and saw the steady, rhythmic breathing of her chest.

Then her eyelids fluttered.

* * *

"Doctor Ludd? I think she's waking up. Daith? Daith can you hear me?"

I don't know—can I?

"Daith?"

The voice reached Daith's ears slowly, as if traveling through a syrupy substance. She struggled to the surface of consciousness, then opened her eyes, which felt more like prying than opening. Focus came slowly.

"Where...?" Her head felt heavy, her mouth dry. She didn't recognize her surroundings. The room was bright with white walls. A curtain hung around part of her bed, white and rippled. Everything smelled clean—too clean. Sterile.

"Easy, now. Go slow," the voice said.

Daith's gaze rested on Trey's face, soft with concern. She tried to push herself up, but he gently held her back.

"You need to rest. You're in the medical wing. Doctor Ludd is your attending physician. He should be here shortly to start you on some medication."

Daith nodded, unable to speak until her salivary glands

moistened her mouth.

Trey sat on the edge of the creaky bed. "Do you remember what happened?"

Flashes of her session in the simulation room flickered through her mind—the particle, the star, the intense heat inside her. "Where's Dru?" Daith asked, her voice cracking.

Trey frowned. "Dru's in his office, going over what happened during the simulation. He's trying to understand why you passed out."

"Oh." She dropped her gaze from Trey's, disappointed.

"Dru sometimes gets more wrapped up in the results of his tests than in his patients." He took her hand. "I'm here though. I came right away." He tightened his hand on hers for a moment before letting go. "Ah—here's the doctor now to give you something to help, right Doctor?"

Dr. Ludd swallowed hard, his lipless mouth a tight line. He took her arm and injected a syrupy brown liquid.

Daith's world dimmed. Her vision tunneled. A sensation of falling settled over her, even though she knew she was lying down. She struggled to stay awake, to ask questions, but her eyelids closed against her will.

"Monitor her closely, Doctor," she heard Trey say in a swirl of overlapping syllables. "And remember, you have less than three weeks to get her back on her feet."

Daith's last moment of consciousness centered around Dr. Ludd, his words so loud they sounded like they were in her head. *I'm so sorry, child. For everything.*

* * *

Trey headed toward Dru's quarters to update him on Daith's

condition and see what progress he'd made with her charts. Hopefully he'd figured out a way to tweak the safety parameters of his program for when she recovered.

If she recovered.

You are killing her. The thought spiked into his brain. He knew the girl's outcome could result in death, but he would do what he could to prevent that. And he'd known she was expendable from the beginning. She had to be.

But you care about her.

Trey stopped cold outside Dru's room. Care? An absurd thought. And yet seeing her lying on the bed in the medical wing, helpless....

Trey bit the inside of his cheek, hard. He used the pain to block his emotions, a technique he'd learned. He straightened and strode into the room without ringing the chimes. Dru, still hunched over his computer console, didn't notice Trey's entrance. Trey cleared his throat and grinned inwardly when Dru jumped.

"I hate when you do that."

"Old habits die hard, I suppose," Trey said. "I thought you might want an update on Daith's condition."

"Of course. How is she?"

"She'll be fine. In fact, the doctor said with some medication, she should be back and ready to go in about three weeks."

Dru rubbed the back of his neck. "Really? I should probably go check on her. I've been here all day."

"It's tomorrow, brother."

Dru rubbed his face and glanced at his timereader. "It's...tomorrow?"

"Technically, yes. But don't worry. I've come from visiting her and she's sleeping. I'll let you know when she's awake, if you want to see her then," Trey replied. "You need to continue to calculate these results and let me know what else happened with this young lady."

"All right."

"Good. When will you have this compiled into a report for me?" Trey asked.

"By morning. I only have a few more details to go over."

"Goodnight, then." Trey left his brother's room and as he strode down the corridor, unwanted thoughts once again crept into his mind.

She isn't Riel, you know.

Trey ignored the thought, determined not to take the bait.

You can't have her anyway.

Trey quickened his pace, hoping his steps would drown out his thoughts.

Why do you care so much if Dru goes to visit her?

I don't care, he countered, denying the accusation. *There is no reason for him to go see her. She's sleeping.*

So then where's the harm in letting him check in on her? his thoughts argued back.

He needs to get that report done.

She is probably going to be in and out of consciousness for the next couple of weeks. He has plenty of time to finish his report.

Trey felt himself getting angry. *He can go when he's finished.*

No sweets until your chores are done, right Trey?

"Enough." Trey said the word out loud. A moment later, a young cadet came around the corner.

"Excuse me, Commander," the cadet said, skirting out of the way.

Trey nodded, realizing he'd almost been caught in a moment of weakness. He arrived at his own quarters and sat quickly before his knees gave way. Keeping control was getting harder.

* * *

Dru waited a few moments after his brother left before slipping out of his office and heading toward the medical office. He didn't care what Trey said, he wanted to check on Daith anyway.

Once inside, Dru stood by her bed and watched as mechanical monitors reassured him she slept peacefully. With a slow movement, Dru placed his hand upon hers. The monitor remained steady.

"I'm here," he whispered. "You're not alone."

Though the beeps stayed even, Daith's mouth smiled.

Chapter 14

TREY'S BODY SLUMPED with exhaustion. He'd gone over several spec sheets down in engineering, scrutinized the new cadet assessments, made a quick check on Daith, scanned through power efficiency levels for shielding capabilities, restocked his dream-deflector supply from Dr. Ludd—although he didn't think he really needed them anymore—and crammed the rest of his cold, half-eaten lunch down his throat for dinner before he kicked off his boots, pulled off his shirt and pants, and slid into bed.

The moment he began to drift away, eager to view another tidbit of Jacin's life, a loud alarm blared through his communications panel followed by a jolt that raced through the ship. The panel on his wall lit up. He jumped out of bed and hit the button on the wall, cursing as he slammed his finger into it.

"Commander Xiven to the bridge crew. Status?"

A crisp female voice responded. "This is Cadet Ikar. We need you on the bridge, Commander. We are under attack."

"On my way," Trey said, shaking his throbbing finger while trying to pull on the freshly pressed uniform ready for the following day. *I wish I hadn't dumped my clothes from today on the floor. I'll have to remember to wash and press them before morning.* Trey ground his teeth at what he'd been diminished to—two uniforms for the whole week. He used to have his choice of three uniforms a day—daily and ceremonial.

He reminded himself the situation was temporary. Things would be back to the way they used to be soon enough.

Trey emerged onto the circular bridge, still a little hazy, and assessed the situation. He scanned the semi-vacant surroundings, the low metallic ceiling, the shiny, circular, center-facing empty consoles around the room. Three crewmembers worked on duty that night: a pilot, one to run tactical, and one to command. The bridge normally ran with eight crewmembers.

"Report," he called out. Another shudder ran through the ship. He strode toward the center of the room, relieving a blond man. He plunked into a plush chair, surrounded by six screens.

A bronze-skinned woman at the piloting console turned her attention to Trey. She answered with the same crisp voice he'd heard earlier in his room.

"We are being attacked by an unidentified ship. I believe they are targeting energy signatures. Aim seems to be fluctuating between our engine room, weapons, and medical. They cannot get an exact energy lock, but the minimal power behind their attack suggests they only mean to cripple us, Commander." The ship lurched again and her amber-colored eyes flicked back to her console.

"Pirates."

Trey swiveled around. The voice behind him belonged to the blond man, Cadet Malco Pitar. A tinge of pink touched his pock-marked cheeks, but he regained his composure and went on with the report.

"Shields down to thirty-five percent efficiency," Cadet Pitar continued, running his fingers over the console in front of him. "We've lost main engines, but backup generators are holding. Our forward weapons have been destroyed. Aft weapons are taking heavy damage."

"Disconnect us from the spaceport. Evasive maneuvers," Trey said.

"I wonder how they found us." Cadet Pitar murmured.

Trey wondered that himself. Pirates usually worked alone, stationing themselves close to trading planets or along familiar trading routes. They preyed on smaller ships, crippling them, boarding them, and taking whatever, and sometimes whomever, they could find. Why were they out here in the middle of nowhere attacking a ship attached to a spacestation?

Trey touched a small button on his chair. In a flash, the six viewscreens adjusted to his eye level.

The ship itself, shaped like stackable crosses, had digital viewing stations attached at six points. These stations relayed their images back to the screens where each showed a different view of space surrounding the ship. With visibility from six angles, the crew could see objects without reorienting the craft. To see something on a larger scale, he simply had to touch one of the smaller screens and the image would be enlarged on the main viewscreen at the front of the bridge.

Taking a deep breath, Trey felt the tension in his body melt as he exhaled. Opening his eyes, he began to work.

He zoomed in on an oval-shaped ship turning to make another pass. The vessel carried no name on its deep blue side, only jagged streaks of silver where the metal underneath shone through. The paint job didn't worry Trey, but rather the double set of Droibid cannons hanging from either side of the ship. The weapons could dole out massive fire power, which meant the pirates would not need to accept any terms except the ones they offered.

Cadet Ikar had been doing an excellent job avoiding most of the oncoming fire, but Trey knew he'd have to think of something else soon because his ship's shields were dropping at an incredible rate.

"Cadet Ikar, initiate our sensor-damping shield to jam their sensors."

With their sensors blocked, the other ship wouldn't be able to pinpoint any of the *Horizon's* systems. And since Trey's ship appeared exactly the same all around, the oncoming ship wouldn't be able to tell the difference between an engine signature and a luxury suite. A desperate move, since it meant the other ship would be firing at random, but Trey needed every opportunity he could get to keep them off his weapons.

Cadet Ikar acknowledged. After the damping field initiated, Trey felt pressure on his body, like being compressed.

Another tremble made its way through the ship, followed by a shuddering.

Trey glanced at Lieutenant Koye, who worked the tactical and weapons console.

"Aim for their cannons, Lieutenant. I need them out of commission." The ship shook again. Trey tightened his grip on the arms of his chair.

"Yes, Commander." Lieutenant Koye answered without the slightest hint of panic in his voice. His fur-covered chest swelled before he started to fire.

Panic was evident, though, in the young officer. His scarred face gave him a gruff exterior, but his voice cracked when he spoke.

"Shields are down to twenty-two percent," he told Trey. "I don't think we can take more than two direct hits." He blew his pale hair from his sweaty forehead, his fingers gliding over his console.

"Get more power to those shields," Trey barked.

"I'm doing what I can, Commander. She's not equipped to handle—"

"I don't want excuses." Anger tinged Trey's tone, though his face remained neutral.

Cadet Pitar's stance straightened before he spoke again. "I've rerouted power from the engines and boosted shield intensity by forty-two percent. We won't be able to outrun them, but this should give us the time we need."

"Good work," Trey said. A light at his communications station blinked. Trey activated the comm. "Xiven here."

"This is Lieutenant Byot in engineering. We lost power to the engines. What's going on up there?"

"Needed it for shields. Stand by."

"But, Commander, we—"

"Commander," Cadet Pitar interrupted, his black eyes wide with alarm. "The pirates fired on our main engineering section. They've disrupted our engine power. We have no shields!"

Trey mentally cursed. They had lost. But he couldn't let this ship fall to pirates. Before he could shout another order, a message came in from the attacking ship. A crackly voice rang through the bridge, its language badly garbled by the translator.

"We know...*hiss*... of your engines and shields...*hiss*... have no power.

"Prepare...*hiss*... being boarded."

Trey gritted his teeth, knowing full well he would blow up his ship before he'd let pirates board. Paranoid thoughts gripped him. What if they knew about Daith and were coming to get her? What if they knew about his plan? Trey's gaze darted around the bridge, assessing the other crew members.

We lost this too easy. They set me up. This was all a trap. Trey clenched his fists, willing the thoughts away. *No. It's all in your head. Everything is fine.*

Everything is FINE.

The main screen changed, showing the oval-shaped ship approaching the side of the *Horizon.* Trey's dark blue eyes flashed. *They think they are going to dock with us....*

"Cadet Ikar. Divert power to the back-up generators from the damping field when they approach. But don't angle our docking port on the first level toward them. Tilt the ship as if they need to dock at our third level."

"Isn't that where our viewing system is?"

"Do it."

Trey didn't even consider his plan could go wrong. He had one shot to destroy those pirates and he had to take it, no matter the outcome. His crew wasn't large enough to handle a boarding. He turned to Lieutenant Koye and quietly gave him an order. A growl trembling in Koye's throat spilled out and his lips curled into a fiendish grin.

Trey signaled Cadet Ikar to reconnect them with the pirates.

"Very well. We submit." Trey waited, all the while watching them on his viewscreen, angled straight into the front of his attacker's vessel. He held until they'd pulled up, nearly to the point of extending their boarding clamps.

"Koye—fire!"

A jolt raced through the bridge as their aft weapons fired. The energy from the exploding ship ripped through Trey's vessel, shorting out systems all over the bridge. The console next to Trey sparked wildly. An arc of electricity slithered up his arm. To his left, Cadet Pitar writhed on the floor, having taken a direct blast of electricity. Flames licked the front of his uniform. Trey called out to Lieutenant Koye to notify Dr. Ludd they had a medical emergency on the bridge. The blond youth's mouth hung open in shock. The upper right side of his charred chest burned a sickly, smoky black. Warning alarms rang and flashing lights momentarily blinded the bridge crew. Trey slammed his hand on the console behind him, turning off the lights and alarms.

"Status," he called, trying to keep his voice steady.

Cadet Ikar picked herself up and limped back to her console, left knee swollen under her ripped pants leg.

"Unidentified ship has been completely destroyed. No escape pods were jettisoned. No survivors detected, Commander."

"Lieutenant Koye, damage report."

Lieutenant Koye was still poised, although Trey could see him shake as his adrenaline dropped.

"Shields and weapons are down," he told Trey. "Engines are offline. A section of our hull tore off during the explosion. Injuries are coming in from that section now. No casualties reported yet, Commander."

Trey motioned for Ikar to come and take care of the wounded man while he sent a communication to engineering. "This is Commander Xiven. Status?"

"Commander, this is Lieutenant Chief Engineer Byot. The explosion didn't do any additional damage to the engines, but I can't say how long until they come back online. Right now we are putting out the last of the fires. No major injuries yet, Commander."

"Keep me informed, Lieutenant. As soon as we can, reconnect us to the spaceport. Xiven out." Trey returned his attention to Cadet Pitar. *What kept Doctor Ludd? I can't afford to lose any more of this crew!*

Trey watched Ikar tend to the wound. She pulled an emergency medical kit from underneath one of the consoles and placed a burn-pack onto the blond officer's chest. The pack sizzled as it distributed painkillers and a cooling gel to slow down the burn.

"I'm going to take look at your wound," she said after the painkillers had taken the edge off. "It will hurt when I take the burn-pack off, but I need to see it." Trey willed himself not to show his repulsion when Ikar peeled off the burn pack. The smell of cooked meat wafted from his chest. A circle of the cadet's skin, about twenty centimeters around, flaked away in black wisps. The edges of the circle were a deep red, but the smoldering had stopped, so the skin wasn't burning anymore. Ikar replaced the pack gently.

"You will most likely have a scar, but the damage doesn't seem too bad. Just a little crispy," she said with a small smile.

Dr. Ludd and a medical assistant droid arrived. The doctor made his way over to the fallen officer, lowering his hovering device so he could reach the wound. He sprayed a foam substance over the charred surface and Cadet Pitar's face showed immediate signs of relief.

"I should be able to fix this without too much permanent damage," Dr. Ludd told Trey. He loaded the cadet's body onto a stretcher. "Some of his nerves may be beyond repair, and I will most likely have to use a skin graft, but I think the burn itself isn't too severe. No sign the infliction penetrated too deeply and I don't think there will be any damage to the lungs either."

"Keep me updated," Trey said. "What about...?"

"She is still sleeping. She had no reaction to what took place."

Trey closed his eyes for a moment. The less he had to explain to Daith, the better.

Dr. Ludd fired the repulsors on the stretcher. He made his way off the bridge with Cadet Pitar in tow, heading back to the medical wing.

Trey had been so involved he hadn't even noticed the assistant droid had sprayed the same foam substance onto his own injured arm and wrapped a surgical bandage around it.

"Please come to the medical wing tomorrow morning to have the bandage replaced." The droid spun its spherical body and zoomed away, without waiting for an acknowledgement from Trey.

Trey gingerly touched his bandaged left arm, surprised at the lack of pain.

Dr. Ludd must have used a pretty strong painkiller. And Trey felt grateful. Even though the fight had lasted only minutes, the damage to be repaired would keep him busy for many hours to come.

Chapter 15

DAITH AWOKE GROGGY, strapped to an uncomfortable white bed. Her eyes adjusted to the brightness of the harsh white lights reflecting off the white walls. The sharp smell of cleaning chemicals filled her nose. A warm feeling pounded through her, like her pulse pumped fire.

"Uhhh?" she croaked. The edges of her mouth cracked with dryness. The door slid open and a jelly-like being hovered across the floor to the bed.

"Good morning!" the being said, his body jiggling. "My name is Doctor Ludd. Do you remember me?"

Daith's eyebrows furrowed. Her head felt fuzzy. She vaguely remembered him and nodded.

"Excellent," Dr. Ludd exclaimed. "At least your memory seems to be working, which is wonderful news, so I'm going to give you a little longer to get your bearings. You seem alert, which is quite remarkable for someone in your condition so I'll be back in a short while to ask you a few questions and to have you perform a few motor skill tests, to make sure everything is still in working order. Nothing unpleasant, mind you. A few things to help me record your progress and to chart how well you seem to be doing and I promise the tests won't hurt at all so there is nothing you have to worry about. I'll let you get a little settled and then I'll come back in a bit." Dr. Ludd started to leave the room but turned abruptly, wobbling on his gravlift at the swift change in direction.

"Oops! I forgot to undo your restraints. You see you were a bit restless while you slept and we feared you might fall off the bed and you know the old saying of 'Better safe than sorry,' right? Unless, you don't know that phrase because you may not remember it or have never heard the saying before because you don't really have any recollections to begin with. At least, before the past few days, because, as you well know, and remember, you still have the memories of the past few days which is a great thing and encouraging in terms of getting your memory back and by that I mean the memory you don't remember, not the memory you have of the past few days which I already said so I'm repeating myself so I'll go now and let you settle a bit and then I'll be back in a little while and we'll talk more then." Dr. Ludd's lips splayed open in a huge grin while he undid the restraints. "Feel free to sit up, but I don't recommend walking because you've had quite a shock to your system. I'll tell you anything you'd like to know when I get back. You relax, take it easy, and I'll see you soon." Dr. Ludd left.

Daith's head spun. She tried to grasp the overwhelming amount of words Dr. Ludd had thrown at her, but her brain didn't want to process anything yet.

* * *

Dr. Ludd stared at the medical charts in front of him with disbelief. The charts showed Daith had fully healed in two days.

It should have taken six weeks—minimum.

The charts showed her body temperature had increased to a feverous state the whole time she'd been unconscious, and she'd been without any other symptoms of illness. And now, she was responsive when she should have been in a coma or dead.

"This doesn't make any sense," he told himself, tapping on the chart. Her body had even rejected the stimulant concoction he'd given her.

Dr. Ludd floated back into Daith's room and stopped at the end of her bed. "Feeling a little more oriented?"

"I feel warm and tired, but otherwise all right."

"Good, good. Well, I have to tell you this Miss Tocc, you are a medical marvel. I was sure you would take far longer to make this kind of progress and yet, here you are, completely recovered and it's absolutely astounding. Honestly Miss Tocc, I have no idea how this happened. I mean, not only are all your basic systems back to normal, but your brain activity has actually increased and this goes against everything I've ever seen. But don't worry because I mean that in a good way and it's just incredible!"

"I'm sorry, but I'm not really sure what you're talking about. Why am I such a medical marvel?"

"I'm the one who should be apologizing," he gushed. He floated over next to her and explained while he periodically tested her joints and checked her vitals.

"Do you remember performing the memory test with the star particle?" he asked, shining a light into her eyes.

"Yes."

"Good. Well, during your test, you released a huge amount of energy, which caused your brain to overload and, in a sense, short circuit. This caused a complete shutdown of your secondary functions, while leaving your primary functions intact."

Daith blinked a few times. "I passed out?"

"Exactly. The problem was, you had expelled such a huge energy output we believed you would sink deeper into unconsciousness."

"You thought I'd go into a coma."

"Precisely. Anyway, most patients in your condition usually don't recover for several weeks, sometimes not even for months. Stand up please."

Taken aback by this sudden change in conversation. Daith took a moment before registering what the doctor had asked. She got to her feet and Dr. Ludd continued to talk while he checked her neck and spine.

"Unless they were given steroid treatments, which would have increased their recovery time, but only by a few weeks at most."

"I've been unconscious for weeks?"

Dr. Ludd motioned for Daith to sit. "That's the amazing part. You woke up after two days. And what's more, your brainwave pattern is more stable."

"How is that possible?"

"I'm not sure. The only conclusion I can think of is whatever part of your brain you used during your test must have triggered and released something chemical inside you and gave you the ability to heal yourself. But none of it makes any sense, medically speaking. I've only seen this once before and I concluded he must have possessed some sort of genetic mutation."

"Genetic?" Daith asked. "Do you think this is something I could have inherited?"

Dr. Ludd swallowed. He couldn't believe he'd nearly revealed he'd worked with her father before.

"It's possible, but the one I worked on before wasn't even your species," he lied.

"I see." Daith's eyebrows furrowed and her forehead wrinkled, like she didn't accept his explanation as true.

"I know this is difficult, but I believe in spite of all these hardships, you will find your path. My best advice for you is to trust yourself. You will know what's right." Dr. Ludd patted Daith on the shoulder. "I'm going to keep you here for observation overnight, don't hesitate to ask if you need anything."

"Actually," Daith said, her hand on her stomach, "I am a bit hungry."

Dr. Ludd slapped his flipper to his head. "Of course you're hungry! The amount of heat and energy you used would cause you to need an addition of nutrients. I had you on a supplemental nutritional feeding line, but I underestimated how much energy you were going to use, not that I could have guessed something like this would have happened, but still I should have thought to ask you right away, but this result didn't match with your condition and I—"

"I don't mean to interrupt, but..." Daith trailed off.

Dr. Ludd let out a gurgling laugh. "Of course you meant to interrupt. I usually don't stop talking unless someone else starts. Irritating habit, I'm told, to your species. Although I believe you tend to use too few words. I don't understand how you can possibly explain everything you are thinking without using all the words I do. It makes—"

"Doctor."

Dr. Ludd nodded at Daith's cut-off. "My apologies again. I will do my best to restrain my flow of words. Now back to the subject of nutrition. I will get a droid to bring something in for you. Do you have any requests?"

"Something served cold? My insides still feel pretty warm."

"I know just the thing." He floated out of the room to place the order. Daith settled back on the bed and waited for the droid to arrive. When it did, it brought something Daith had never seen before.

The small bowl contained a ball-shaped substance about the size of her fist. Daith tried a bite and found the food pleasantly sweet and creamy. Though light, it sated her appetite. While she ate, she felt the heat in her body recede. A yawn escaped her lips and her eyelids drooped. The bowl tumbled to the floor with a clatter. Her head fell back onto the pillow and she fell into a deep and dreamless sleep.

* * *

Trey's vision blurred. He felt hate toward his office and all the time he spent there. Maybe he should return to the meeting room and process all these reports?

His body groaned in protest, too tired to move. Trey readjusted himself in his chair and flipped through all the reports: crew injuries, power shortages, engine malfunctions, shield glitches, weapon failures, communication delays—the list seemed endless.

He squeezed his eyes tight. Between commanding the ship, keeping his plan on track, making sure everything with Daith flowed smoothly, and having to read every report from every single station because there simply wasn't anyone else on board who could do it, Trey wouldn't be able to maintain his control much longer.

He continued with the ship's reports. The damage could have been much worse. Lieutenant Chief Engineer Byot had assured Trey the silari engines would be back online within a few standard days. The hull would be fixed by tomorrow, and the electrical systems, running on back-up generators, would be good as new once the engines worked again.

The bad news was the young cadet who'd been burned on the bridge hadn't survived his injuries. Dr. Ludd had said he'd had an allergic reaction to the burn pack. The ship wasn't stocked with the right supplies to keep him from succumbing to allergic shock.

Another soldier lost.

Trey could hardly stay awake. His head drooped and he snapped it back up. He tried to read the report again, but exhaustion won. His head fell onto the stack of datapads on his desk. Even before his face hit the cold plastic, Trey had fallen asleep.

Trey could see his mentor in front of him, watching a special news update. He remembered the update—a few years after Jacin Jaxx had visited Trey's home planet, Sintaur, and stopped the civil war he'd been forced to fight in. The bulletin referred to Jacin's wife who'd been attacked by some protesters who'd rallied against Sintaur's new government, claiming Jacin had corrupted the individuals by using mind control.

It put Jacin about five years after the previous memory, but his aged face, tired eyes, and premature hair loss made time passed appear at least three times longer....

Elor had been attacked? Guilt gnawed at the edges of Jacin's thoughts. How could he have been so stupid? He should have realized his family would be targeted.

Deep down Jacin knew what really would have stopped this—if he'd been home like he'd promised. But he couldn't admit to that. If he did, then the beings he'd helped, the power he'd accumulated, the energy and sweat and pain he'd put toward his work—all of his effort would have been for nothing.

Rage swelled inside him. The situation wasn't his fault. The protesters had done this. He'd been so patient with them. He hadn't forced them to join him. He hadn't made them change their minds about him. Obviously they weren't as innocent as he thought. Jacin knew they had to be taught a lesson. How could they hurt Elor? She had nothing to do with his work.

Jacin slammed his fist into the wall of his quarters. Bones cracked, but he didn't care. He could repair the injury later with his mind. Right now, anger consumed him. He flung open his door and stormed down the ship's corridor. He fumed, pulling apart the walls around him with the energy built up inside him, a hot torrent of flame.

They have no right. She didn't have anything to do with it. They deserve to be hurt, to feel what Elor felt, to feel pain! He reached the bow of the ship, shoved the pilot aside, and manually plugged in the coordinates to Lameer.

Once there, Jacin raced into the crowd which had gathered around the hospital. He roared and threw bodies aside with his mind, bent solely on getting to his wife. One large man stepped in front of him and took a swing. Jacin ducked. With his mind, he pushed at the man's broad chest and sent him flying. The man fell to the ground.

Jacin tore past the screams of the crowd and found his wife's room, her discolored face asleep on the pillow.

He ordered everyone out and began to work.

The next day, Jacin awoke in his home to the sound of a newscast on the vidlink.

"Good afternoon. This is a special news bulletin being broadcast globally around Lameer. We have received an official report regarding the riots outside Lameer Main Medical Hospital after Elor Jaxx's admittance. We bring you live to an interview with Officer Laack, who witnessed the demonstrations."

"—there were several injuries and one death during yesterday's riot. There has been no official report on who is responsible. As for Jacin Jaxx's involvement, there have been contradictory statements from several witnesses. Charges against him have not yet been filed—"

Jacin turned off the vidlink.

He put his hands to his face. The officer's words ran through his head. Someone had been killed.

And Jacin knew he was the culprit.

He remembered the man who would not get out of his way. The man he'd shoved backwards with his mind. The man who lay limp on the ground, unable to get back up.

Jacin dropped his hands. He'd killed someone.

If Jacin had used his hands to push the man instead of his thoughts, he would never have killed him. His gift had gotten out of control.

But another thought crept in—the man had deserved to die. He had been one of the protesters, one of the ones who had put Elor in the hospital in the first place.

Jacin observed his wife, preparing lunch for him and the girls, completely healed after Jacin had fixed her. But he couldn't erase the memory of her in the hospital bed—jaw shattered, battered face, left leg propped in a gel splint.

"The galaxy is better off without someone like him in it."

Trey awoke, his desk and cheek covered with vomit, his chin crusted with blood. The darkness in Jacin's voice surprised him—the sneer on his lips. Trey had never known Jacin had killed a man at the hospital.

And yet Jacin had been right. The removal of that man's existence made the galaxy better. He'd had every right to protect his family. Those protesters should not have attacked Elor.

Trey took deep breaths to calm himself and made his mind go

blank. His doubts faded. He was in control again.

This dream reaffirmed Trey's initial belief that Jacin should not have had control over his own powers. He let his emotions interfere.

Except Trey could use that instability to his advantage with Daith.

A blinking light to his left caught his attention. Dr. Ludd had left a message: Daith had recovered and would be released in the morning.

A grin bloomed across Trey's face, the stretch causing the dried mess on his cheeks to crack. He took a few moments to clean up, reorganize his datapads, and dove back into reading the injured personnel report.

Everything was going to be fine.

Chapter 16

DAITH STARTED THE next morning refreshed and full of energy. After a final inspection by Dr. Ludd, she was released from the medical wing. She'd felt uneasy around him when he spoke about others who'd had the ability to heal quickly. Waves of energy emitted from him and when they hit her, they felt— *wrong.* The same as she'd felt when she believed Trey had been lying.

But she'd also been extremely groggy and perhaps her unconventional recovery had left some side effects. Dr. Ludd assured her she would be fine and reminded her to continue taking her evening pills. In a week, he would check in to see how her nerves responded under the conditions of her memory-work.

When Daith returned to her quarters, she found a couple sets of new clothing, and noticed her communications panel blinking.

"Hello, Daith," the message began. *"This is Dru. I checked in on you this morning and Doctor Ludd said you would be out of the medical wing later today. When you feel up to it, would you mind*

stopping by my office? I'm sure you have a lot of questions about what happened."

A smile touched the corner of her mouth at his voice. She felt immediately more at ease simply hearing him speak.

Daith took a quick shower and dressed. The ship's computer told her the location of Dru's office and made her way there. She rang the door chimes and, after Dru told her to enter, walked in to disorder.

Papers strewn all over, empty food trays piled on the edge of the desk, and towers of datapads leaned at precarious angles.

Dru glanced up from his computer. "Hey!" He paused. "You look great."

"I'm sorry?" Daith asked.

"You show no physical signs of fatigue or stress. I would have never known you'd just gotten out of the hospital."

Of course. He meant as a doctor. Daith wondered at the thought. What did it matter how he thought of her? "Thanks. I feel pretty good, too."

The two of them stood in silence. Daith fidgeted under his gaze.

"So," she asked, "you wanted to talk to me about something?"

"Oh, yes. Yes," Dru remembered, motioning for her to join him at his desk. "This is your chart."

Daith tiptoed around the piles on the floor. She examined the graph, full of lines and numbers. "Of course this is my chart. Keep up the good chart-making work."

"Sorry," he replied with a grin, picking up on her teasing tone. He sat on a wobbly stack of books to give her his chair and pointed to the different graph lines. He leaned across her and she could smell his scent, earthy and sweet. The smell triggered something inside her—a sense of safety and comfort.

"This graph," he said, circling the whole screen with his finger, "is a numerical diagram of the maximum mental energy output you produced. The exercise we did stimulated particular areas of your brain to generate the maximum amount of energy output possible. Meaning, how much brainpower you have. You can see here the highest energy outputs belong to empaths and telepaths. The highest score came from a patient who had both empathic and telepathic traits. You can see his mark here at point one hundred forty-three."

"Where am I?"

Dru extended the chart and showed her a point right below 400.

"Does that mean I won?" she asked jokingly.

"Truth be told, I've never seen anything like this before," he said. "But I don't think it's necessarily a bad thing. Having this kind of power could give you access to many types of abilities."

"What kinds of abilities?"

Dru ticked the list off on his fingers. "Telekinesis, elemental control, mind-control, healing abilities—the list goes on."

Daith stared at the graph, dumbfounded. A week ago she had no idea who she was. Now she may be able to move things with her mind or control someone's thoughts.

"How do I know I have any of those abilities? And if I do, how do I use them?"

"You find out what you're capable of and then focus and improve those abilities, like any other motor function."

"I wouldn't even know where to start. Besides, even if I did, what would keep me from exerting too much energy and ending up unconscious again?"

"I would," Dru offered.

"Maybe you forgot, but you are the one who put me in the hospital to begin with."

Color tinged his cheeks. "The computer was programmed to shut off if you exerted beyond your maximum amount of mental energy. Apparently, the energy you gave off wasn't more than your brain could handle, just more than your body could. That has never happened before. Honestly, I didn't think it could happen. But I would modify those safety parameters to make sure you remained safe."

Daith thought about it. The idea tempted her, even through her fear. These abilities sounded pretty powerful. How could she know if she could handle them? "What about my memories? Would I still have time to work on getting those back?"

"Actually, we can do both at the same time. Strengthening your mind in these skills will get you in touch with blocked areas of your brain. Since your memories are also blocked, we will be able to unlock those areas faster." Dru shifted his weight.

"You think that will work?"

He swallowed. "Yes. I know I'm asking a lot, considering you haven't known me very long."

Daith stared into his eyes—gray with flecks of cloudy blue. There wasn't any real reason to trust him, considering everything she'd been through. But there was something about him—his smell, his presence, his words—she did feel safe with him. She knew, somehow deep inside her core, he genuinely wanted to help her.

"Let's try. It's pretty scary, but kind of exciting, too. I mean, only a few days ago I was a blank slate and now—who knows?"

Daith glanced at the old food trays piled on Dru's desk. "Listen," she said, blurting out the words before she could stop, "I don't really know anyone except you and Trey, and of course Lieutenant Koye, who doesn't seem interested in making friends, and the Doctor, but he doesn't seem like he really has time to leave the medical wing.... Okay, so I know a few crewmembers, but you seem to be the most convenient..." Daith paused. "I didn't mean it like—I meant—oh, this is coming out all wrong." Daith took a deep breath. "I'm tired of eating alone. Would you like to have dinner with me?"

Dru hesitated.

Oh, great. He thinks I mean a date. "I mean, I want to talk to you about what kind of things to expect during our sessions," Daith added quickly.

"I don't know," Dru said. "I have a lot of work to do and others might—" He shook his head. "You know what? I'd love to."

"Really?"

"Why not? I've been cooped up in here too long. Having dinner company would be—refreshing."

* * *

Daith stood in front of her reflector-unit, her dark emerald eyes scrutinizing her appearance. She had the option of black, slim pants and a green long-sleeved ribbed shirt or black, slim pants and a blue long-sleeved ribbed shirt. Not much of an option, but she preferred it to the one-piece jumpsuit.

"I don't know why you are making such a fuss about this," she said while sliding on the blue shirt. "It's not a date." Checking her time-reader, she realized she'd be late if she didn't leave soon, so she glimpsed her reflection one last time, ran her fingers through her long, russet hair, and left.

Less than a standard minute later she rushed back in, stripped off the blue shirt, and put on the green one. "It fits better," she told herself.

Liar. You want to wear this one because the green in your eyes stands out.

"Be quiet. It's not a date."

Daith trotted to the simulation room. Glancing up at the computer panel, she noticed Dru was already inside. She stepped through the door and stopped, stunned.

An intimate, dimly lit restaurant filled the space. Its dark gray ceiling reached high and arched into points, punctuated with divots of shadow. A trio of dancers writhed and twirled on a stage to the left, while the musicians moved around the room. Dru had even simulated other patrons so Daith didn't spot him at first.

As she weaved toward him, the food smells intensified. Some sort of spice tickled her nose, causing her mouth to water. The lights shifted from gold to amber. The music changed, a quicker tempo. The dancers accelerated their steps to musical pulses, their hoofed feet stomping and clicking.

"Welcome," Dru said, gesturing for her to take a seat.

The cream-colored silky chair molded to her body. "Thanks." Daith noticed he wore the same clothes he had on earlier and felt foolish at how much time she'd spent on her outfit. "This program is incredible."

"It's a recreation of a restaurant I used to go to when I was younger," he said. "The species are called Manachs," he said, in reference to the dancers and musicians.

"Manachs?" Daith recalled. "Trey spoke of them the other day. He said he lived with two Manach families in his housing structure."

"I know," Dru said.

"You know he told me about his childhood?" Daith asked, surprised.

"No. I know he lived with two Manach families. And a Grassuwerian one."

"Trey told me he'd never told anyone the story of his past."

"He didn't have to tell me. I was there."

"What do you mean?"

"Trey is my older brother."

Daith stared at him for a moment before she mentally kicked herself for not realizing the connection before. The resemblance between the two men wasn't strong, but they both had the same angular jaw line and pointed noses.

"I can't believe I never put it together," she said. "So you're the younger brother Trey mentioned."

Dru nodded. "What did he tell you?"

"He mostly talked about how the war changed your world." She didn't know if she should mention Trey had spoken about their mother's death. Even though Dru would know about the incident, she still felt voicing it would be betraying Trey's confidence.

Their food arrived shortly, plates of creamy white sauces smothering thick, warm puffed starches. A dense and rich meal, but not so heavy Daith couldn't have seconds.

"What was being in a war like?" she asked. She bit her lower lip. "I'm sorry. Is that too personal?"

"It's okay. I don't mind talking about it. I didn't see much action. The war started when I was eleven. For three years I worked in the weapons factories before the government drafted me to fight. I stayed only on the front lines for a year, unlike Trey who was there for all four. But then Jaxx came and ended the war."

"He ended a whole war? How'd he manage that?" Daith asked.

Dru choked on a piece of food. After a few frightening moments, he swallowed. "Guess it went down the wrong way."

"It happens to everyone."

"I suppose," he said, his cheeks flushed. "But lucky for you, you can't remember embarrassing moments like that."

Daith noticed even the simulated patrons had stopped their meals to see what had happened. "True, but I wouldn't mind if it meant I could remember something."

"I don't know," Dru said. "There are definitely some things I'd like to forget."

"Oh? Juicy and embarrassing moments from your life, huh?" she teased. "Well, since I don't have memories of my own, I insist you tell me yours—the more outrageous, the better."

Dru laughed. "Well, one time, at eleven years old, I came across an itsu bird, screeching...."

"Do you think you'll need another day of rest," Dru asked after dinner, "or do you feel ready to start our work tomorrow?"

"No, tomorrow's fine. How does mid-afternoon sound?" She patted her stomach muscles, though satisfyingly full, hurt from laughing.

"Sounds good." The two of them paused at Daith's quarters. The door slid open with a squeal.

"Well," Dru continued, "thanks for the invitation to dinner. I had a great time."

Daith mumbled something in agreement. Her gaze flicked around the corridor, avoiding Dru's stare.

"Um..." Dru said. "I guess this is goodnight, then."

Daith swallowed hard. "Uh-huh."

Dru took a half step toward Daith. Though they didn't touch, Daith could feel energy emanate from his body, like heated static electricity.

Dru cleared his throat and quickly stepped away from her. "Well, see you tomorrow." He strode down the corridor.

"Goodnight," Daith called out after him. She went inside and flopped down on the bed. Her insides squirmed. What had just happened? She couldn't remember ever feeling that type of sensation. Her whole body reacted toward him, but not solely as a physical attraction. The energy inside her wanted to touch his.

She shook her head fiercely. That didn't even make sense. *Get a grip! You only met him a week ago.*

Daith's head spun. Here she was, no memory, no family, no real friends, and getting wrapped up in silly dinner stories and being called a medical marvel.

She needed to stay focused and figure out her identity.

Though Dru had said working on her unique abilities may help retrieve her memories faster....

Then I'll push my abilities to their limits if it helps me remember who I am.

A yawn escaped her lips and her stomach gurgled with digestive contentment. Her eyes protested staying open. She stripped off her pants, popped a pill from the vial Dru had given her, and slid under the warm covers. The moment her eyelids slid shut, she fell asleep.

Chapter 17

DAITH GROANED AT the ring of her door chime.

"Go away," she called out, pulling the covers over her head. Her bare feet stuck out at the other end.

The chime rang again.

Daith pushed off her covers and rolled off the bed. The sound continued until she staggered to the door and opened it. A gush of recycled air from the corridor blew her hair from her face.

"I was asleep," she said. "What do you want?"

Dru stood there in silence, mouth slightly open.

"*What*?" she asked.

Dru averted his gaze. "Maybe you should get dressed."

Daith glanced at herself. She wasn't wearing pants. "Oh, space!" she cursed. She pressed the panel to close the door.

Daith grabbed the wrinkled ball of black slacks from the floor and slid them on over her underwear. Running her fingers through her hair, which stuck out in kinked angles, she opened the door again.

Dru had taken a couple of steps away.

"I-I didn't know if you wanted me to wait," he stammered.

Daith blushed. "Maybe you were right. I probably could have done without the memory of this embarrassing moment." She let out a couple shaky laughs. "Why are you here so early?"

Dru bridged the distance between them. "You wanted to meet this afternoon. It's close to dinnertime."

"Dinnertime? What are you talking about? I barely laid down." She stifled a yawn.

"That was last night."

Daith glanced at her timereader, which indicated the lateness of the day. "Wow. I guess I needed rest."

"You are obviously still recovering from your trauma."

Daith let out an impatient sigh. "I feel fine. I needed sleep, that's all."

Dru scrutinized her. "Maybe. But I'd like to run it by Doctor Ludd first."

"If you think it's necessary. But really, I feel fine."

"I insist. Give yourself a little time to wake up. Meet me in Doctor Ludd's office in a standard half hour?"

"Sure."

* * *

After he'd left, Dru knew he shouldn't be thinking about it, but he couldn't get the image of Daith's barely dressed body out of his head—slim hips, smooth thighs. Even her bare feet enticed him.

I can't be attracted to her. I'm her doctor. It's unethical.

But he couldn't really blame himself for his response. She *was* half-clothed.

This is ridiculous.

He couldn't deny her allure. And he'd felt the energy reaction from her the night before. How was he supposed to explain that? He'd never even felt that with Riel.

Sharp guilt stung him. How could he even think of comparing anyone else to Riel?

He couldn't. He would simply dismiss any interest unless purely professional.

* * *

Daith met Dru outside the doctor's office. They waited until Dr. Ludd finished with a vidlink call, their gazes wandering across the walls splattered with pictures from his children, diplomas, and letters from patients he'd helped. When he glanced up at the new visitors, the doctor's pink eyes blinked twice before he broke into a smile.

"Ah, Miss Tocc. Back so soon? Everything's okay, right? No dizziness or nausea? No cramping or fever? No—"

"No, Doctor Ludd," Daith interrupted. "I feel fine."

"Good, good. Then, to what do I owe this pleasant visit?"

Dru stepped forward. "Actually, I had a quick question I'd like to run by you."

"Of course, Doctor Xiven," Dr. Ludd said. "What would you like to know?" He adjusted his gravlift so he could meet Dru's eye line.

"Daith's energy output during her session ran exceedingly high. I would like to know, especially based on the negative way her body responded, if she is healthy enough to continue along the same path of tests. Provided, of course, the tests would only target specific brain functions, not her maximum output like before. She did recently sleep six standard hours beyond a normal-length sleep cycle so I'm worried she may be negligent about her own health in order to proceed more quickly."

"I appreciate your coming to ask me, doc, especially since my advice is not always sought. However," Dr. Ludd added quickly, "I understand there are deadlines to be met."

Deadlines? Daith watched Dru's eyebrows furrow. She wondered if he knew any more than she did.

"I think working with Miss Tocc to test her mental and emotional abilities is fine," Dr. Ludd continued. "I'd like a summary of the tests you plan to run beforehand, but I know *you* will be careful, so I don't foresee any problems."

"Thank you, Doctor. I will write up a list and will bring them to you tomorrow. Today, I thought I'd work on some basic telepathy skills."

"Sounds fine, doc," Dr. Ludd reaffirmed. "As long as she doesn't feel too tired or have a headache or a fever or nausea or aches or—"

"Doctor!" Daith and Dru both cried out in exasperation.

"Well then good luck with your tests, Miss Tocc," Dr. Ludd finished with a gurgle. "And if you have any other problems, poor sleep or too much sleep again or no appetite or—"

"I will let you know," Daith reassured him.

"And thank you, Doctor Ludd," Dru added.

"Of course. If you'll excuse me." The doctor gently motioned for them to leave when a crewmember staggered in, her normally greenish skin a pale pink with illness.

The two of them exited and made their way to the deck below, the corridors quiet. While they moved, Daith wondered about the conversation between the two doctors. She wanted to know more, but she would bet Dru wouldn't tell her out right.

"I'm glad I got the doctor's approval," Daith said, her tone casual. "Even though I feel alright, it's reassuring to have someone else tell you you're in good shape."

"One reason why I wanted to check with him first." Dru nodded at a crewmember who scuttled by.

Daith ignored the crewmember as he gave them a wide berth. "I guess you aren't that kind of doctor."

"No. I received basic education in medical science, but my main studies focused on neuroscience and psychology. That's why I'm going to stress you tell me or Doctor Ludd if you experience any unpleasant side effects during your tests. The areas we will deal with are taxing by themselves—adding memory loss may complicate things."

"How so?"

"The brain is like a computer," he explained, "programmed to function by interpreting information, sending information down specific pathways, and relying on all its parts to perform tasks. Memory loss may not affect any abilities, like telepathy or empathy, but since this is something not yet fully explored, we can't know for sure. In your case, while we tap into these areas, we may stimulate the memory portion and, in a sense, shock your memories back into your conscious self."

Daith thought about it. "So—without memories, my abilities may be blocked or the abilities could bring them back even faster?"

"Yes. Or not having memories may not affect things either way."

"I see. Guess that means I'm the 'trial and error' type of patient." Another crewmember, this one younger than her, squeaked when he noticed her, and then turned abruptly down an adjacent corridor, trotting on all fours. Daith gritted her teeth.

"I suppose you could consider yourself that type of patient."

"Oh, now I'm reassured," she said, sarcastically, bringing her attention back to Dru.

He smiled. "Sorry. Remember I'm not good at the bedside manner thing."

"At least you don't talk for ten standard minutes about something like congratulating me on waking up."

Dru let out a laugh as they took the stairs to the floor below. "Doctor Ludd does ramble a bit, doesn't he?"

Daith seized the opening. "Has he always been this way?"

"For as long as I've known him, but I haven't seen him in years. It's a trait of his species. They claim it prevents miscommunication. If you talk long enough, you'll say everything you're thinking, so no one can misread what you've said or claim you're holding anything back."

"Interesting...so you've worked on this ship before? With Dr. Ludd?"

Dru stopped in the middle of the corridor. "Uh...."

While Daith watched Dru, warmth spread through her body. Not like what she felt the night before. This time her stomach turned and rolled, nervous. Her skin beaded with sweat and she felt lightheaded. Dru reached out and grabbed her arm to steady her.

"Daith, are you okay?"

The warmth receded. "Yeah, I'm fine."

"You looked like you were about to faint."

"Really, I'm okay. I just felt..."

"Felt what?"

"I don't know exactly. Nervous then hot and then—I don't know."

Dru hesitated before he responded. "I think we should postpone our session."

"Please don't. I really am okay. Doctor Ludd even said so."

"Doctor Ludd didn't see what happened. If he had, I'm sure he'd change his mind."

"No." Daith's body trembled. "You don't understand."

"Yes, I do. I—"

"No, you don't," she said. She pulled away from him and continued toward the simulation room. "I have nothing. No memories, no family, no anything. There's no one I know to tell me I will remember them and they love me and this is my life. I am surrounded by strangers who keep secrets and scurry away at the sight of me. And now I have the chance to learn more about myself and get my memories back and you want to keep me from doing that? How much longer do I have to wait before I know who I am? How many more 'tomorrows' until tomorrow becomes today?"

Dru caught up with her. "Daith, you're scared—"

She whirled around. "Yeah I'm scared. I'm terrified!"

They'd arrived at the simulation room. "I wish I could help answer all your questions," Dru said, "but I don't know many of the answers myself. I don't know what deadlines Doctor Ludd spoke of or why you were attacked. I can't answer about your family and I don't know how long any of this might take."

He put his hands on her shoulders and made her face him. "But I do know I will help you find those answers. The one thing I won't do is put your life in jeopardy to do so. Knowing who you are, where you came from, what to do with your life—these things are all important. But what use are they if who you are right now gets damaged? Your past and future won't matter if you get lost in the present."

Daith's shoulders sagged in defeat. A heat emanated from his hands. She relaxed. "I just want to know what's going on."

"And you will, but the process will take time. And I promise I'll be here to help you through it."

Daith let out a huge breath. "Okay." She couldn't imagine doing this without him.

"Do you still want to work today?" he asked.

Daith nodded. "I need to do something. Alone in my room, staring at nothing, trapped in my own thoughts—yeah, I need to do something."

Dru opened the door to the simulation room. "We'll go slow. Computer, please call up program X-Dru-two." A beep before a circular patch of sand bubbled up under their feet. A small table with two chairs sat in the middle of the sandy area and all around them stretched a vast body of water, its surface calm and a bluish- purple. Large, green, feathered creatures soared above them in an intricate pattern, cawing in the distance. Daith breathed in the salty sea air. Her tension seemed to magically melt away.

"I've always been fascinated by oceans," she said as she took a seat. "I mean, when you gaze out across the water, the surface is calm and peaceful. But below, there is so much happening. I think individuals are that way too—putting on a calm exterior to cover up the chaos underneath."

"When did you first make that analogy?" Dru asked.

"I'm not sure. I don't remember ever seeing an ocean before. But it's so familiar." Daith snorted. "I must sound crazy."

"On the contrary. It's a good sign. It shows some of your memories may still be intact." Dru paused, pointing at a stack of datapads on the table. "The stack contains various numbers, words, and pictures. You will use them to work on your telepathic ability."

"How do you want me to do that?"

"Hold up the first datapad so you can see it, but I can't."

Daith flipped it up. The word on the screen was 'ocean.'

"Now," Dru went on, "picture the word clearly in your mind and project it toward me. In theory, I should be able to see the word in my mind and will then say it out loud."

Daith felt a little silly, but agreed and closed her eyes. She held the image of the word and mentally pushed it toward Dru. She wasn't sure what else to do. Before she could open her eyes a warmth centered in the pit of her stomach, like a fiery ember. The sensation reminded her of what she'd felt during the star-particle session. Frightened she might over-exert herself again, she opened her eyes.

Dru's eyes were still closed, his dark hair moving with the breeze. Daith cleared her throat and his eyelids fluttered open.

"Is something wrong?" he asked.

"I'm not sure." Daith explained the "warmth" she'd felt. "I was afraid the same thing might happen when I went to the medical wing."

"Of course. This is entirely my fault." He flipped his hair off his face and sat back into his chair.

"What do you mean?"

"I should have told you what to expect during this exercise."

"You mean, I'm supposed to feel that way?"

"Yes," Dru assured her. "The 'warmth' you felt is a surge of energy. In our first session, you had no control over it, no focus. When the warmth spreads, squeeze it all together. Then you should be able to pull or push the focused energy where you want it to go. For this exercise, you'll want to push the energy behind the word toward me."

"How do I do that?"

Dru hesitated. "Well, see, I'm not exactly sure."

"Haven't you ever done this?"

"Me?" Dru asked. "Oh, no. You are at a much higher skill level. I only have some basic empathic abilities."

"Empathic. Does that mean you can sense my emotions?" Her body shivered with tension.

"Sometimes, but only if they are really strong. And nothing more than glimmers. Ready to try again?"

Daith nodded and closed her eyes, forcing herself to push aside her nerves. Instead, she imagined how incredible the moment would be when she remembered her past.

Holding the image of the word 'ocean' in her mind, she again felt the surge of warmth in her stomach. This time though, she concentrated on the feeling and kept it from spreading further throughout her body. To her amazement, the energy stayed tightly together. She directed the concentrated power upwards, through her chest and throat, like a floating hot ball of light, and up into her head. With a gentle push, she sent it toward Dru with the word 'ocean' attached. Daith could feel the instant when the image reached Dru's mind.

"Stars, Daith," Dru cursed. "Ocean! The word is ocean!"

Daith's eyes flew open, stunned. "What?"

Dru's fingertips rubbed his temples. "You don't have to yell the word."

"I—I didn't. I just pushed it toward you."

"Really? Wow. I've never had such a strong connection with someone. You have a lot of power."

"Maybe it's just you," she said. She meant the words as a joke, but the tension spike in the room scared her.

"How do you feel?" he said, changing the subject.

The heat in Daith's body had receded, but she felt fine. "Good."

"Great!"

"Can we try some more?" she asked, eager.

"Of course."

The two of them kept working, with quicker results. Soon, Daith could send whole sentences.

"What comes next?" Daith asked.

"Next is dinner and sleep," Dru replied, rubbing the back of his neck. "We've been at this for three standard hours. I'm exhausted and my head is throbbing."

She put her hand on his. Heat immediately flared between their skin. "Is that my fault?"

"No. I haven't worked with a telepath in a while. It's like going for a run without warming up first. I'll be more ready next time." He glanced at their hands, chewing his lower lip, before he drew his away. "How do *you* feel?"

Daith took in another deep breath of salty air. "I feel pretty okay. A little tired maybe."

"Good. You show real promise, Daith."

She grinned, happy she'd done so well, and pleased by his reaction.

They decided to meet back the same time the following day. Daith toyed with the idea of asking Dru to dinner again, but fatigue settled over her and the thought of being social sounded exhausting.

Once Daith arrived in her room, she went to put an order of food in through her console, and stood staring at it. She popped one of her pills while she thought about what to order, but sleep seemed more enticing. She changed into some comfortable clothes and lay down, falling asleep before her head hit the pillow.

Chapter 18

DAITH BOUNCED OUT of bed when she awoke. The once unfamiliar surroundings now felt like a comfortable place of refuge. Though she'd still overslept a bit, she found pleasure in the fact she had nothing more than a slight headache from her work with Dru the day before. Daith threw on an outfit, then inhaled her breakfast before hurrying to the simulation room. When she arrived, the computer indicated Dru's presence inside, and Daith wondered what sort of scenario she would be in for this time. To her disappointment, the room contained an ugly green chair in the center and a few other pieces of furniture scattered about.

"A little bare, don't you think? Guess you shouldn't have used all your interesting programs so soon," Daith joked.

"You will be working with real objects today, not simulated ones, and the empty room will keep you from distraction."

"Sounds boring."

"Hopefully, it won't be too bad." He examined her face. "How do you feel this morning? Headache, bloody nose or ears, fever, dizziness? Anything out of the ordinary?"

"No. My head feels a little heavy, but none of those other things." She paused, her eyebrows crinkled. "Are those other symptoms likely? I mean, I thought you said I would be safe developing these abilities."

"You will be safe in my simulation programs." Dru indicated the chair. "However, working your body's energy and expanding your mind's limits can take a physical toll. The most common thing I've seen is headaches. They are the first sign you are pushing too hard. The other symptoms are a result of overextending your abilities. Those sometimes develop after the testing is over. If you ever notice things like blood on your pillow in the morning or if you wake up sweating or with chills, these could be latent responses to being overstimulated. I think if we take things slowly, you shouldn't have any problems."

"Sounds like I'm taking a risk either way." Taking things slow might prolong her memory loss while going too fast could cause injuries. She didn't like feeling stuck at a fork where either path could lead to making her life more difficult.

"Yes, but I think you'll be up for the challenge."

Her anxiety melted away. "Thanks, Dru. I'm glad you are here to help me."

"Can't think of anywhere else I'd rather be."

Daith cleared her throat, hoping the heat in her face wasn't physically noticeable. "Okay then, let's get started. What are we working on today?"

"I thought we could continue with your telepathy training."

Daith eyed the old chair. "You want me to send thoughts to furniture?"

"Not quite. Telepathy isn't simply sending your thoughts or

reading someone else's mind. It is a link to the objects around you, without using your normal five senses. You can tell what someone's actions are in another room or you can decipher the inner workings of a machine. You can understand and give understanding to others around you without having to explain anything."

"Sounds intense."

"It can be. But I believe access to telepathy gives one of the greatest rewards: a better connection to the universe."

Daith pointed at the chair. "Why am I using something not alive then?"

"It's easier to focus when you don't have to worry about emotions. With something animate, the being's emotions can be stronger than their rational mind, unless they've learned how to control them. If you started with living things, you would have to deal with their thoughts and their emotions at the same time."

"But you and I worked together yesterday on telepathy and you aren't inanimate."

"True, but I also have a strong control of my emotions. I worked with you instead of against you, and I've had experience receiving impressions before."

"I guess that makes sense. How do I start?"

"I would like you to find out what's wrong with it." Dru guided Daith behind the chair, the heat between them instant. He stepped away quickly.

The piece of furniture seemed normal, except for being painted a hideous shade of green and sporting a large crack in the wood.

"And how am I supposed to do that?"

"Use your mind to connect with the chair. Search its fibers, its different components like wood, wax, oil, or paint. Then find any breaks, chips, cracks, or other parts that may be broken and tell me what they are."

She closed her eyes. *I feel ridiculous.* Daith stood for a few moments, waiting for something to happen, but nothing did. All she could hear was the hum of the ship and her own heartbeat. She opened one of her eyes and peeked at Dru.

"Concentrate," he said.

Daith closed her eye and let out a long, slow breath. She placed her hands on the back of the chair and let her fingertips slide over its top. The wood beneath her hands felt curdled and knobby, the paint flaking away.

This makes no sense. How am I supposed to have a chair tell me things? It's not going to say 'Hey! Did you know I once lived in a house with six children? Once, while playing a game, the oldest knocked me over and broke one of my legs. They thought they could fix me with glue, until their father came home, sat on me, and broke me again!'

Though the story sounded silly, Daith could *see* the image in her mind—the children laughing, their horror at the broken leg, when they hid as their father bellowed after rebreaking it.

'And of course', she imagined the chair continued, *'the huge fire where I got charred to a crisp. I was one of the lucky ones. The couch didn't stand a chance. They tried to sand me and repaint me, but can you believe what color they picked? It's hideous.'*

Daith could taste the acidic smoke of a fire and smell the scent of fresh paint drying.

Startled, she opened her eyes and knew she had witnessed the chair's history.

"But how?" she gasped, after telling Dru what had happened. "I mean, the chair didn't actually say anything. But I could see and smell what had happened."

"Every object emits energy," Dru explained. "You felt the life energies connected to the chair. The energies left a mark and you were able to, in a sense, relive those marks. Think of them as energy fingerprints."

Daith's body vibrated with excitement.

"Are you okay?" Dru asked.

"I'm fine," she said. "It's a lot to take in at once. I just had a conversation with a chair." She paused. "Do you think I knew about these abilities before my memory loss?"

"I wouldn't be surprised. The type of skill level you've displayed is quite high."

"Do you think I had better control over them? Or greater abilities?"

"I suppose it would have depended on how much training you'd received and how hard you'd practiced."

"I want to work on these abilities more, then. Really find out what I can do." Her tone bubbled with eagerness.

Dru hesitated. "Why?"

"I don't know. It's just—incredible. Such a rush."

"It can lead to a lot of power," he said.

"Power?"

"The tests we've done so far have been passive. If you continue on with training, you will be able to test for active powers also."

"What's the difference?"

Dru indicated she should move to the next piece—a warped reflector unit. "Passive powers are the willing exchange of energy while active powers require a forced change. For example, our test of sending words was passive—you sent me an image and I received it. An active way would have been for me to pull a thought from your head without your consent or for you to implant a thought in mine. You could dig through someone else's memories or thoughts without their knowledge, learn their secrets, or manipulate them into doing anything you want."

Daith shivered. “Sounds like mind control.”

“In some cases, it is. But what if it’s to force a hysterical being to calm down or retrieve the dying wishes of someone who is in too much pain to speak?”

“I see what you mean. I suppose it comes down to how someone uses that power.” Daith paused. “Will I be able to do those things?”

“I don’t know.” Dru averted his gaze. “We can test your active powers later on, if you want.”

Daith caught her reflection in the reflector unit. “I want to.”

“What if you found out you could do those things? Would you?”

“Why not? I could use those gifts to help others.”

Dru didn’t respond.

“Right?” Daith asked, feeling less sure.

“How would you know you were helping?” he asked, slowly. “Say you retrieve a dying man’s wishes from his mind and tell his family. What would you do if they said that wasn’t what he told them he wanted? And how could you tell if his wishes were really what he wanted or if his thoughts had been altered due to the stress of dying or dementia?”

“I don’t know.”

Dru’s words came out rough. “Or what if you stopped a civil war by destroying all the weapons on the planet, but then an outside force comes and conquers the world because the civilians have no way to fight back?”

“I-I don’t know.”

“Or what if you think you’re doing good, but others disagree and turn against you? Are they the ones you now need to fight against, or are they victims, too? Do you reverse what you did or stick to your path?”

Daith had never seen him this intense. “Where is this coming from?"

"What?"

"These examples seem specific. Have these things happened before?"

Dru didn't respond right away. "Some of those who have power cannot accept responsibility for it. I've seen how wanting to help can get twisted. There is no line between right and wrong, only perspective."

Daith sat, unsure of what to say. Dru seemed lost in his own thoughts. The two of them continued with her tests, and even though hours had passed, Dru hardly seemed to notice.

When they'd finished, Dru excused himself, saying they'd meet again in the morning. Daith watched him leave. Her stomach muscles pinched together, her eyes watered. She felt bleak, alone, unsettled.

So much sadness. Startled, she realized she wasn't upset. He was.

She could feel Dru's emotions.

* * *

Dru left the simulation room, lost in thought.

Why did I blurt out those questions? But he couldn't help it. The similarities between Daith and her father were too parallel. And he couldn't lead Daith down the same path.

But did he really trust himself with this responsibility? He hadn't been able to save her father—what made him think he could save Daith?

If only Riel were here.

Except Riel was dead.

Dru stumbled in the corridor. He reached out to steady himself against the cool, metallic wall. It had been close to a year since her death, but the pain from the loss hit him fresh. He'd been ignoring his grief since he'd boarded the ship.

Entering his quarters, he sat on his bed, his forehead pressed against his hands.

Please. I don't want to remember her right now. But the memories came anyway—moments like sharp lighting.

Eighteen years old, fresh out of school. Off of Sintaur, away from the war, and waiting to start his new job at PRIN, the Psychology Research Institution on Neoron, when Riel showed up. Short red hair, a halo of sunset to her sunshine-yellow skin. And her smile...

Flash forward two years. Dru remembered the vidlink call from Trey, his dark blue eyes flitting back and forth. *I need your help, Brother...something is wrong with Jacin... I've read about your work at PRIN with Riel...you two are the only ones who can help....*

A few weeks later, Dru and Riel aboard the *Enforcer.* They'd met with Jacin, but both agreed he might be too far along for help. They decided to try one last time...

Trey showed up instead, face eerily blank.

"Jacin's dead. He killed himself."

Dru and Riel sat, stunned. Riel reached over and took Dru's hand—the touch a source of comfort. A stark contrast to the contempt on Trey's face at their touch.

After they'd left, Dru tried to contact his brother, but with Jaxx's death and the disintegration of the Aleet Army, the whole galaxy changed overnight.

And Trey would not respond.

Seven years later—married to Riel—in love—and then the worst moment of Dru's life...

Riel ignored Dru while she picked out clothes for the trip. Dru never liked being without her.

"The convention will be boring anyway. I know you don't want to go." He'd given her the best 'sad-eyes' he could muster. She'd thrown a pillow at him, laughing, telling him his cheap tactics wouldn't work.

"But Riel!" he gushed in a joking voice, "you can't leave me here all alone!"

She had stopped. "You sound like your brother."

Dru had been taken aback. When he asked what she meant, she said his brother had told her the same thing the night before Jaxx had committed suicide.

Dru was floored. He'd had no idea.

"Trey told me he'd fallen in love with me the moment he met me. When I told him I didn't feel the same, he said I couldn't leave him there all alone," she said. "And then Jaxx's death happened and you and I left the ship."

"Why didn't you tell me this before?"

Riel shrugged. "It all happened so fast, I guess I forgot. We were only there a few days."

Dru's eyebrows rose. "You forgot? You reject my lonely brother, his idol commits suicide, he sees you and me together—and you brushed it off?"

"You think that's why he hasn't answered your contact requests?" Riel's eyebrows contracted. "I suppose that could have been the case. He wasn't exactly stable. It's probably better you've been separated from him."

"Of course he wasn't stable. You know our family was torn apart piece by piece. Trey always had to do the fighting while I got to go to school and transfer off the planet. We could have reconnected on the mission with Jacin."

Riel shoved the remaining pieces of clothes into her bag.

"Really? Did you not see how unhinged your brother was? If he got that upset over something so trivial, then I did you a favor. He needs help, not you."

Dru's anger gushed over. "Leave."

Riel swallowed, hard. She snapped her suitcase closed and stalked out of the room.

The next morning Dru received a telegram. Riel's transport ship had malfunctioned while landing and crashed.

She was dead.

Just like that.

Six months later, he'd received a message from Trey. His message simply read "I heard about Riel. I will have a job offer for you soon."

Dru raised his head and regarded his quarters on Trey's ship. Nearly a year since Riel's death and he still hadn't forgiven himself. He didn't think he ever could. He knew all the psychobabble texts told him her death wasn't his fault and he needed to let it go, but how could he?

And now, Daith—the one woman he could give that second chance to. But what if she couldn't handle the power?

What if she ended up like her father?

Chapter 19

TREY SCRUTINIZED HIS brother across the office desk. Bloodshot eyes, paled skin, unkempt dark hair—Dru was a mess.

"Are you all right?"

"Sure," Dru said, rubbing his fingertips across his puffy eyelids. "No, yeah. I'm fine."

Trey's brow furrowed. "Fine, huh?"

"I guess so."

"What's the problem?"

Dru absentmindedly traced circles with his finger on the immaculate desk. Trey held his tongue at the streaked smudges left behind. He couldn't have his brother fall apart. Not now.

"Dru?" Trey prompted.

"Sorry." He ran his fingers through his hair. "It's just...I'm worried about the direction of Daith's sessions."

Trey's fingers spasmed under his desk. "Meaning?"

"Meaning I don't think she's taking things seriously enough.

I'm concerned about her safety, about the rate at which we're progressing, and...," Dru paused. "And how much she sounds like her father."

Trey's hands relaxed. "It's to be expected."

"It makes me wonder if I'm actually helping her. Everything I've done so far has been in a controlled environment. It's been too easy for her."

"I agree."

"You do?"

"I do." Trey laced his hands behind his head, the stiff-backed chair preventing him from leaning backward. "I've been giving her tests a lot of thought. I knew Jacin better than most. He never had anyone to guide him—show him how the use of his powers could cause harm. I wonder if he had known, if he would have done things differently." He swallowed. "If so, he might still be alive."

Dru leaned forward, his head bobbing quickly. "Exactly! She could be headed down the same path."

Trey pulled fragments from his last dream about Jacin—when he'd killed the rioter in the crowd without realizing he'd done it. "What you need to do, Brother, is create a situation causing emotional distress. It's in this area Jacin would lose control. I assume his daughter would respond the same way."

Dru's eyes were open, but he didn't see Trey anymore. "Yes, I thought that after our session yesterday." He paused, letting out a sigh of resign. "I think I know what I need to do."

* * *

Daith headed back to the simulation room to meet with Dru for her next session, hoping he would be more at ease this time. He'd seemed genuinely shaken at the comments she made about wanting to learn more about her abilities. But hadn't he been the one to encourage her in the first place?

Dru's erect stance when Daith entered the white room contrasted sharply with his drawn and pale face. With a quick wave, he gestured to three different objects on the floor: a rope, a metal bar, and a wooden board. Each item had been split lengthways into two parts.

"I can tell right now they are all broken," Daith teased.

"I want to see if you can fix these objects with your mind," he told her, his tone flat. "Our last session had you sensing inanimate objects' energy. This test will determine if you can manipulate that energy." He yawned and tapped something on his datapad. "It's a boundary between passive and active powers: active because you are controlling the energy, but passive because these objects don't have a will of their own. If you can do this, the results could help to reconstruct your own damaged memories."

"No pressure, right?" Daith kidded. Dru's mouth curved for a moment into a half-smile, but fell quickly. She gave up.

Focusing on the task instead, Daith took up the piece of rope and stared at the two frayed ends. Her eyes unfocused. Her mind wandered. She envisioned the fibers. Each part ragged and split where they'd been severed. Concentrating on the ends, she focused the heat inside her, winding the energy toward the tips of her fingers, and tried to meld the ends of one half to the other.

Nothing happened.

"I can't do it," she said.

"Uh-huh. Keep trying." Dru didn't even glance at her.

Daith's jaw tightened at his lack of response. She tried a couple more times with the same results. Frustrated, she dropped the rope and picked up the metal rod. She focused on the rough edges where the two halves of metal split and tried to make them merge into one rod.

She felt the same warmth flow through her and she concentrated on the metal, willing the two pieces to come together.

Still no luck.

Daith growled softly, wiping roughly at the sheen of perspiration on her forehead. She glanced over at Dru, but he was still tapping away on his datapad.

"Bored?" she asked.

His gaze remained on his notes. "No. Continue."

Squeaks from her teeth grinding together reached her ears. She directed her aggravation toward the wooden board. She tried to mentally pull, twist, bend, burn, melt, tie, and connect the two splintered sides anyway she could. She focused all her energy into a tight beam, feeling the warmth surge through her body. The beam grew, welling up until it squeezed into a tight point aimed directly at the spot between the two boards.

The board remained split.

Daith dropped the broken board to the floor with a thud.

"I can't do it," she repeated. Her body felt drained, her mouth dry.

"I wondered."

Daith's head pounded. "You wondered what?"

"I wondered how far your abilities stretched." Dru typed in a few more things and raised his eye line to Daith, who was rubbing her temples. "Are you all right?"

"Yeah. Just a bit of a headache."

He pursed his lips. "We should take you to see Doctor Ludd."

"No, really, I'm fine," she lied, her head pulsating. She dropped her hands to her sides.

Dru raised an eyebrow. "Let's not work anymore today. Go back to your room, eat a big dinner, and then head to bed early. We have a full day tomorrow, and I want to make sure you're up for it."

His attention returned to his notes.

Daith stared. Why the orders?

Dru looked up at her. "You can go now."

Daith paused at the dismissal. "Fine," she said, the word clipped. She stormed from the room. *What is wrong with him? Is he still upset from yesterday? Or just disappointed I couldn't fix those stupid things?*

Daith dismissed that last thought. Dru couldn't have been upset because he seemed to know she would fail. Though she didn't know if him *knowing* infuriated her as much as the fact she *had* failed. She should have been able to fix those things. Dru had said her energy output outreached anyone else's. So then why couldn't she do this?

Daith returned to her room and flopped down on the bed, facing the gray ceiling. Letting out a sigh, she pressed her fingers to her temples to ease the pain. Why was she so irritable? Did she think she'd be perfect at everything? After all, Dru hadn't said he expected her to fail, he only wondered what her limitations were. Maybe other patients of his had had problems in this area. Maybe everyone failed. Maybe telling her beforehand would have ruined the test.

Daith could think about "maybes" all night and not accomplish anything. It wouldn't get her out of this foul mood. And staring at the ceiling wasn't going to help.

Chapter 20

DAITH LEFT HER quarters, determined to shift her focus from her frustration with Dru. She knew from the schematics the ship had five floors—one above her and three below. Since she didn't have the desire to run into Dru downstairs near his quarters, she headed up a floor instead. Dr. Ludd had always been kind to her and right now she could use some of that kindness.

"Why hello, Miss Tocc!" Dr. Ludd said when she strolled into his office. "What brings you here? Nothing wrong, I hope."

"Not at all," Daith said before he could ask her a dozen questions. "I thought I'd stretch my legs."

"If you're bored, you can always go to one of the simulation rooms. There are some fascinating programs available."

Daith thought of all the work she'd been doing there. Somehow, the simulation rooms didn't sound relaxing. "I think I need a break from those for today."

Dr. Ludd rested his mushy pink chin on his flipper. "Tough

session?"

Daith rolled her eyes. "To say the least. I failed miserably. And Dru completely dismissed me like I was only his patient and not...."

And not what?

"And not," she continued, "like someone with feelings. He seemed distracted and I can tell he's keeping something from me, like Trey, and—" Daith shut her mouth. What if Dr. Ludd told Trey she was complaining? She would seem so ungrateful after he'd saved her life. And what if Dru found out she was talking behind his back? Would he stop his work with her?

"Don't worry," Dr. Ludd said. "I won't tell either of them."

Daith breathed a mental sigh of relief. She took a seat in the plush, green chair in front of his desk when he gestured for her to sit. The cushion molded to her body, as the chair had done when she'd gone out to dinner with Dru. Daith pushed the pleasant memory from her mind, wanting to remain angry with him.

"Besides," Dr. Ludd continued, "your irritation with Commander Xiven is completely warranted, as is your annoyance with his brother. Both of them have offered you little information and in return they ask for complete trust and unquestioning obedience, which of course is completely unfair to anyone, but especially someone vulnerable like you; not meaning you're incapable of handling yourself, but without your memories you have nothing to fall back on."

Daith felt stunned.

Dr. Ludd gently flapped the back of her hand with his flipper. "First and foremost, I'm your doctor, not their employee."

"How did you know I felt all that?"

A gurgle resembling a laugh resonated in Dr. Ludd's throat. "I'm the physician on this ship. I know the moods, habits, and medical history of every member of the crew. And I've dealt with memory loss patients before.

"It seemed pretty obvious to me," Dr. Ludd went on, "you would begin to get irritated at not knowing any more about yourself, nor having access to anything to give you information, and on top of that, I'm sure you feel as though you're being treated like a child, constantly being told what to do and when to do it."

"Amazing. And it's refreshing to have someone be straightforward with me for a change," she said, probing.

Dr. Ludd didn't take the bait. "Please don't expect me to tell you things Commander Xiven hasn't because it's not my place to divulge things he doesn't think you should know. I am in charge of your healthcare, not Commander Xiven's goals. But—!" Dr. Ludd said quickly before Daith could protest, "there are many things I *can* tell you. And since you seem keen on stretching your legs, have you toured the ship yet? I'd love to take you around, although I don't have legs of my own to stretch, so to speak," he joked, wobbling deliberately on his gravlift.

Daith smiled, her headache dissipating. "Sounds wonderful. I haven't exactly had crewmembers begging to be my friends. In fact, most of them seem intent on avoiding me at all costs."

"This crew has been through a lot. They have reasons not to trust. But that is not your fault, nor should they treat you as if it is."

As the two of them left his office, Daith told the doctor she'd explored her floor with the mess hall and the one below her with the simulation rooms and meeting rooms.

"Oh good," he said, his eyes twinkling. "You've left me with the interesting decks. In fact, let's head all the way downstairs to the first level and start with Engineering."

They reached the engineering bay, which sat in the center of the first floor. The large door slid open and Dr. Ludd introduced Daith to Chief Engineer Byot. He was about a head shorter than her and his ashen skin matched his white hair.

"Welcome, welcome, to the cave of wonders," Byot said. The room's floor opened like a concave bubble, with the floor carved out below them. The ceiling hung just above their heads. They headed down a ramp toward the center of the floor, which glowed amber. "Well, more like a cave of loud machinery."

Daith laughed and craned her neck, peering around. Dark coppery walls surrounded them, smooth and shiny. Bundles of black wires snaked their way across the sleekness, winding down into the ship's belly below them. Blue electrical currents sparked where panels had been removed for repairs. "I bet you know every nut and bolt in this place."

"Actually, I got promoted a few days ago, so I'm a bit new to the whole 'Chief' thing, but I'm getting the hang of it." He turned toward Dr. Ludd. "It appears you are having a few difficulties yourself."

Dr. Ludd struggled in the doorway with his gravlift, desperately trying to keep his balance.

"Too many currents all at once, I suppose, not that you aren't keeping things in tip top shape, of course, I just mean—"

"I understand," Byot said, interrupting. "I have no problem giving Daith a quick once over of our engines if you want to wait outside?"

"I'd be grateful." Dr. Ludd turned abruptly. His left side slid off the edge of the seat, but he managed to shift sideways as he floated from the room.

"He's definitely a character," Byot said. "But he's an amazing doctor. Although he couldn't be anything else."

"What do you mean?" Daith asked. She raised her voice to be heard over the humming-chunk noise of the machinery.

Byot continued down the ramp. "I don't know the exact details, but I guess on his homeworld, he knew he would be a doctor from the day he was born, or I guess concocted? I don't know if it's a genetic thing or what, but I guess he can't be anything else. You'd have to ask him for specifics, but whatever way you slice it, he's a great doctor."

Byot gestured for Daith to follow him. Relief washed over her at how comfortable he seemed around her. She hated everyone tiptoeing around her, making up excuses to avoid her, changing directions when they recognized her in the corridors.

Byot stopped in front of her, at the edge of a large, circular pool. "This is what we call the Engineering Bubble. And these," Byot said, motioning toward two long, spiraled machines on either side of the pool, "are our engines. I call them Bola and Bida, which are the names of my two daughters back home, and boy, they sure do act like them. Bola always needs more silari gel and Bida—"

"More *what* gel?" Daith interrupted.

"Silari."

"What is that?"

Byot indicated she should lean her head over the side of the railing next to the first engine. A deep pool, at the lowest point of the bubble, glowed a rusty orange. The substance rippled in a seemingly random pattern, quivering from the motions of the ship. Long tubes carried the gel into the spiraled engines, casting the amber hue to the underside of the mechanical beasts. The edges of the pool were overhung with huge roots. Sap bled into the container from two large, violet-orange trees towering behind the engines.

"So what does the gel do?"

"Fuels the engines," Byot answered. "It's a fairly new discovery—only about fifty standard years old. This ship was one of the first designed to use it. The gel is processed from Silari trees, grown on Sintaur. This fuel is what gives us the ability to travel the distances between planets a thousand times faster than normal space travel, even without a TimeSphere.

"The trees have been protected ever since, but the Allied Planets have decided to attempt growing Silari in other places and see if they'll flourish, so this gel can be used more often."

"Is that what the aroma is?"

"Yep," Byot said, inhaling deeply. "Sort of a nutty, wet-dirt smell. It's the best smelling engineering section I've ever worked in, I can guarantee you." Byot hummed a sigh. "You know, I used to hate space travel—all recycled air. It got to me. I always felt so closed in, surrounded by machines. But this room?" He took in another deep breath. "It's alive, you know?"

Daith nodded. Even though she'd been in several simulations, there was something different about the reality of two beautiful, living trees.

Byot and Daith made their way back to the main door so she could exit.

"If you don't mind my asking," Byot said before Daith could leave, "how are you doing here?"

Daith's heart felt close to bursting. Someone actually cared about her. And not a doctor. A myriad of thoughts whirled through Daith's mind. She wanted to tell him everything, open up about all her problems, her worries about the crew, but she bit her tongue. She thought it best not to have their first real conversation be a mass of complaints. "Fine, I suppose."

"Well, I can't say I know everything you're going through, but if you ever want to take a break, feel free to come and visit."

Daith blinked back her tears. Byot could never understand how much those few words meant to her.

"Thanks, Chief. I appreciate that. Although, truth be told, I don't know how long I'll be on this ship." She hesitated, but the words spilled out. "Dru and Trey have been wonderful, but if they can't help me get my memories back, I'll think I'll go back home. Even though my house was destroyed and my family killed, maybe I can find something or someone to tell me who I am."

"Then you're not staying to help us?"

Daith's eyebrows rose. "Help you? With what?"

Byot jerked his knobby fingers through his short, white hair. "Oh. I guess I heard wrong. Forget I said anything."

Before Daith could protest, the door opened, where Dr. Ludd waited on the other side.

"Enjoy the rest of your tour." The door closed.

Daith stood for a moment, incensed. Did that really happen? She'd finally felt she'd met a crewmember willing to talk to her and then he closed off, too? What was *with* this place?

"Are you ready to continue with our tour?" Dr. Ludd asked.

"Yeah. Sure. Whatever." The two of them circled around Engineering, but Daith's attention wandered. They visited the cargo holds, which were mostly empty. Single-pilot and four-passenger shuttles occupied the shuttle bays. Since Daith didn't understand half the technical jargon Dr. Ludd explained to her, she simply felt more irked.

The two of them left the first level and made their way up to the second. They began with the bridge, located in the center. Daith watched surprise cross the faces of everyone there, except Lieutenant Koye, who scowled.

"Doctor Ludd and Daith Tocc, why are you on the bridge?" Koye demanded.

"I am giving Miss Tocc a tour. Would our presence be too much of an inconvenience if I show her around?"

Koye eyed Daith suspiciously, but made no protest. His was not the only gaze Daith felt follow her around the room.

"Ignore them," Dr. Ludd whispered. "They aren't used to civilians, especially on the bridge."

"Sure. I bet that's the reason." She noticed the red-haired, bronze-skinned woman at the piloting console—the one who'd snubbed her in the mess hall.

Dr. Ludd pointed out consoles which controlled different aspects of the ship: weapons, engines, navigation, shields, and communications. He then indicated the six screens in front of the center chair.

"Each of these screens connect to six different transmitters on the outside of the ship; one on the bottom, outside of engineering, one on each of the four ends of the third level, and one above the fifth level, which I'll show you when we get up there."

"You are taking her to the observatory? But wouldn't you have to go through the—restricted area?" Lieutenant Koye asked. This was the first time Daith had ever heard the Lieutenant falter with his words.

"I plan to use the side access tunnel, Lieutenant. Don't worry," Dr. Ludd said.

Another restricted area? What a surprise.

Dr. Ludd continued explaining the six screens. "Each screen receives a one-hundred-and-eighty degree view of space from its transmitter. The advantage of this is the ship doesn't have to reorient itself when at a new arrival point. Most of our dealings are in the vacuum of space so there's no need for an aerodynamic ship. When we have any dealings planetside, we take a shuttle."

"Uh-huh."

Dr. Ludd must have noticed her lack of interest. He stopped talking and led her off the bridge. They moved quickly past Armories A and B, since Dr. Ludd didn't have security clearance to access the rooms. They made their way around the bend and came upon Trey's office. Daith rang the chime, but no one answered so they moved on.

Since Daith had previously explored the third and fourth levels, the two of them made their way up to the fifth. Daith assumed they would start with the center room again, but was surprised when Dr. Ludd started at the medical wing and worked his way around, skipping the center.

"These sections are Holding Blocks A and B and the ones on the other side of the center are Holding Blocks C and D. These are our prison cells and they hold one hundred individuals per Block. Each cell is half the size of your quarters so the section can accommodate twice as many individuals. The ship holds a compliment of four hundred crewmembers, but we are also capable of carrying four hundred prisoners. Of course, all the cells are vacant right now since adding extra guard duties on top of everything else would be impossible."

Holding cells? Prisoners? What kind of ship is this?

"We've never filled all the cells at once," Dr. Ludd rambled on, "although at one point we carried over two hundred and fifty prisoners. The noise was so obnoxious up here I could hardly keep my patients resting. Honestly! Whoever built this ship lacked a medical degree, I can assure you, but I suppose if they did capture someone and that someone sustained an injury, the easiest thing would be to treat them and then move them quickly to a cell on the same floor, instead of transferring them to another part of the ship. I suppose that's why they put the center room up here, too. Easier for me to go in and work on someone and then transport them to the medical wing, claiming illness or injury, than to move them about through the ship and have other crewmembers ask questions. But still, I could have used all the space in the center for my own equipment, instead of the monstrosity they set up in there."

"What *is* in the center room?" Daith asked.

Dr. Ludd whipped his head around, tottering on his lift.

"What? Oh! Nothing. Nothing at all. Just ah—cargo space."

Daith clenched her teeth. "I should have figured. Probably something you can't tell me about, right?"

"Of course not! It's cargo space. I would show you, but I don't have access. Remember, Lieutenant Koye said it was restricted."

Daith glared at the doctor. "If you can't tell me what's in there, fine. But don't lie to me."

"I'm not lying," Dr. Ludd said softly.

"And I am not stupid. You just finished telling me you have gone into that room, worked on someone, and then transported them to the medical wing. So you obviously have access and it's obviously not cargo space. Stop treating me like some kind of naive child!" Daith's hands flew to her head. Pain pounded inside her skull. She squeezed her scalp to try and muffle the sound.

"I'm sorry," he told her, his voice trembling. "And you are absolutely right. I should have been honest with you." He paused when she let out a ragged breath. "Are you all right?"

Daith's trembling hands moved to cover her face. She felt so embarrassed, having blown up at the doctor when he'd been so nice to show her around the ship. She slid her hands away to apologize, when Dr. Ludd's expression made her stop.

"What's wrong?" she asked.

"Your nose is bleeding."

Daith brushed her fingers across her face. They came away bloody.

Dr. Ludd got her to his office and gave her something bitter to drink. By the time the flow of blood had stopped, Daith had gone from slightly embarrassed to completely humiliated. Dr. Ludd suggested taking a break from her sessions with Dru for a day.

At first Daith wanted to tell him she felt fine, but truthfully a break sounded wonderful. Once she returned to her quarters, drowsiness hit her. She had meant to go see Dru and tell him Dr. Ludd ordered her to take tomorrow off, but the thought of making her way down another floor to his office sounded unbearable. Instead, she popped one of the pills from her small vial and slid into bed.

Chapter 21

"COME IN!" TREY barked at the door chime. He forced his balled-up hands to relax. Dr. Ludd's bulbous figure floated through his office door.

"You wanted to see me, Commander?" Dr. Ludd asked. He maneuvered his gravlift next to the chair across from the commander's desk.

"Yes, Doctor. I wondered why you thought taking Miss Tocc on an unauthorized tour of my ship was appropriate." Trey's words held an icy tone.

Dr. Ludd cleared his saggy throat. "Miss Tocc approached my office, Commander, and seemed distraught. She felt considerably bored and troubled by the lack of progress in some of her sessions. I realized some of this irritability could be a side effect of the dream-deflector pills and since she'd already explored part of the ship on her own, I believed a supervised tour would be a better alternative. I didn't want to call for your permission because Miss Tocc was waiting, and it would have damaged the concept of trust if she felt she had to ask to investigate the ship. We even stopped at your office to see if you were in—"

"You should have waited," Trey interrupted. He gestured wildly with his hands. "Distracted her in the simulation room for a while or ran some tests on her until you reached me." His fists came down, hard. "You are not aware of all the details surrounding this girl. The bridge, for example, is no place for her, at least not yet. And of course, the M.M. room should never be accessed. You are responsible for her health and well-being only. Clear?"

"Of course, Commander," Dr. Ludd said. "It won't happen again."

"No, it won't. And remember, Doctor, she is not the only one being monitored."

Dr. Ludd swallowed. "I'm fully aware, Commander."

"Good." He paused. "What?"

"On our tour, Miss Tocc became extremely distressed. During this moment, the walls around her...well, they quivered, Commander."

"Quivered."

"It's as though they rippled or vibrated or...I'm not sure how else to describe it. When she calmed down, the activity stopped."

"Did Daith notice this?"

"No, Commander. Her hands covered her face."

Trey's stomach rolled with excitement. "Thank you for the update. You are dismissed." After the door closed behind the huge, pink, wobbly blob, Trey returned his attention to his computer screen, which held a view of Daith in her room, fast asleep.

Trey traced the lines of her face with his finger.

He'd recently finished reviewing one of the latest recordings between Dru and Daith—their telepathy session on the beach. Daith was indeed progressing quickly. And like he'd thought, her emotions were tied to her actions, like her father's.

Trey turned off the vidlink, exhausted, and stretched his arms over his head. He'd watch their next session the following day. Having these dreams about Jacin kept him from getting a good night's sleep, but like an addict, he yearned to see the next memory. He thought he'd known so much about his mentor, but these personal life moments fed him like juicy morsels.

Trey lowered his head onto his desk, too tired to go to bed, and the world swam away into Jacin's memories...

Trey watched in his dream. Jacin Jaxx stood in front of a wooden podium before a crowd of large, dark, furry creatures, huddled in a tight circle.

"Citizens of Puffair," Jacin said, his voice amplified over the dozens of beings. "I'm here to answer any questions or concerns you may have about me or my work." His skin shimmered with wetness from the humid surroundings.

Puffair, a densely forested planet, lived under equal parts rain and sunshine. Multiple types of tress grew at all different heights, creating a criss-cross canopy of shadow and light over their heads. Jacin tried to remain at ease, ignoring the constant movement of animals darting throughout the treetops.

A Puffairian in the front row squeaked out Universal in a high-pitched voice. His yellow pupils, slit vertically, grew larger in his excitement. "How can the use of mind control help these governments? You are taking away their rights and their freedom to choose what they want to believe." The crowd murmured in agreement.

"Let me explain. I do not use mind control methods. I implant ideas to—"

"Implanting your own ideas is mind control!" yelled out another Puffairian, waving his paw through the air. "How do you know the ideas you put into their heads are what they should be thinking? This freak mutation you have doesn't mean your beliefs are perfect or give you and your soldiers the right to control everyone and rule the galaxy. You call yourselves the Aleet Ambassadors? More like the Aleet Army!" The Puffairians screeched and yelled, pointing at Jacin, nodding to each other.

"No. Please! Let me explain. Everything will make sense if I could explain." Jacin raised his hands to calm the crowd.

A female Puffairian cried out. "He's trying to control our minds right now. I can feel him inside my head!"

Chaos erupted. Most of the group scattered in fear. Jacin's soldiers came in to block the oncoming crowd, but a few Puffairians slipped through, jaws partly open, claws curved.

Jacin ran. He could hear them following him through the dense foliage, calling out with piercingly high sounds. He stumbled over a large root hidden in the shadows and fell. Fear engulfed him. He knew he would have to face them. They knew the area much better than he did. He stood and turned to confront his four attackers.

The first of them emerged from between the leaves. It lunged. Jacin panicked. In an instant, he broke its left thigh bone with a thought. The creature sprawled to the ground, the side of its head slamming into a protruding rock. The Puffairian did not get up.

The next two approached from either side to trap him. Jacin was too fast. He jumped back and focused on a branch above one of the Puffairians. With one thought, the limb snapped in half and fell, landing on the creature's head. Its neck crunched and twisted.

Jacin shifted his attention to the next attacker. Focusing the energy within him, he cracked the Puffairian's collarbone and the creature went down in an earsplitting howl of pain.

"Stop!" Jacin pleaded. "I don't want—"

The fourth attacker rushed Jacin from behind and tackled him to the ground, pinning his arms behind him. Hardly able to breathe, Jacin struggled uselessly against the Puffairian's strength. With his mind, he hurtled another branch toward it. The creature let out a bark as the branch struck his shoulder. The blow loosened his grip. Jacin pulled his arms free. With a twist he rolled onto his side. Peering into his attacker's eyes, he used his mind to make them explode inside its head. One of its paws went up to the bloody sockets while the other paw took a swipe at Jacin. Jacin darted to the side. He missed the direct hit, although one of its claws left a long bloody scratch down his chin and neck. Jacin, now filled with rage, glared at the blind Puffairian. Seeing into the inside of its chest, he ripped its heart in two. Within seconds, the creature slid off Jacin. It fell dead on the forest floor.

Smeared with a mixture of their blood and his own, Jacin pushed himself to his feet and stepped over his last attacker. He stumbled over to the one hit by the branch and felt for a pulse. There was none. The third Puffairian, the one with the broken collarbone, lay a couple of meters off, panting loudly through high- pitched wheezes.

"Everyone will know what you've done here," it whistled through its teeth. "It won't matter if you call it self-defense. The fact that you killed others by using your mind–the mere idea will discredit you forever. And for that reason alone, our plan worked, and my companions have not died in vain."

Jacin regarded the Puffairian blankly until he registered what it had said. They never wanted to listen to him. They had used this opportunity to get him here so they could frame him. A fury rose inside him. The warmth inside his stomach churned, licking his insides, desperate to be unleashed. These rioters attacked his wife for no reason, they refused to listen to his explanations, and they lured him here to make him appear the villain.

"I'm not naive anymore." Jacin crouched down, his face close to his victim. "Your plan to blacken my name has instead blackened my heart. And to think, I used to pity you protesters. No more. Now I know you are not only ignorant, but malicious and loathsome creatures.

"I have never killed before except in self-defense. You wanted a murderer? Congratulations." Jacin used his mind to unwind the fibers of the Puffairian's brain stem and it slumped over dead, face firmly impacted into the muddy ground. Jacin limped away, his head pounding. Blood trickled from his right ear.

Trey snapped awake, unaware of the blood that trickled from his own ear. His heartbeat raced. He could feel the adrenaline drop in his body, panting as if he'd killed the Puffairian himself. The one who had dared to set him up.

Trey reminded himself he hadn't actually done anything. He'd been watching, nothing more.

Trey had never known why Jacin had used violent means against his protesters. Never confiding in anyone, even in Trey, Jacin simply came aboard the ship and changed his orders.

"But now I'm learning all your secrets," Trey whispered to the darkness. "Now I know what it took to turn you. And I'll use what I learn to mold your daughter into what I need."

Chapter 22

DAITH RINSED HER pillowcase in the sink, scrubbing away the dried blood. When she'd woken, she took a moment to remember her bloody nose from the day before.

She glanced into the reflector unit—her emerald green eyes lackluster, her eyelids puffy. Although she wanted to continue working, she was glad the doctor had requested she take the day off. Besides, she still felt upset at the way Dru had dismissed her.

Daith got dressed while she waited for breakfast to come through the chute, then ate quickly before making her way down to Dru's office to tell him they'd have to postpone their session.

Yawning, she rang the chimes to his office.

"Come on in Cadet—" Dru answered as the door opened. He paused and blinked. "Daith? What are you doing here? Our session doesn't start for another two hours."

Daith could tell he had recently gotten up, since he was shirtless and spoke to her through a mouthful of food. Daith had never noticed the leanness of his body.

"I know. That's what I came to talk to you about. Am I interrupting something?"

"Not at all. Just waiting for some data. I'll be right back."

Dru maneuvered his way through the mess and entered a door at the back of his office. Daith peeked through and could make out a bed, the edges of a closet, and stacks of clothes and datapads on the floor.

Daith took a seat in front of Dru's desk while he emerged from his quarters. She forced her gaze around the room as he slid a shirt over his head, embarrassed by the fact she wanted to glimpse his bare skin.

"What's going on?" he asked, interrupting her thoughts.

"I spoke with Doctor Ludd and he told me to postpone my session with you until tomorrow."

"Why?"

"He thinks I've been overworked. I can't say I disagree. My head has been feeling a little—raw."

Dru frowned. "You should have told me this. I would have given you the day off."

Daith fought the shout at him. "I know. I don't think I noticed the discomfort myself until last night. The work excited me. I guess I ignored the pain."

"That's foolish of you, Daith," he said. "You should be more aware of what's happening to you, otherwise you could get hurt."

"Really?" Sarcasm soaked the word.

Dru nodded, like he hadn't noticed. "Oh, yes. Make sure you tell me next time. Go relax. See you tomorrow." He dropped his gaze to his plate, shoveling in another bite of food.

Daith clenched her jaw. Did he think she didn't know this? She wasn't a child. "Fine. I'll make sure to tell you in the future."

Before Dru could respond, Daith stalked out of the room.

* * *

Dru wanted to call out after her, but what could he say? He didn't want to push her so hard, but to make sure she understood the severity of her power, he had to. And he knew the side-effects from the dream-deflector pills weren't helping her frustration levels.

Dru stared at his breakfast, his stomach cold and tight. He pushed his plate away with more force than he meant. The meal flew off the edge of the desk. Food splattered onto the floor.

Dru expelled a forced breath. He couldn't blame her for being upset. He'd been ordering her around and scolding her about things she already knew. If he could only tell her about his plan....

He dug the heel of his hand between his eyebrows. This test was so important. If she failed, they could all be in danger.

Especially him.

* * *

Daith let out a long sigh, sinking deeper into the bath's muck. Sloppy, pale orange bubbles popped in the air around her. She'd had the best day she could remember—literally. Daith spent most of her time in the simulation room. She'd gone for a stroll in a tropical forest dotted with waterfalls, the spray kissing her face. Cool water caressed her skin during her swim in a crystal clear pond. The sound of her footsteps echoed while she explored an underground cave, dotted with glittering chunks of jeweled rock. Now immersed in a tub full of a slimy peach-colored mass, which according to the ship's computer, would relax her muscles, clean her body, and rehydrate her skin.

She emerged and the goo slid off her body, leaving her skin soft and smooth.

Getting dressed, she wondered what she'd order from her quarter's food chute when a sudden urge hit her. She didn't know why, but she felt she should go to the mess hall instead.

Daith cautiously entered the area. She hadn't been back since she'd been snubbed by several crewmembers. At the counter, she ordered a plate of lutari, which released bursts of a heavy, flowery scent. She glanced around the room and took a seat at the end of an empty table.

Scooping a heap of the small, round pods into her mouth, Daith inspected the area. A cluster of ten young cadets congregated in one corner, all highly involved in some sort of game using information on datapads. Other tables were sparsely populated, with smaller groups of three or four. One group, which appeared to be officers, included a muscular man who conversed quietly with his companions. Daith heard someone call him Lieutenant Commander Cenjo.

While she chewed, she stared at him, fascinated. He appeared to be the eldest of the group, which wasn't saying much since he seemed only five or six years older than she, with velvety black hair combed back severely over his scalp. The harsh, artificial lighting made his olive skin seem sickly, but his deep brown eyes sparkled, alive and healthy. His biceps pushed against his shirtsleeves, barely contained. She had a feeling she'd seen him before, but she didn't remember meeting him on the ship.

He stood to leave and Daith felt the same strange urge she'd had to go to the mess hall, but this time to follow him. She downed the rest of her food in three huge gulps and trotted out behind him. He headed for the simulation rooms and went inside Room Three. The panel next to the door read "Advanced Combat Training."

Daith meant to leave when two cadets entered. She peeked

through the door. The room contained several mats and oddly-shaped obstacles. Lieutenant Commander Cenjo stretched in the background and nodded at the two crewmen who arrived. He caught Daith's eye and raised an eyebrow at her. Daith pulled her head from the room, blushing furiously. Why had she followed him?

Daith proceeded back toward the stairs to go to her room, but when she turned the corner, she bumped into someone.

"Oh, excuse me," she said, not really paying attention.

"No problem, Miss Tocc."

Daith glanced up and, although she hadn't thought it possible, blushed even harder.

"I'm sorry," Daith burst out. "I didn't see you standing there... I mean, I wasn't looking where I-I mean..." she stammered.

Lieutenant Commander Cenjo smiled and Daith wished the floor would swallow her.

"I wondered if I could help you?" he asked her. "I noticed you following me."

Daith stood, trying to think of something, *anything*, to explain her actions. "Honestly? I have no idea."

The Lieutenant Commander patted her on the shoulder. "It's all right, Miss Tocc. I'm only having a little fun. I caught you eyeing me in the mess hall, and was surprised to see your head peering into my class. I cut around the other way, it's a bit quicker, to head you off." He had a relaxed dialect, not clipped and proper like Trey and other crewmembers from Sintaur. Daith liked him immediately.

"I didn't mean to take you away from class. Are you the instructor?"

"I'm in charge of combat training and hand-to-hand military tactics," he said, the pride evident in his voice. "I was real lucky. The skills I have are invaluable to this ship, 'specially 'cause we are always bringing on new recruits. It's good to have someone a little more seasoned, in order to teach the 'newbies' a thing or two."

"You can't be that old." She cringed at her bluntness.

"I'm not, but on this ship, I'm practically ancient. Me and Commander Xiven are considered relics at thirty standard years."

"Why are so many of the crewmembers so young?" Daith asked.

He tapped the end of her nose with his finger, like an older brother teasing his younger sister. "A long story and I've got a class to teach." He paused.

"Something wrong?" she asked.

He hesitated. "No, Miss Tocc. You just...ah, well. I've got to run. See you around, Miss Tocc."

Exasperation bit into Daith's mind. Another crewmember keeping something from her?

She'd had enough.

Chapter 23

DAITH TOOK A moment outside the simulation room to collect herself. Her mouth felt dry when she swallowed. Confrontation wasn't an appealing option, but she didn't have another choice. She'd grown tired of Dru's dismissals and condescending tones, sick of crewmembers like Dr. Ludd and Engineer Byot feigning friendship while keeping secrets from her. Even Lieutenant Commander Cenjo seemed upset about something.

No matter the outcome, she wanted some real answers.

Dru spoke first when she came in, catching her off guard. "Daith, I want to talk to you about something." The program featured a meadow next to a small stream. Tiny white flowers peppered the grass, filling the room with a sweet, creamy smell. Blue, fronded trees swayed in the breeze around them, bending into the stream to drink. He motioned for her to sit on the bank next to him.

"I know you've been upset with me lately," he continued, his attention on his hands as she sat. "And I want to apologize. I've barked orders at you, expected obedience, and haven't given you a single good reason why. I've also been putting strain on you, physically and emotionally, and expecting you to deal with these added stressors like you've been practicing your abilities for years.

"You've exceeded all my expectations, and I've done nothing but push you harder," he continued. "Before we start today I want to make sure you know how impressed I am, not only by your skills, but also your ability to handle such a chaotic situation."

Dru waited for a response, but Daith sat, silent. Had Dr. Ludd told Dru what they had talked about? How else could he have known what she'd been thinking?

Thoughts whirled through her head. She had so many things she wanted to say, wanted to ask. But the question that spilled from her lips took her by surprise. "Why is everyone afraid of me?"

Dru blinked, but didn't respond.

Daith continued. "I mean, it's not like they run screaming in the other direction when they see me, but most of the crew avoid me or make up excuses not to talk to me. Is there something about me I don't know? Something to make them scared?"

Dru paused. "I want to pretend I have no idea what you mean, but that's absurd. The wariness of the crew stems from these unique abilities of yours. There is a risk if your abilities surface without you controlling them. Even though we've been working on them, your control is still minimal, and I'm afraid some of the crew worry you could be dangerous."

Daith thought about it and understood. She could be compared to a live bomb—never knowing when it might go off.

Her shoulders dropped. "Why didn't you tell me in the first place?"

Dru paused again, but somehow he seemed strange. He stopped moving, even breathing, for a moment before he answered. "I worried about pushing you too hard. Without your memories, I wasn't sure how you would respond to the tests."

Doubt crept back in, tensing her muscles. "But we haven't worked on getting my memories back. I mean, I haven't remembered anything new. All of our sessions seem to revolve around these abilities."

"You did say you wanted to work on them."

"I know I did, but I also want to remember who I am."

He placed a hand on her knee. It felt dense and cold through her pant leg. None of the warm energy she'd felt before. "And you will," he reassured, "in time. I really do think this route is the best to take to maximize your potential and restore your memories."

Daith felt confused. She believed Dru, but she felt hurt by the fact he still kept her in the dark. "Thank you for telling me," she said, "but please stop holding things back. Being a blank slate, I can't trust myself. I need to feel like I can trust you."

This time several moments passed before he found his voice again. "I understand. And I agree. Trust is important and hopefully will come more easily for both of us after today." He removed his hand. "For now, if you're rested and ready, I'd like to start on today's session."

"Sure." Daith wasn't exactly happy with the way the conversation had ended, but she supposed his explanation was a start. And at least he'd seemed willing to be open with her.

"Good. We're going to start with . . ." Dru stopped talking and became completely still. Not frozen this time, he still breathed and blinked, but he stopped moving. The color in his face bled away. He grabbed his chest. Gasping, Dru fell backward onto the soft grass.

Daith crawled over to him. "Dru! Are you okay?"

He clawed at his shirt, blinking rapidly. "It's my heart," he gasped.

Daith's body felt numb. "I'll call medical."

"No." Dru grabbed her hand. "No time. You can fix it. You can save me."

"I-I can't." She tried to get up, to call Dr. Ludd, but Dru held her in a tight grip, her skin dimpling under his cold fingertips.

"I won't make it. You can do it." Dru's eyes rolled back into his head. Convulsions rippled through his body.

Trembling, Daith knelt next to him. She took a shaky breath, closed her eyes, and concentrated on Dru's chest. Pictures of his pain-filled face flashed through her mind, but she forced them away. She needed to focus.

Daith imagined the inside of Dru's chest, filled with organs, fluids, and tissues. Heat built inside her, growing, eager to be released. She placed her hands on his chest, letting the energy flow through her, using her mind to connect with Dru's body.

A huge, black hole. An empty body. There was nothing inside.

What? She opened her eyes. Dru had stopped stirring. His mouth hung open. White sockets met her gaze.

What had happened? Had she done something wrong?

Daith shook the limp body. "Dru!"

He didn't move, didn't respond.

Horror filled her. "No you can't be dead." She shook him again. She needed him. No one else could show her who she really was.

"Someone..." she called out, her voice cracking. "Someone, please, help me."

The door to the simulation room opened.

Dru entered.

Daith gaped at him. How could he be standing there?

"Very interesting," he said, typing something on his datapad.

He's alive?

Dru told the computer to end the program. The meadow and

stream vanished, along with the Dru who had been lying dead at her feet. White walls and emptiness surrounded her.

"You're not…but you were…this was all fake?" she asked, gesturing.

The real Dru nodded. "I knew you had the ability to reconstruct animate tissue, but I had to show you can't save everyone. Hence the simulation. With nothing real for your mind to connect to, simulated Dru would die no matter what you did."

Daith could see Dru talking, but she couldn't hear his words. He stood there, calm, chatting as if nothing had happened—like she hadn't had to watch him die in front of her. Her head pounded with fury.

"This was all a test? A way to teach me a lesson?" Her anger intensified at the bored expression on his face.

"I needed to prove a point."

Daith's vision tunneled. She felt the warmth creep through her body, but this time she didn't try to control it. She didn't care. "All those things you, or the fake you, or whoever said were all lies. You don't care about me. You don't care I had to watch you die."

The heat increased, powerful inside her. Her rage wanted to come out. To explode. Daith let it. She was so angry she paid no attention to her energy burst. She didn't even realize he hurt until he screamed.

Dru's hands pressed against his throat. His veins bulged as his face purpled.

Daith stopped. The warmth subsided.

"I'm sorry! I didn't mean to," she pleaded, but she knew it wasn't true. She had wanted him to feel pain, the way she had felt moments ago.

Dru shook, his breathing erratic. "Did you enjoy it? Making me feel pain?"

Daith couldn't say anything. Tears streaked her face.

Suddenly Dru's face softened and he put a hand to Daith's face, wiping away the salty tracks. The feel of his warm fingertips made her cheeks tingle. "I'm sorry about this. It was the only way." He hesitated and brushed his fingers above her lips. They came away dark with blood. "I think you should go see Doctor Ludd."

Daith nodded, pressing her sleeve to her face. She barely remembered leaving—her mind filled with tumbled emotions and she hurried from the room, her blood-saturated sleeve dripping onto the floor.

When she reached the medical wing, Dr. Ludd ordered her to go more slowly in her sessions.

"Like it's *my* fault," she snapped at him.

Dr. Ludd patted her with his flipper. He made her drink the bitter medicine to stop the nosebleed and told her to sleep for a couple of standard hours.

She stumbled through the empty corridors to her room. Once inside, she crashed onto her bed, dizzy from the session and blood loss. She fell asleep instantly, legs hanging over the side, face smashed between the bed and the wall.

Chapter 24

THE AIR PASSED in and out of his lungs. Dru rubbed his chest with relief. He had to admit he'd been afraid she wouldn't stop suffocating him.

He took a few moments to collect himself before he turned to leave the simulation room. He couldn't believe how strong Daith's anger made her. On his way to his quarters to update his data—and decide exactly what to say to Daith so she would trust him again—he found his path blocked by a crewmember.

"Excuse me...?" Dru trailed off, unsure of the man's name.

"Lieutenant Commander Cenjo," the olive-skinned man replied.

"Right." Dru searched his memory. "Combat training, correct?"

"Yes, doc."

Dru paused, an awkward smile touching the corners of his mouth. The officer hadn't moved. "Uh, is there something I can help you with?"

"Actually there is." Cenjo took a step closer. "You can watch how hard you are running Miss Tocc."

"Excuse me?" he repeated.

Cenjo's dark eyes narrowed. "You heard me. She just flew by here, face and shirt smeared with blood. Whatever you're doing to her needs to stop."

Dru squared his jaw. "No offense, but you have no idea what you're talking about." He tried to brush past the Lieutenant Commander, but Cenjo blocked his path, planting his muscular body firmly in front of him.

"I may not know how to treat a patient like her, but I do train the crew and I know you are pushing her too hard. She's an incredible woman with amazing gifts like her father, and we all know what happened to him." His voice, though low and steady, tinged with intensity. "He was like family to us, so she is, too. She is your responsibility, Doctor, and if I find out you've been neglecting her health to feed your own timetable, you'll have to answer to me." Cenjo knocked against Dru's shoulder before he strode down the corridor.

* * *

Daith's time-reader beeped. She peeled her face away from the wall. With a slow roll, she quieted the noise, and rose from the bed. In the washroom, she sighed at her reflection—a large pink mark stretched across her face.

While patting the splotch with cold water and trying to smooth the wrinkles from her crumpled clothes, the chimes rang. She blinked the last of the sleep from her eyes and went to open the door.

Dru stood there, his face gaunt and pale. "Hi."

Anger boiled up inside her, but she kept it at bay. "Yes?" she asked, her voice icy.

"How are you?"

"Fine," she lied.

"Oh, um, good." He shifted uncomfortably. "I checked with Doctor Ludd. He told me he treated you for the nosebleed—"

"I'm finding it hard not to punch you in the face," she interrupted. "What do you want?"

Dru's cheeks flushed crimson. "I came to explain."

Silence enveloped them. A crewmember slunk around Dru in the corridor, her hair tendrils rising toward them to overhear their conversation.

"Come in," Daith said, waving him in. She glared at the crewmember who skittered away.

"I know you're angry," Dru said, "but there is a reason for what I did."

She crossed her arms. "I'm sure there is."

"You aren't the first patient I've worked with that has had telepathic or empathic abilities. Most of the time I worked with those who never received training or thought they could learn how to control their abilities on their own. The results were usually disastrous.

"Some went insane, others are in prison for unspeakable crimes, and there are a few who couldn't deal with the pain they'd felt or caused. They took their own lives." Dru made a move to sit on the bed, but Daith's glower made him pull back.

"I approached Trey a few days ago," Dru continued, "with another report on your progress. We were both worried about your advancement, even with me there to help guide you, and that you might not be prepared for all the consequences.

"I thought up a test, involving a scenario you couldn't win, no matter what. I had to know if you could handle real loss. And betrayal."

"Mission accomplished," she seethed.

Dru swallowed, hard. "So I started acting cold, dismissive. Anything to provoke you, put you off guard. Once you felt angry enough at the way you were treated, I turned your emotions against you, apologizing, returning to my old self. A cheap trick, I know, and I feel terrible, but you had to feel not only loss, but betrayal. Like everything I'd said had been a lie. You needed to be angry enough to hurt me. And the more you cared about the person, the stronger the reaction." Dru's voice quieted. "That's why I chose myself."

Still furious, Daith willed herself not to blush.

He continued at her silence. "I couldn't really put myself in danger, because I had full faith you would save me. The only thing you couldn't save was a simulation."

"Oh. Well, now it's all better," she said sarcastically. The warmth inside her returned. She'd felt like such a fool. "I thought you died," she said. Her sight became blurred from moisture. "I had to watch you die. Don't you understand? You're my only chance...the only way...and you were gone."

He reached out, tentative, and when she didn't pull away, he put his hand on her elbow. Energy surged between them, but he didn't break the connection. "I know. I'm so sorry."

"You're sorry. I thought I'd let you die and you're sorry."

Dru removed his hand. "It was the quickest way to unsettle you, make you upset enough to lose control. You needed to know, first-hand, how powerful you are. And how dangerous."

She wanted to still be upset about being lied to, but she remembered how quickly she'd hurt him, how she had wanted to hurt him. Without her last-moment restraint, she would have killed him.

Daith's shoulders slumped and her arms dropped to her sides.

"I really hate to say this, but I think you may have been right." She rubbed her face, feigning fatigue, but actually wiped away tears.

"I think we've both pushed ourselves to our limit today. How do you feel about taking the rest of the night off?"

"You're asking me?"

"Of course. I only ordered you around to get you angry at me."

She paused. "Dru?"

"Yes?"

"This is the end of the tests dealing with emotional upheavals, right?"

"Right. No more tests like that."

"Good. Because I'm still mad at you." Her words were harsh, but her tone soft.

Dru placed his hands on her shoulders, his touch immediately calming her.

"I promise you, I only care about your wellbeing. I told you we would do this together and we will."

Chapter 25

WHILE DAITH MADE her way to meet Dru for their next session, she wondered what sort of scenario he'd have planned. She was surprised to find the simulation room empty. After she waited fifteen standard minutes—listening to nothing but the buzz of the ship recycling air—she turned to leave when she noticed a datapad near the door.

The screen hummed to life. Blue words appeared across the screen.

"Welcome to the 'Hunt For Dru' game.
The datapad contains a clue to lead you to a different area of the ship, which contains another datapad and the next clue.
Each clue will become increasingly difficult.
I advise you to bring the datapad along for a reference.

I was told by the evil Doctor Henchman (a.k.a. Dr. Ludd)
you received a tour of the ship.
I hope for Dru's sake you paid attention.
You have one standard hour.
I have Dru trapped in my evil lair and it's up to you to save him.
Ha Ha Ha. Good luck."

Daith laughed out loud and read the first clue.

"Your first clue is:
Hiding here where things aren't real
Can be a little unnerving
Go to the place where crew members eat
And someone is always serving"

Daith smiled. She knew the answer right away. Trotting up one floor to the mess hall, she headed toward the serving counter and searched for the datapad. One of the small three-legged creatures approached her and squeaked, the next clue balanced delicately on its top. She thanked it, although she still wasn't sure if it had ears, and turned on the datapad.

"Congratulations on solving the first clue.
Can you find Dru in time or will he remain in my evil clutches
for all eternity?

"Clue #2:
I feel empty, although once I was full
I wish I held more
Shall Dru remain captive by the creatures up high?
Who knows what they have in store?"

Daith reread the clue. Her first thought centered around the cargo holds, because they were so empty, but she noticed Dru was being held captive and "up high" could mean the upper deck, so she reasoned the clue referred to the prison cells on the fifth floor.

Daith raced upstairs. She bolted past Dr. Ludd's office and came to the prison door, the datapad propped up against the wall. Quickly, she snatched up the next clue.

"You're doing well, better than I thought, so things will be tougher. The one hint I'll give is you have three clues left, although by now you should already have won.

"Clue #3:
Bring your sweet self closer
You've almost figured it out
Otherwise Dru is gone
The beginnings will help you out"

Daith stared at the clue. She had no idea what the words meant. "The beginnings?" she muttered.

Maybe 'the beginnings' meant her room—the first place she remembered on the ship. Or maybe it referred to the meeting room where she'd initially met Dru?

Daith's eyesight blurred. She sat there, the words on the datapad slightly out of focus, when the answer jumped out at her.

"The beginnings will help you out." Daith read the first letter of each sentence. They spelled B-Y-O-T. She was supposed to get the next clue from Lieutenant Byot.

Daith took off, flying down four flights of stairs to engineering. She approached Lieutenant Byot, out of breath.

Lieutenant Byot handed her the next datapad and smiled. "I knew you'd get this far. I've got a bet going with Lieutenant Koye. Don't let me down!"

Daith turned on the datapad, realizing she had less than a standard half hour left and still two clues to go.

"You're making me nervous, and I don't want to lose, so this next clue is going to be really hard.

"Clue #4:
I connect those at the top
Without me you cannot cross
You'll plummet if you fall from up above
But if I'm up, you're at a loss"

"I connect those at the top" didn't seem to help her so she moved to the line "without me you cannot cross." She knew the ship's levels were spread out in 't' shapes, so she figured the clue meant one of the rooms in the center, which you would have to go through if you made your way straight across from one side to the other. The next line "you'll plummet if you fall from up above" made her think the location was on the upper level, but then "if I'm up, you're at a loss" really confused her. She took a moment to go over each center room: the engineering room, in which she currently stood, so that couldn't be it, the mystery room on the fifth floor which she didn't have access to, so one more crossed off the list. Fourth floor had the mess hall, where she had already gotten a clue, and below that the simulation rooms, where she had started. That left the bridge.

"Of course! I connect those at the top, meaning the bridge lies between Trey and Lieutenant Commander Cenjo's offices. If you fall off a bridge you'll plummet into the water below, and if the bridge is up, you can't walk across it." Daith said all this out loud while she raced upstairs to the bridge. She had about fifteen standard minutes left.

Lieutenant Koye handed her the datapad without a word, glowering. Daith waited until the screen lit up and anxiously read the last clue as she left the bridge. This one ran longer and the words appeared different.

"You've done well, but you're being distracted.
Dru will be lost forever and you will have failed.

"Last and Final Clue:
Nothing is what it appears to be
You've realized this through your time here
There are many who lie, deceive, and trick
Preying on doubt and fear

You're being betrayed, it's all a lie
Your life is just an illusion
In your mind is the truth
To break through your confusion."

A chill ran up her spine. Something bothered her about the message, but Daith couldn't place it.

Daith's stomach churned with unease, but she shifted her focus on the words. She thought she knew the answer, but her conclusion didn't make sense. The clue made her think she should return to the simulation room, which contained things that appeared real but weren't. Except she'd already been there.

Daith didn't have any other choice—she was nearly out of time.

She ran to the simulation room and hunted around for another datapad. Empty. She reread the clue again, searching for what she had missed, when she remembered something. Sifting through the five datapads, she found the one with the first clue and read the first line.

"Hiding here where things aren't real..." Daith eyed the empty room. "Computer, end program." The room's width grew by three meters and there stood Dru, grinning. He had created a program to make the room seem smaller.

"Congratulations," he said. "You saved me from the clutches of evil."

"That's what clue number three meant," Daith said, suddenly realizing it. "It told me I should have already won. The line about 'beginnings' meant I should have checked the first datapad again. I could have won right there!"

"Yes, but you figured out the answer anyway. I'm impressed. It took me quite a while to come up with clues I thought would be hard enough."

Daith handed Dru the datapads. "You did well. But why the game at all?"

"Thought this might be a fun version of a test. Problem-solving and making connections in your mind from words to images to reality." Dru pushed his hair from his face. "I don't know about you, but I'm famished. Want to grab something to eat?"

She half-bowed. "Anything for the man I rescued."

Chapter 26

DAITH NUDGED SOME stacks of datapads aside with her foot and settled into the chair across from Dru's desk. Her stomach growled with anticipation while the food chute hummed. When their meals arrived, Dru handed her a tray.

"What is it?" she asked.

"It's called ulah uun. It's a fungus from Sintaur. I was happily surprised when I noted the dish on the menu, but Trey did love it growing up, so I understand why it's here."

Daith cut through the prickly, green growth and placed a bite in her mouth. The morsel crunched and an explosion of tartness hit her taste buds. The back of her mouth ignited in protest as her lips puckered.

"That is so bitter!"

Dru placed a vial of creamy yellow liquid in front of her. "You're supposed to pour this sauce over it."

Unconvinced, Daith dribbled the sauce over the fungus and

took a smaller bite. To her amazement, the tartness balanced with sweetness.

"Much better," she said through a full mouth.

Dru grinned. "I'm glad you like it."

"I do. It's a perfect end to a fun day. The 'Hunt for Dru' game was really great. The exact break I needed." She paused. A quiver of warmth, which had nothing to do with her meal, filled her stomach. She knew she could ask about the sadness she'd felt from him after their furniture session. "You seemed to have needed a break, too."

"I suppose I've been 'investing' in our work a lot."

"Because you're excited? Or is there something else?" Daith held her breath.

Dru swirled the sauce for the fungi around his plate. "I lost someone close to me a while ago. It's been—difficult. Working with you has been a good distraction."

Daith let the silence hang. She wanted to ask him about it, know more about his life outside this ship, but she felt guilt twisting in her gut. She had no reason to feel guilty, but the stronger the feeling became, the odder it felt, like the sensation pressed on her.

Daith changed the subject. She thought about the final clue Dru had written—about how uneasy the words had made her feel.

"Maybe I read too much into it, but were you trying to tell me something with the final clue?" she asked. "I mean, other than where to find you?" The guilty feeling subsided when Dru looked up.

"No. Why?"

"I don't know. Something in the wording." Daith pointed at the last datapad.

"It seems pretty straightforward to me," he said. He read the lines out loud. "'Start at start and end at end, follow the way to find me, I can see you standing there, but it is I you cannot see.' Not the most elegant wording I suppose."

"Those words aren't right," she said. "I read something different."

"Are you sure?" He pressed several buttons on it, flipping through different screens.

"Positive."

"What did it say?"

Daith's words caught in her throat. "Something about where things aren't real. That's why I thought of the simulation room. I don't remember the rest." Her tongue felt thick in her mouth at the lie.

Dru frowned. "Maybe a previous file got loaded by mistake. I'll check the archives later."

Daith let the subject drop, the words of the last part of the clue running through her head. *You're being betrayed, it's all a lie; your life is just an illusion; in your mind is the truth; to break through your confusion.* If Dru hadn't written the clue, someone had, and they meant for her to read it. But why?

Dru smirked.

"What?" she asked, still distracted.

"There's something I want to show you."

Her stomach gurgled. "I don't know if I can take much more fun and excitement today."

"Don't worry. I swear this will be completely dull and boring," he joked.

"Oh, boy," Daith muttered. The two of them left his office and headed up to the fifth floor. They passed through a door next to Dr. Ludd's office and climbed a vertical ladder. The cramped tube caused Daith to knock her knees and elbows more than once.

"Could they have made this access shaft any smaller?"

Dru laughed from above. "It's not convenient, I know, but it's the only way to get where we're going. The usual way is restricted right now."

"Restricted?" she asked, trying to sound nonchalant. Maybe Dru would tell her about the mysterious center room.

"Yes," Dru said. He reached the top of the tube, pulled on a latch, and the hatch above him opened outward. "I'm not sure why. Trey only told me the room contains some kind of delicate mechanics." He pulled himself out of the tube and offered his hand.

Daith meant to ask what he guessed might be in there, but the words died on her lips. Her head rolled upward to the ceiling—a ceiling that wasn't there.

Her hands went to her mouth in shock. "Dru?"

"Welcome to the observatory."

Daith gazed through the transparent protection above her into the vastness of space.

"Doctor Ludd told me you two hadn't made it up here on your tour so I thought I would surprise you."

Though she'd been in the simulation rooms, something felt different about the real thing. Knowing only a thin layer of clear material separated her from the void made her heart skip.

The sight included a partial view of Dru's ship, the *Reminiscence,* and a portion of the spaceport where they were docked. The rest—utter blackness, so dark the stars blazed with pure whiteness.

And the universe stretched forever.

"Dru," she said, turning to him. Her fingers quivered.

"Daith, what's wrong?"

"I don't know, I just..." She paused. "I come from somewhere out there. And everything is so far. So many things I loved are lost and I don't even remember them. How will I ever find out who I am?"

Dru pulled her into his arms. She buckled under his support, taking in his warmth, his safety.

"I'm so sorry," he told her. "I didn't think—"

"No, this is—it's wonderful. Really," she insisted. "I just...I want to know who I was. Who I am." Her chest still hurt, tight with fear. Energy poured from her, mixing with his own, crackling like static.

Dru's face hardened and he pulled away to look into her eyes. "You may not know who you were, but I think I know enough to tell you who you are. You are an independent, strong, gifted woman who I think will accomplish anything you set your mind to. If you want to find out who you used to be, you will, but don't ignore how amazing you are, even without that knowledge." Dru gestured toward the cosmos. "You've done so much more than anyone I've ever met in your condition. And no matter how big the galaxy is, you will be able to decide who you are, past or no past."

A calm settled over her and her muscles relaxed. "You really believe that, don't you." The words were a statement, not a question.

"I do." He smiled, but it seemed reserved.

"What is it?" she asked.

Dru turned his face away and peered into the vacuum of space. "It's—it's nothing."

Daith placed her hand on his arm. Warmth spread upwards into her fingertips. The energy flowed between them—comforting, unique. "Dru..."

Dru's eyes closed and he gently covered her hand. "Daith, this has been difficult for me. As your doctor, I care about your well-being, but as a man, I shouldn't...I shouldn't care this much." He turned toward her, his face crinkled with sorrow. "There is something so special about you, your abilities, your gifts. I don't know if it's the fact I'm slightly empathic and we've been working so closely together or because of my grief..." he trailed off, unable to continue, and Daith watched him struggle with his thoughts.

"Please," she said, her stomach somersaulting. She could feel the energy from his body pulsating off him in waves. "Tell me."

Dru straightened, removing her hand from his arm. "My contract to work with you is near completion."

Taken aback by the abrupt change in subject, Daith's stomach muscles clenched. "Okay…?" she said.

"I will be your *doctor* until then," he said, stressing the word. "And our sessions are already intense. I can't let it be more than that." He held up his hands to keep her from interrupting. "What I mean is, it's my job to help you, make sure you are safe, but if I cross that line…. I won't allow it. It's the code of ethics I live by, a promise I made when I took an oath to be a doctor."

She hesitated, her heart beating in her throat. "And after your contract is over?"

Dru pushed a lock of hair away from her forehead. "Right now, it's not over."

Her skin tingled at his touch. "I understand."

Dru clasped his hands in front of him. "Well, now you know how to get to the observatory. Feel free to come any time you want."

"I will." Daith followed him down the access tube. Something had changed. Undefined, yet their connection was more than doctor and patient.

Chapter 27

THE FOLLOWING MORNING, Daith made her way to Dr. Ludd's office for her nerve-tracing pills check-up. She thought about Dru the entire time and although she tried, she couldn't wipe the grin off her face. The more she resisted, the harder her cheeks flushed.

Not that her daydreams mattered. Nothing could happen between them. He was her doctor. And yet, a man existed underneath the title—imaginative, clever, attentive, fun. Not to mention attractive. Plus he truly cared about her and really wanted to help.

Perhaps when she left the ship to search for her past he would want to come with her. The thought made the warmth in her belly purr.

Daith blinked rapidly to clear her mind of these thoughts as she arrived at Dr. Ludd's office.

"Please come in, Miss Tocc," Dr. Ludd said after she knocked.

"I'll be with you in a moment."

The bare walls stood out—a striking contrast from the clutter he usually had pasted around the room: pictures of his children, the newest articles on medical marvels, his credentials.

"Are you painting?" Daith asked.

"No, Miss Tocc. I'm retiring."

Daith gaped at him. "I thought you loved medicine?"

"More than you know. But I miss my family and I'm tired of compromising." Dr. Ludd hesitated before he spoke again. "Commander Xiven is a wonderful leader, but he and I don't always agree."

"So why not work for someone else?"

"It's not that easy. I've made mistakes in the past and...let's just say I'm not as desirable anymore."

Daith wanted to ask what he meant, but the question seemed too personal. "When are you leaving?"

"Tomorrow."

Daith's shoulders slumped at his sudden departure date, but said nothing. She took a seat in the examination room and waited.

* * *

Dr. Ludd squirmed while he postponed his examination of Daith. He knew what Trey had ordered him to do, but he couldn't bring himself to do it. At the current rate of Daith's sessions, Trey would kill the girl. Dr. Ludd still hated himself for letting Dru continue on with his tests, even though Daith's headaches, nosebleeds, anger, and loss of control all pointed to being overworked.

Except that's exactly what Trey wanted. He needed her to be unstable and on edge. Well, Dr. Ludd wouldn't help anymore. He'd done his share of wrong, but always on those who'd volunteered, never on someone innocent.

Dr. Ludd reentered the examination room. He took blood and tissue samples, checked Daith's vitals, and told her he'd be back shortly with the results.

Dr. Ludd threw the samples away. He hadn't tested anything. The charade was an excuse to keep Daith on the dream-deflector pills. He'd been ordered to go back in the room and tell her she needed to keep taking the pills, under the pretense they would continue to monitor her nerve reactions for another week.

But he couldn't.

No matter the price.

Dr. Ludd floated to back where Daith waited, took a deep breath, and smiled.

"Everything looks perfect. You have no need to take those pills anymore."

Daith smiled. "Great!" She paused and placed her hand on his flipper. "Thank you, Doctor Ludd. For everything. And I'm really going to miss you."

"I'll miss you, too," he said, patting her hand. "Good luck, Miss Tocc." He watched her leave. "And sweet dreams."

Dr. Ludd returned to his office and let out a wobbly sigh. Now or never. He picked up the microchip with his flipper and slotted the device into the ship's computer through his medical terminal. The ship scanned the chip and confirmed the doctor's genetic pattern.

Dr. Ludd hit the communications panel and called Cadet Milastow to the medical wing. Milastow wasn't fully trained, but she'd have to do for the time being. He didn't trust anyone else with his crew.

Dr. Ludd gurgled a laugh. After all this time, he still thought of them as his crew. His responsibility. But how could he protect them when he knew what Commander Xiven really had planned?

He felt like a coward—running away when he should stay and fight, but what could he do? He was a doctor, not a warrior. His training didn't include combat. And if he couldn't help others...

"I wouldn't be me anymore," he said to no one.

A few moments later Cadet Milastow arrived.

"Can I help you, Doctor?"

"I am feeling a bit drained from some events today, Cadet, and would like for you to cover my shift for its duration."

"Of course." Milastow frowned, her large, maroon ears perking slightly. "I have to admit, doc, I've never known you to be ill. I do hope you get better."

Dr. Ludd patted her on her third appendage, which sat relaxed, wrapped around her elongated neck. "This fatigue has plagued me for quite some time, but I will get the rest I need and be fine." He paused before he exited. "Take care of them."

"You can count on me. Goodnight, Doctor Ludd."

"Goodnight, Cadet."

Dr. Ludd floated through the dimly lit deserted corridors to the cargo room with the escape pods. No one could leave the ship without consent—a protocol introduced years ago by Commander Xiven—but Dr. Ludd knew a way around it. Executive orders could be bypassed by the head physician. The process had been instituted by Jacin Jaxx—a safety-net, in case the commanding officer wasn't available. Trey didn't know the bypass existed.

Dr. Ludd punched in the override code and wobbled off his gravlift, sliding his massive body into the shuttle. Once settled, Dr. Ludd started up the shuttle, opened the cargo room doors, and shot out into space. He plotted his course and settled back for the standard week-long trip to meet his new ship, the *Nuadu.* He'd managed to link with the previous attacking pirate ship and "piggybacked" a signal to a nearby medical freighter. Dr. Ludd put in a request for new work—they asked few questions, desiring a capable medic over credentials. Coordinates had been exchanged and Dr. Ludd sped on his way to meet his new ship, his new crew, and to start his new life.

The *Horizon* sped out of view and Dr. Ludd thought once more about Daith. There was nothing else he could do for her now. But hopefully, she would dream....

Chapter 28

***THE GALAXY STRETCHED** out in front of Daith, its hugeness dwarfing her. She raised her arms to touch the stars. They bowed, extending their points of light toward her, bleeding into their surrounding darkness.*

She laughed, feeling fire pour from her fingertips into the vacuum. Her hair stood on end, floating all around her, like she was suspended in liquid.

"Come to me," she cooed. "Come and play with me and I will rewrite everything."

The stars trembled, but their light reached closer. She turned the reaching beams into diamonds and flame and dewdrops and tears. The sky whirled into shadows of lilac and blue, crimson and gold. The stars no longer shone like chips of white, but stretched and bent in shades of liquid silver and flesh.

"The galaxy is beautiful," Daith said, the words taking shape in wisps of web-like smoke. "And it is all mine."

"You mustn't."

Daith turned, her hair swirling.

"Who are you to keep me from my destiny? This galaxy is mine."

She filled her lungs, her veins, her whole being with fire and unleashed her power upon the intruder. Pain, pure pain shot from her hands, engulfing the one who'd spoken.

"This galaxy is MINE!" she screamed.

The fire died. A body lay limp on the floor, small compared to the vastness of space.

Daith overturned the corpse with her foot, to stand triumphant over the one who would stop her.

Eyes white. Skin reeking of burnt meat. The taste of smoke in the air. Bone exposed through black, curling flesh.

And yet she still knew the face's identity....

Daith bolted awake. She shook so hard beads of sweat quivered on her arms. The image of Dru's dead body lingered in her mind.

She jumped at the sound of her room chimes.

"Who is it?" she called out, her voice cracking.

"It's Dru."

Relief rushed through her. He was alive. "Come in." The door slid open. Tousled and uncombed hair reflected Dru's tired appearance.

"Is everything okay? I heard you scream."

"I did?" Daith asked. She wiped her sweaty hands on the blanket.

Dru sat next to her on the bed. "I was on my way from the mess hall to my office when I heard you."

Daith grasped at the remnants of her dream—the stars, the flames, the pain she inflicted. "It was terrible. I know the dream wasn't real but—"

"A dream?" Dru's eyebrows furrowed with concern.

Daith wrapped her arms tight around her body to stop from shaking. "More like a nightmare."

"You're still having nightmares?"

"No. In fact, this is the first dream I've had since the day we met." Daith watched Dru scan her room. "What are you looking for?"

"Hmm? Oh. Where are your nerve pills?"

Daith frowned at the abrupt change in subject. "Doctor Ludd told me earlier today I didn't need them anymore. Why?"

"You stopped taking them?"

"Yes."

"And Doctor Ludd told you this was okay?"

Fear crept into her belly. "Why? Am I supposed to still be taking them?"

Dru chewed on his bottom lip. "I'm not sure. I wasn't aware he'd changed your medication."

"He said my tests all seemed fine."

Dru's forehead creased. He stood and headed toward Daith's communications panel. He sent out a request for Dr. Ludd to respond. When no response came, Dru asked the computer to locate the doctor.

"Doctor Ludd is in the medical wing," the computer answered.

Dru turned toward the door to leave. "I'm going to see what's going on. It's not like Doctor Ludd not to answer a call. He doesn't need to sleep and he's always in his office. But maybe he's in surgery..." Dru trailed off. "Regardless, you need to go back to sleep."

"Yeah right," she countered, searching for her pants. "Like I'm not coming with—"

"Doctor's orders." He touched her shoulder, stopping her.

"But—!"

"We still have another session tomorrow and I want you at full strength."

"You expect me to sleep after this?"

"Yes. I bet if you lie down you'll be asleep sooner than you think."

Stubborn, she sat, blanket clenched tight around her waist. His hand remained on her shoulder, gentle. Energy poured from him.

"I'm not tired and I want to know what's going on." The words came, but her eyes felt grainy. His touch soothed her. She blinked repeatedly.

"You'll know tomorrow."

"But—" Daith tried again, but the statement lacked conviction. The adrenaline rush from her dream drained out of her. And at the expression on his face, full of concern, she knew she didn't want to do anything else to hurt him. Not after what she'd done in her dream.

"Sleep," he said. "I'll see you soon." He left.

Daith lay down, remembering the feel of his fingers on her skin, afraid one day they'd be flaky and burnt and the fault would be hers.

"I'll never let that happen," she whispered into the darkness, her eyelids sliding closed. "Never."

* * *

"He's *what*?"

"He's gone." Dru spoke to Trey over the communications panel. "I'm in his office right now. The computer says he's here, but there's no sign of him. I don't understand how—"

Trey tuned his brother out. Dr. Ludd—gone. How? HOW?

"Dru," Trey interrupted his brother's words, "get down to my office."

The moment the panel went silent, Trey smashed his hand into it. The buttons bowed inward with a pop. Static hissed from the broken console. He paced while he waited for Dru.

How could this have happened? And when? Doctor Ludd was under surveillance like everyone else on this ship.

Trey went over to the communications panel and hit one of the broken buttons. "Commander Xiven to—" He cursed at a loud squeal from the panel, followed by a puff of acrid smoke. He'd have to go to the bridge himself after his brother showed up.

As he thought it, his chimes rang.

"Enter!" he bellowed.

Dru strolled in, shaking his head. "It doesn't make any sense."

Trey dismissed the comment with a wave. "It doesn't matter, it's already done. I will figure out what happened later, but first I want to know how this affects Daith."

"He took her off the dream-deflectors and she had a nightmare. When I went into her quarters to check on her, she seemed distraught, but all right."

Trey chewed his tongue. Dru was in her quarters?

It doesn't matter. Focus!

"We should get her back on them immediately." Trey headed into the room adjacent to his office. He returned shortly with a large bottle of pills. Opening it, he shook several into Dru's hand. "These are extra dream-deflector pills."

Dru raised an eyebrow, but took the pills silently.

"I'll leave their administration up to you, *doctor*. With Doctor Ludd gone, she is entirely your patient." Trey put his hand on his brother's shoulder. "She is at a critical point and I need you to see this through. I'm counting on you."

Dru hesitated, but he set his jaw and nodded.

Once Dru left, Trey made his way to the bridge to find out exactly what had happened with Dr. Ludd—and who would take responsibility for this mistake.

Chapter 29

THE FOLLOWING MORNING, Daith rang the chimes to Dru's office. She wanted answers. Once she'd fallen back asleep, she'd slept restlessly. Dreams of a blond man lying in a hospital bed plagued her. She knew he could tell her who she was, but he wouldn't respond. Once she awoke, the concern and confusion she'd felt about her medication and Dr. Ludd flooded back and the images of the blond man bled away. Why didn't anyone else know the doctor had left? Why had he stopped giving her those pills? And why had Dru been so worried about it?

Daith came back from her thoughts at Dru's invitation to enter his office.

"Morning," he said. "How did you sleep after your nightmare?"

"Night—?" Daith's mouth went dry. She'd forgotten. Her control over the stars, her desire to remold the galaxy, her retaliation at Dru for wanting to stop her. She backed away, colliding into the wall behind her. Images of his burnt corpse filled her mind.

"Daith!" Dru grabbed her. "Daith. Focus on my voice. You are in my office. You are safe. You are with me. You are *not* dreaming. You—are—safe."

The dream faded and Daith stumbled into Dru's arms.

"It was awful!" she blurted out. "You were dead and I-I killed you. I don't know—everything is turned around like your death already happened, but it couldn't have happened because you are here and alive and…"Daith burst into tears. She clung to Dru.

"It's okay. You're safe with me. It's okay."

Daith's sobs subsided and she pulled back from Dru. "It felt so real!"

Dru led her to one of the chairs. "It was only a nightmare."

Daith shook her head, but didn't say anything.

"I know it's hard," Dru said, "but talking might help."

"I was molding space around me, but you didn't want me to do it. And then I felt so angry, and there was heat, and flame…." She couldn't bring herself to tell him what had happened, what she'd done to him.

"Let's not push it. I'm here. I'm okay. And you're here and you're okay. Right?"

Daith let out a ragged breath. "Right."

"Do you still want to work today?"

She nodded, looking into his gray eyes, so relieved they shone alive and healthy. "I could use the distraction."

Dru gestured for her to lead the way and they strolled through the corridor toward the simulation room—a path she now knew quite well. They stood outside for a few moments as the program loaded before Daith remembered why she'd shown up early at his office to begin with.

"Dru?"

"Yes?"

"What happened with Doctor Ludd last night?"

Dru acknowledged a passing crewmember. "Ah, yes. A miscommunication. My brother forgot to inform me Doctor Ludd had left. No one told me you didn't need to take the nerve-dye anymore."

"Oh." Daith's gut squirmed. Something didn't seem right. "They didn't think to tell you?"

"His departure was sudden. Trey said he'd planned to tell me in the morning."

"Oh." Her next question died on her lips as the scents in the simulation room hit her in a waft of mixed fragrances. A multitude of flowering plants reached into every corner—some higher than she could stretch, others peppered around her feet.

"Little heavy on the perfume, don't you think?" she asked, clearing her throat from the pungent smells.

Dru smiled. "Different senses are controlled by different parts of your brain. Today we'll be working on focusing your senses when one is over stimulated."

"Let me guess, sense of smell is first?"

"Can't put anything past you, can I?"

* * *

Dru completed his report back in his office. Fingertips found their way to his temples to ease his headache. The sheer effort of continually opening up to her while keeping his thoughts blocked, drained him. But the headaches and fatigue were worth it.

Dru had studied Jacin Jaxx's file and ran through a listing of all Jacin's abilities: the power to heal damaged living tissue, the ability to pull apart objects, the technique he used for implanting thoughts, the way he could feel others' emotions, even Jacin's description on how he could remain connected with other minds even when they weren't in the vicinity—sometimes for years.

Through each of their sessions, Dru had tested Daith on each of these abilities with interesting results. She had the ability to heal living tissue—she had demonstrated that with her recovery from her coma. Like her father, she could not reconstruct inanimate tissue, shown by her failure to reconnect the broken board, metal rod, and rope. Unlike Jaxx though, she didn't seem to be able to sense emotions, which Dru knew was a good thing. If Daith could feel the crew's emotions or even his own...

Dru sighed. He thought of how he'd handed Daith the dream-deflector pills after their session—this time under the guise of sedatives to help her sleep through the night. The pills had rattled inside their new bottle. A fake label printed across the side explained how often and how much of the medicine to take. The rattling sound now echoed in Dru's mind.

He pushed his chair away from his desk, nauseated. *Get yourself under control. Those are the same pills she took before.*

Dru caught a reflection of his face in the shiny surface of his desk.

"Do you want to keep doing this?" Stray thoughts flitted through his mind.

I don't want to hurt her.

Can I can keep lying to her?

I can't let Trey down.

Remember what Trey said. This could give Daith a second chance at life.

"Yes. I want to keep doing this," he told his reflection. He would keep a close watch on her to make sure she stayed within healthy limits. He would only lie to her if absolutely necessary. And if he succeeded, perhaps this would help him and his brother find peace.

Chapter 30

TREY STARED AT the report, eyesight grainy, unsure exactly how to feel. He re-read everything uncovered about Dr. Ludd's 'escape,' from the microchip left with his genetic imprint so the ship would still think he was on board, to the way he'd gotten off the ship by using an old medical emergency code, and finally the encrypted messages sent to a passing transport ship to pick him up after he'd jettisoned from the *Horizon.* On top of everything else, Dr. Ludd had wiped both his and the central ship's computer of all his reports, his patient's files, and his surgery results.

Trey sat back in his chair. Dr. Ludd had outsmarted him. And since so much time had passed, pursuing him would be useless.

He'd have to increase security, of course. He'd have to scour the computer for any other old codes still active and install more security cameras, with a personal review of each recording. He'd pay more attention to his crew, judge any hesitation or resistance on their part, and then make sure they couldn't be a threat. He would eventually find Dr. Ludd and deal with him accordingly.

He could do it.

He could because he couldn't rely on anyone else.

Trey nodded at his resolve, but the motion caused him dizziness. His head spun, too full, and his body overrode his mind's plan to stay awake. Trey's eyes rolled into the back of his head and he fell forward onto his desk, sound asleep....

Jacin stood at the front of the *Enforcer*—he and the crew he commanded were headed to Milla Vance IV. Before they arrived, Jacin received a disturbing report.

His daughters could not be located on Lameer.

Concerned, Jacin made inquiries to the soldiers on watch.

"We aren't sure what happened, Commander. The day before they were home with their mother and the next day, they were gone. We searched all the logs for departing ships, but none held records of anyone matching the two girls' descriptions. We questioned their mother, but she refused to answer and demanded we leave the premises."

"Tell the captain to plot a course for Lameer. The other ships may continue on to Milla Vance IV. We'll catch up with them later."

"Aye, Commander."

Jacin sat in his chair, puzzled. What could have possessed Elor to send away his guards? Didn't she know they were there for her protection? Maybe she'd been forced to. Maybe someone kidnapped the girls. Perhaps held them hostage.

Jacin's mind crawled with ideas. Flesh and bone would be no obstacle when he found those who'd hurt his family.

Five standard hours passed before the shuttle docked at Lameer's main bay. Jacin and two of his guards caught the first *Anywhere And You're There!* vehicle and headed to his family's house. When they arrived, Jacin ordered his guards to remain outside.

Elor sat at the table, facing the entrance as he came in.

"Elor!" Jacin cried. He started to rush to her to sweep her into his arms when her hardened look stopped him in his tracks. "Love, what's wrong? Where are the girls? What's happened to them? Are they okay?"

"I knew you would come," she said coolly.

"Of course, Elor. If you sent the guards away, something had to have been wrong."

"Oh, really? Is that all it took for me to get you to come home? Simply dismiss the guards? I should have kicked them out a long time ago."

Jacin's temper rose. "Elor, please don't tell me you brought me all the way here to have this same argument again." Jacin took a seat next to her. "You know my work is hard, and I know I don't come home as often as either one of us would like, but—"

"No. That argument is over. And so are we."

Jacin blinked. He must have heard wrong. "What?"

She spoke slowly, her face turned away from her husband. "I can't do this anymore, Jacin. I'm so alone, always alone." Her eyes filled with tears. "Did you know Valendra turned sixteen last week? She has a boyfriend. And Daith graduated from Lameer Young Adult School last month and took first place in her school's running competition." Elor's composure wavered, her voice shaking, although tears still did not fall. "Did you know I was sick in the hospital for three weeks? I tried to contact you, but they told me you were too busy and to try back in a few days. Every time I called, they gave me the same response."

Jacin's heart pounded. This couldn't be happening. He knew he'd been absent a lot—had missed a few family things—but Elor would never leave him. She was probably tired of being stuck home with the girls while he flitted around the galaxy, making a difference.

"Elor—" he said, a smile on his face.

"You think this is funny?" Elor asked. "You actually see humor in this? Great. I hope you still find this situation funny out in space by yourself. The girls and I will be fine without you. Better in fact without protesters and reporters everywhere we go."

Jacin's heart raced, but still he clung to denial. "Elor, you don't know what you're saying. Let's talk about this. I promise things will be better—"

"You promise? You promised you would take some time off. You promised to stop working once we had enough money. I'm done with your promises," she said, spitting the words at him, "and I'm done with you."

The grin on Jacin's face faded. She was serious. Not a trick to get him to come home more often. She wanted him gone. But he needed her to stay.

Jacin forced his fear to recede, to keep his mind clear. "I'm sorry. I know I wasn't home often, but I'm here now. You haven't lost me."

"You want to bet?"

Jacin raised an eyebrow, waiting for her to finish.

"Have you seen yourself?" Elor said. "You look terrible. It's been two years since I've seen you and you seem to have aged ten. Your hair is thinning, your eyes are bloodshot, and your skin is practically hanging off your face. You've lost a lot of weight and your clothes—"

"I know my appearance isn't perfect," Jacin interrupted, "but my work is demanding. I can't help someone and then take a break when they need me the most because my clothes are dirty." His words came out harsh, a reflection of his pent up anger. "You have no right to dictate how I should look when you have no idea how hard this has been. I can't abandon them because I feel tired and have bad headaches. And I have all those stupid protesters to deal with. I don't know why they can't understand I'm helping!"

"You talk about helping those who need you and doing whatever it takes for them, but what about your family? We needed you and you've let us down time and again. Who are we supposed to depend on? We were a team and you broke us apart. And the 'troubles' you have because of those protestors? Maybe if you stopped to check yourself you'd see you don't seem like you're helping anyone."

Jacin's anger blossomed. "You don't *agree* with the protesters, do you?"

"You have to admit your policies have changed over the last year. I mean, Jacin, you've allowed your soldiers to beat and kill innocent beings—"

"Innocent? That's what they want you to think. They don't care about me or the reasons behind my work."

"What reasons?" Elor challenged. "You've become more interested in proving yourself right than doing what's best for others. When's the last time you healed just to heal? When's the last time you helped instead of forced?"

Jacin couldn't believe it. His own wife had turned against him. She, when all others had abandoned him, was supposed to stick by him through any problem, any decision.

Sweat trickled down his forehead. *Maybe she really doesn't love me anymore. I can't live without her. I need to know for sure.*

Using the technique he'd perfected to penetrate the thoughts of hundreds of others—to stop war, to end prejudice, to change governmental ideas—Jacin pushed forward to comb through her mind.

Nothing.

"Why can't I read you?" he asked.

"What?"

"Your mind—I can't see what you are thinking."

Elor's fingernails dug into the tabletop. "What, now you're trying to read *my* thoughts?"

His eyebrows contracted, perplexed. "No one has ever been able to stop me from reading before. How did you do it?"

"Is that all you care about? You used to ask me what I thought."

"I need to know how you did it. What if others can do this? I need to know so I can counteract it." He breathed heavily as he inched forward.

"Jacin," Elor whispered, "what's happened to you?"

All at once, Jacin felt her fear, like a rush of cold nausea. She had never been afraid of him before. But he had to know how she had counteracted his efforts. Still feeling her fear, he softened his features.

"I'm sorry, Love. I thought I could understand better if I could see what you are thinking. I should never have done that."

"No, you shouldn't. It's a good thing Daith showed me how to block my thoughts." She bit her lip.

Jacin glared at Elor. "Daith has my abilities? How could you not have told me?"

"You think after my attack I would let anyone know about Daith?"

"You had no right to keep that from me," Jacin snapped.

"I don't have to tell you anything. We aren't a family anymore. I don't love you, not this monster you've become. Now get out!"

Jacin's chest tightened, his stomach a pit of ice. He couldn't lose her. Something must be wrong with her. She must be sick. He would go inside her. He would fix her. Then she'd love him again.

Jacin built up a larger amount of energy and pushed against her mind. Her blocking bent and folded beneath his momentum. Once through, a huge burst of energy struck him, a wave of heat, knocking him back into his own mind.

"How dare you!" she screamed, backing away from the table.

He licked his lips, rising. "I can fix this. I can fix us."

Jacin reconnected with her mind. Elor fought back, mentally blocking him again. She put the chair between them.

"Stop it!"

"You're confused," he told her, his voice filled with desperation and fierceness. He disregarded the chair. It wouldn't stop him. "Don't fight me on this. Just let me in and everything will be the same as before, the way it should be."

"Do you really think if you force my mind to change you'll get me back?" Elor's words fell on deaf ears. He tried to connect with her mind and again a wall of energy forced him out. But her resistance felt weaker this time, and they both knew it.

"Please, stop," she pleaded. Her breath came in gasps. Her fingers curled around the useless furniture.

Jacin pushed again, further inside with every try. Elor used up more energy every time she shoved him out. Tears streaked her face. Jacin ignored them, convinced he could help her, fix her.

With one last thrust, Jacin plowed inside. He went into her memory core. Nothing. He couldn't find anything wrong. All her circuits seemed normal. Her thought processes appeared sound. But how? There had to be something he could change.

Suddenly, everything went dark. Jacin felt no force as he slid out from her mind.

Back in himself, he looked at his wife. Slumped over the back of the chair, hands limp at her sides, terror etched on her face. Her mouth lay open, slack. No light shone in her deep, emerald eyes.

"Elor?" Jacin's throat tightened.

She didn't move. She didn't blink. She didn't breathe.

Jacin screamed.

In seconds, his guards appeared.

"Is everything all right, Commander?"

Jacin whirled toward the intruders. "Get out!" he bellowed. The guards stumbled back. Jacin gazed through his tears at the body of his wife, his love.

He swept around the table and gathered her lifeless body into his arms. "What have I done?" Silence answered him.

A thousand thoughts raced through his mind. He couldn't understand what had happened. The only person who'd ever supported him, ever believed in him, was gone.

But she didn't support you. She didn't believe in you. She gave up and tried to leave you, alone. The thoughts stabbed at him. Tears of despair falling down his face became tears of bitterness and resentment. Jacin let go of Elor's body.

"You tried to leave me. You said you wanted to understand, but you lied." The words poured out, as years of frustration with his work, his life, his gifts overwhelmed him.

"The only thing I knew would always be there was my family." Elor's body fell off the chair and thudded onto the floor. Jacin didn't even blink. The heat inside him raged.

"I had you. And you wanted to leave. Not only that, but you hid our children..."

Jacin stopped. His children. Elor had said Daith had his gift. Maybe she could help him? Maybe they could help worlds together, as a family?

Jacin left the house, absentmindedly wiping the blood that trickled from his nose, already focused on the task of finding his daughters. "Dispose of the body inside," he told the guards. "Make sure nothing is left of it or the house."

Trey awoke, shaking. Blood had dripped from his nose onto his desk, trailing across the datapads on which he'd been reading about Dr. Ludd.

Trey felt sick. He had not chosen that version of Jacin Jaxx to follow. Jacin had been so out of control, and then in an instant, flipped his emotions to make himself correct. He'd killed his wife and left her dead without a second thought.

It wasn't right.

Elor had been innocent. One of so many.

Trey knew Jacin had failed because his powers consumed him. But with Daith, if controlled by someone else, her abilities could be harnessed and channeled. The innocents could be saved and the wrongdoers punished.

Trey pushed himself away from his desk, his hand sliding in the blood. He knew now the plan he'd dreamed of since he'd been younger, since what had happened with his mother, had to be put into play.

Dru would never go along with it—Trey knew this. But perhaps he could use his brother in a different way.

Chapter 31

DAITH SMILED AT the sight of Dru, who sat cross-legged on the simulation room floor, his brow furrowed in thought. She loved the way his hair fell over his face, casting shadows across his stormy eyes.

"Good morning," she said, willing her mind to move away from these thoughts.

"Morning! How did you sleep?" He patted the floor next to him.

"I slept wonderfully," she replied, sitting. "I feel great."

"Good because I think I'd like to try something new today."

"Don't we try something new every day?"

"True, but this will test the next level of your abilities. How do you feel about an attempt to use active powers instead of passive?"

Daith tucked up her legs and wrapped her arms around them. "Active. That means a forced change in energy, right?"

"Exactly.

"I'm game. What's the test?"

Dru loaded his program and the room filled with simulated beings—tall, short, different skin textures, different species. Bodies took up so much space Daith couldn't see the walls or exit. Dru handed her a datapad with a grid, labeled in rows and columns from one to six, which represented the room.

"I'm going to mix in with these simulations," Dru said. "I will think of the grid square I'm in and once you've read the location from my thoughts, touch the appropriate spot on your pad. If the spot turns blue, it's me. A red spot means try again."

Dru stood and melted into the crowd. The simulation started and the beings moved all around her, scraping or stomping their limbs on the floor, chatting in incoherent languages. Daith closed her eyes. She concentrated on the pad, trying to determine his location. She waited for Dru's thought to come, but didn't sense anything. Her ears filled with the incessant noise from the simulations moving, talking, laughing. Daith pursed her lips. She reminded herself active powers required a forced change in energy. If he didn't send her the coordinates, she would have to find them.

Daith thought of Dru. She pictured him in her mind; thought of his gray eyes, his calm voice. A tremble in her stomach ignited as she thought of the surge of energy between them when they touched. She imagined him, could feel him move around the room. She searched for his mind. Warmth grew inside her—unrelated to her quivering insides—and she directed the energy toward him. The sounds around her diminished, muffled, and she could hear his voice inside his head.

Five-five.

Daith's eyelids flipped open and she pressed the designated spot on the datapad. The spot turned blue, the simulated images faded, and Dru stood by himself.

"Not bad," he said, after she explained how picturing him had helped her connect with him. "Now you have to find where I am," he explained, "but I'm going to feed you false coordinates."

"How am I supposed to find you then?" She stretched her legs out in front of her and bounced them, waking them up.

Dru paused until he found the right words. "Once you've made your connection, try to push against what I'm telling you. You should be able to feel a difference compared to the truth."

The simulation restarted. Daith connected with his mind in a few moments.

Five-five.

But the thought felt different. She could press against the number and it felt flimsy, as if made out of thin gauze, not solid like before. Daith mentally pushed at the gossamer shell and it stretched, thinning. Leaning harder on the thought, Daith's mind moved past the barrier and found a second set of coordinates which seemed clearer.

Four-six.

She opened her eyes and pressed the button. The spot on the screen turned blue.

"Wow," he said. "I thought that would take longer. Okay, let's see if you can handle the next level. You have to find me, but I won't know where I am. You will have to reach into my senses. See what I see, feel what I feel. In this way, you can tell where I am from my surroundings."

Daith closed her eyes, waited a moment so he could find his spot, and concentrated on Dru, thinking about how he'd see himself in the room.

Suddenly, she could see through his eyes, but the view appeared different. The colors were brighter and the edges of the room blurred. Spots of light danced in front of her and the distortions made focus difficult. Daith concentrated harder and after a while she adjusted enough to interpret what Dru saw. She studied his surroundings, noticing the simulation room door, and felt confident she could pinpoint his position.

Daith began to disconnect her mind from his, when she felt his gaze move and stop, resting on her. A surge of emotion flooded through him, knocking Daith out of his mind.

She'd felt heat, desire, guilt, and concern. They felt like electricity—bolts striking her core.

Shaken, and embarrassed at uncovering his personal feelings, Daith quickly pressed the button and stood. The simulated crowd disappeared. Dru came over quickly.

"What's wrong? Is everything okay?

"What? Yes. Everything is fine. My leg fell asleep," she lied.

"Okay. Well, tell me what happened."

"Nothing happened," she said quickly.

"Well then, how did you find me?"

"Oh!" The heat drained from her blushing cheeks while she told Dru what she had sensed in his mind, excluding his personal feelings.

"You've done very well," he said.

Daith smiled a thanks and then stopped. Something about what he'd said sounded familiar. The words stuck in her head, but she couldn't place them. She tried to dismiss the phrase, but it persisted, repeating itself over and over again. She couldn't even concentrate on Dru's words.

And then she understood. A line from the final clue during the "Hunt for Dru" game—the clue that had left her feeling unsettled. 'You've done very well, but you're getting distracted.'

Distracted from what?

Daith gazed around the empty room. All the tests they'd

worked on—sending her thoughts, testing her senses, making her fix broken objects—had nothing to do with her memory. She hadn't remembered a thing about herself since she'd been here.

"Dru, I need to ask you something."

"Of course."

"Why are you helping me develop my abilities?"

"To exercise your mind and memory so you can remember your past."

She scrunched her brow. "I don't believe you."

Dru's face tightened. "What do you mean?"

"We haven't worked on a single memory program. You haven't even asked if I've remembered anything. All these sessions have been tests, a way to see how far you can push me, or wanting to know how I respond in critical situations. I want to know what for."

He hesitated. "I want to tell you everything you want to know, but I don't think it's my place. You should ask Trey."

"You're the one testing me so I'm asking you," she countered.

While Daith glared at him, a strange feeling came over her. She felt confused, torn by a decision. She realized she could sense Dru's emotions again. Wanting answers, she concentrated on those feelings, to see what Dru hid from her. But something stopped her, a kind of wall in his mind which blocked her access. She hadn't even noticed he'd continued talking.

"...so that's why it's better for you to speak to Trey first."

"Yeah, sure," Daith said, dismissing what he'd said. "Well, I'm pretty worn out, so I think I'll lie down for a while."

"All right," he said slowly. "Do you want to have dinner later, you know, to go over today's work?"

"I don't think so," she said. "I'll see if Trey wants to have dinner." Daith could see the hurt on Dru's face, but she didn't care. She was too upset. If Dru wouldn't tell her what she wanted to know, then she would find someone who would.

Daith left the simulation room angry and ashamed. She wasn't really mad at Dru—confined by restrictions, he could only tell her so much—but ease came from blaming someone else.

She wanted answers.

And no matter what she had to do, she was going to get them.

Chapter 32

WITH QUICK STRIDES, Daith headed to Trey's office. Halfway there, she stopped. No good would come from her approaching the commander irritated. She wanted answers, but she had to go about getting them in her own way. First, she needed practice. And to practice, she needed someone to practice on.

Changing course, Daith headed to the fourth floor and into the mess hall. Still sparse, but enough crewmembers congregated to satisfy her needs. She ordered something from the front, not really caring about her choice, and plopped down within close proximity to a couple of cadets, sloshing the contents of her bowl as the edge hit the table's surface.

Daith stirred the hot liquid around and focused on the two young men. She listened in for a moment on their conversation—they discussed one of the female cadets on the ship. The first male, tall and trim with black fur and dark red eyes, spoke about the female cadet's last report on weapons' efficiency. He chatted with an air of arrogance and seemed displeased with her report.

"I mean, really, how can Commander Xiven even consider her for a bridge promotion?" He dabbed at the corners of his mouth with his elongated fingers. A black, forked tongue darted out to lick their tips clean.

The other male, shorter, with dark amber skin, bright orange hair, and three golden eyes tall enough to touch his hairline, nodded and added murmurs of agreement whenever the first male stopped to take a breath.

Daith slurped up a spoonful of her meal. She chose the taller male to focus on first, recalling what she'd done with Dru during their session. She pushed her mind forward, darting in and out, searching for a way to connect with him.

And then, like skimming a datapad for a specific phrase and having the words jump out, she felt him.

The sensation felt similar to her link with Dru, but not quite the same. This male's energy was sharper, like the contrast on a photo frame turned to maximum. She started with his thoughts. He projected the same thing he gossiped about, issues with the female cadet, but Daith couldn't seem to push past these thoughts. Loud and intense, they dominated his mind. A further probe resulted in nothing but blackness.

She changed her strategy and focused on his emotions. Jealousy stood out stronger than the others. Daith wondered what spurred the jealousy, but couldn't figure out a way to connect the emotion to a thought.

Still, the whole concept delighted her. She'd moved through his thoughts and emotions and he hadn't even noticed.

With a boost of self-confidence, Daith turned to the shorter male. This male was much easier to connect to. She found the same problem with extracting any thoughts besides those he talked about, but his emotions floated right at the surface. His feelings were gentler and brighter. In fact, this male projected affection and attraction toward the arrogant cadet.

Daith suppressed a laugh. The shorter male was in love!

Pulling her mind away from his, Daith shoveled another spoonful of food into her mouth and thought about what had happened. She had scanned Dru's thoughts so easily during their tests, but perhaps because they were right at the surface. Maybe searching for older thoughts, like memories, or sub-conscious thoughts needed a different method.

She still wanted one more test. Daith searched the room. A few tables away sat three higher-ranking officers, including the combat trainer, Lieutenant Commander Cenjo.

Daith dug in and connected with Cenjo. His sensations were hazier. Although a strong connection, she couldn't sort through his thoughts. She could perceive bits and pieces, but nothing whole. She sensed his thoughts had something to do with her and a mission, but she couldn't be sure. They blurred—like someone trying to read without their glasses on. Once again, she switched to emotions. Also fuzzy. She got impressions of pride, guilt, and contentment, but without knowing exactly what he talked about, she couldn't make sense of them.

Daith, engrossed in her fascination, hadn't realized she stared. Until she realized he caught her.

Panicked, Daith abruptly stood, knocking her half-eaten soup onto the table. She hastily mopped up the spill when Cenjo approached to help her clean.

"That's really not necessary," she said, averting his gaze.

"It's no trouble. I noticed you eating by yourself and wondered if you'd care to join us?" To her horror, Cenjo steered her toward his table.

"Oh no," she told him, embarrassed. "Really. I'm pretty much done anyway."

"But you seemed so interested in my appearance. I thought you wanted some company."

This was the second time Daith wanted the floor to open and swallow her. "It wasn't that..." she stammered. *Think, Daith, think.*

"Well, what then?"

"I wondered..." *think!* "I wanted to ask you something, but I didn't want to interrupt." As Cenjo ushered her to the table, the other two officers watched her with interest.

"By all means, ask away."

Daith could feel the heat in her cheeks. "I thought—if you have time..."she said, stumbling over her words while she stalled. And then something popped into her head. "Is there any space available in your combat class? I'd like to join." She heard a snicker from the officer next to her, but Cenjo didn't smile. In fact, he seemed intrigued.

"I have no problem with you joining one of my classes, but I'll have to talk with Commander Xiven first. He's in charge of the combat roster. Although I think it's a good idea. Never know when you might need to defend yourself."

Cenjo signaled to the other two officers who rose. "Well since that's all, we'll leave you to finish your meal."

"Oh, of course. Let me know what Trey says."

Cenjo acknowledged her statement and left. They weren't far when one of the officers, the one who'd snickered, muttered to Cenjo under his breath "she calls the commander *Trey,* does she? What a joke."

Daith stood there, stunned. *A joke? What did he mean?*

Shaken by the encounter, but not deterred, Daith left the mess hall and headed down two floors toward Trey's office, feeling confident with her new ability. She rang the chimes to his office. The door opened and she took a seat. He signaled her to wait while he finished his vidlink call.

"To what do I owe this nice surprise?" Trey asked after he'd disconnected.

"I have a few things I'd like to talk to you about."

"I understand. I assume you've noticed things are a bit hectic, crewmembers are tense, and I have been preoccupied and not able to see you as often as I'd like."

Daith pursed her lips in response, unwilling to soften.

"I think it's time to open the door the rest of the way. Can we meet later? I will answer all your questions then, I promise. I just don't have time right now." As if on cue, the communications panel on his desk lit up.

"Yes?" he answered.

"Commander, we need you on the bridge. Sensor malfunction."

"I'm on my way." Trey pushed the button to silence the command and nodded his head toward it. "Never seems to end."

Daith didn't want to wait, but realized she didn't have a choice. "Fine. How about we meet for dinner?"

Trey lit up. "Dinner? Sounds great. Here, in my office? Say in about three standard hours?"

"See you then."

Chapter 33

THREE HOURS LATER, Daith rang the chimes to Trey's office.

"Enter!"

Daith went in and paused at the change in the room—dimmed lights, a black cloth laid across his desk. A whiff of the piquant, sweet scent from the spread of food reached her nose. Trey stood behind the makeshift table, his appearance immaculate as ever, a toothy grin on his face.

Palpable tension filled the room—Daith didn't even need to use her new-found ability to sense it.

"Please," he said, gesturing to the seat in front of her. "Sit." He pulled his own chair out with a screech and winced at the noise. "Sorry."

She sat, admiring her plate: long, thin, cream-colored tubes lay in swirls under yellow and orange chunks, drizzled on top with a dark green sauce. There was a puffy white pastry in the middle of the desk and two glasses filled with smoky blue liquid.

"Help yourself."

Daith tried a bite.

"This is delicious." The flavor reflected the sweet and spicy scent in the air. Her beverage, also sweet, possessed a hint of smokiness which lingered after she swallowed.

Trey dug into his own meal. "It's a dish my mother used to make. I taught the recipe to the cooks in the mess hall. It's been a crew favorite for years." A moment of silence while he swallowed, but when he opened his mouth again, nothing came out. He cleared his throat and shoveled another mouthful. Daith's interest spiked at his seeming unease.

"So how are things on the ship?" he asked.

Daith put down her utensil. "You know how they are. Elusive. Secretive. I think I deserve some answers." She readied herself to enter his mind.

Trey nodded and his shoulders relaxed. "You aren't stupid, Daith—far from it. I knew you wouldn't be satisfied with the paltry information I'd given you. I wanted to protect you and I thought sparing you the truth would make things easier for you here, help with your adjustment to your new life." Trey paused, his voice catching in his throat. "I care about you, Daith. I want you to be happy here. I realize keeping you in the dark was wrong. The time has come for you to decide for yourself."

Her eyebrows rose. "Decide what?"

Trey held out his hands. "Let me start with the explanation. Then you can worry about the decision." He let out a breath. "We are at war."

Daith propelled her mind into Trey's, hunting for stray thoughts and emotions to help her determine his honesty. After a moment she connected and sensed feelings of confidence, spite, longing, and—

—and then nothing.

Blackness.

Daith disconnected her mind. *What just happened?* She didn't sense a wall or block. Just a void.

Trey continued. "There are several small factions fighting, but the two main groups are the Aleet Army, which I command, and the Controllers."

Daith tried once again to get a feel for Trey's emotions, but she found nothing to grasp onto—like a vertical shaft with slickened sides. She feared pushing too hard, afraid he would notice.

"A little over twenty standard years ago," Trey went on, "a young man found he had abnormal and unique abilities. He used these abilities to help strengthen and unite many governments that had fought for years. He brought peace and hope to many caught in endless cycles of violence and restored a harmonious way of life."

The familiar words brought her back from her failed attempts. "He did this for your planet, didn't he?"

"Yes. The war I fought in on my home planet, Sintaur, was a war he helped stop. After I decided to join his cause, I became a member of the group he'd started, the Aleet Army."

Trey continued, methodically unfolding then refolding the cloth on his lap. "Some of those who originally controlled the governments, or who profited from the wars, lied to the citizens of these planets. They said our leader had corrupted them, that he wanted to control them, and he wanted power over their worlds."

"Afraid of change, they recruited their own soldiers by propagating the idea they needed to be set free from tyranny and oppression. They called themselves the Liberators," Trey sneered at the name, "but those who wanted peace and supported our leader called them what they truly were, the Controllers. Because of their wealth, the Controllers had no trouble funding their campaign. They viewed our leader as the main threat to their way of life and did everything they could to tarnish his name and image.

"Not everyone believed these lies," Trey continued. "Beings from different planets, different ages, and different backgrounds, sent in their requests to join the Aleet Army."

"You mentioned you are in command of the Aleet Army, so what happened to this leader?" Daith asked.

Trey's lips pursed for a moment. "He's dead."

Daith's chest ached with pity. "I'm sorry. How did he die?"

Trey took a moment to respond. "I suppose in the end the pressure was too much for even him to handle. He'd helped governments all over the galaxy, expanding and pushing his mental and emotional abilities to their limits. I think he finally just—stopped wanting to live." An expression of anguish passed over Trey's face, but disappeared quickly.

"What happened after he died?"

"Everything he worked for, we worked for, fell apart. Chaos broke out on many of the planets he'd helped and the Controllers seized this opportunity to reestablish themselves. Without our leader, the Aleet Army wasn't strong enough to withstand the Controllers. Many members of our group became victims to their propaganda and some of them became double agents. A former recruit double-crossed us and gave away the location of our main base. Hit hard, we lost more than half our soldiers. Many families and civilians were killed, too. Those of us who managed to escape with our lives regrouped, but it's been eight standard years and we are still rebuilding what had been broken."

Daith took a drink from her glass to hide her nerves. "What does this have to do with me?"

"The Controllers sent out teams to find any others who had

gifts like our leader. They heard about your abilities and tried to persuade you to join them. When you refused, they threatened you. Fearing for your life, your family hired my group to protect you. When we arrived on your home planet, you were already under attack.

"Since you had refused to join them, you'd been deemed a threat. They burned down your house, thinking you were at home with your family."

Daith's anger flared at the mention of her family's murder. *How could they do such a terrible thing? How could they take away my past?* Daith felt the desk tremble under her hands.

"The dreams I had," Daith said, quietly, "about the ship and the heat and someone grabbing me—they are my memories?"

"Yes. You may have noticed you haven't had any dreams since you've been here. We did this on purpose."

"You did what?" Heat inside her flared, matching her sparked anger.

"Daith, you aren't the only one with these types of abilities, just this level of power. When the Controllers learned about our leader's death, they not only hunted you, but anyone who possessed gifts like yours. They kidnapped dozens of low-scale telepaths and empaths, using them to search for you, to pry into the thoughts and emotions of others to gain an advantage.

"We learned recently they've been searching minds while an individual is asleep—a way to access their thoughts when they are most vulnerable. They search for clues about someone's whereabouts to find them."

Daith remembered how Dru had asked her where her nerve pills were after she'd had her nightmare about his death. "The pills," Daith said in realization. "You gave me the pills to keep that from happening."

"They help suppress the mind from dreaming. Giving them to you was the only way I could think to stop the connection. We don't know how far these individuals can reach. If we pass too close to another ship or planet.... We didn't want to take any chances."

"Then why did Doctor Ludd tell me not to take them anymore?"

Trey's nostrils flared in disgust. "Doctor Ludd turned against us. And now that he's gone, it's a pretty good bet the Controllers are aware of our location, and of our plans."

Daith's thoughts swirled. "Why didn't you tell me this from the beginning?"

Trey stood, clearing the dishes. "Three reasons. First, we weren't sure if you were an undercover Controller agent. That's what all the tests with Dru have been for. If they'd hired a telepath or empath to take your place, the imposter would not have had the range and power you have.

"Second, if you knew who you were, you would be determined to go back home, and I knew you wouldn't be safe there. I thought keeping you here would be better. Not fair, I know, but I believed it best. Until you could go with confidence in your abilities, of course."

"And the third reason?"

"I didn't know who I could trust. Doctor Ludd is a perfect example. The only ones I do trust are myself, my brother, and you. Doctor Ludd was with us since the beginning. To know he could turn..." Trey twisted away from her, placing the plates near the food chute.

Daith sat back in her chair. None of this was fair. It wasn't her fault she had these abilities. And just because some man in the past had the same abilities as her didn't mean these Controllers could use her like a toy in the middle of their idiotic war. They had no regard for life. They'd killed her whole family on the chance she'd been with them. They wanted to kill her because she wouldn't join their cause.

"What does all this mean?" she asked.

"I suppose that depends on you." Trey sat, reached across his desk, and took Daith's hand. "We would like your help. I know it's a terrible thing to ask, after everything you've been through, but we are out of time."

Daith focused on their hands, the pressure warm and a bit sweaty. "I don't know. What do you want from me?"

"I'm not quite sure yet. It'll depend on how comfortable you are with your abilities. But Daith, there's another part to this—a part I hate to ask, but I truly believe is necessary."

"What is it?"

"You would have to stay on the dream-deflector pills. I know it's the best way to get your memories back, but your dreams may end up being a full-access pass to our whereabouts. I cannot let that happen. Your memories may still resurface on their own, but I can't have you dream. And Dru of course would still be here to help you, if he decides to stay."

Daith's head throbbed and her tongue felt thick. How could she give up the best way to get back her memories? But how could she let the Controllers get away with what they've done? She reached for her glass, nearly knocking it over, and brought the container to her mouth. She swallowed an awkward mouthful.

"What happens if I decide I can't help you?" she asked.

Trey let go of her hand and gestured away from himself. "You can go wherever you wish. The training will have to stop, of course, since you will be dreaming again, but we will drop you off on the nearest inhabitable planet with enough currency to make your way wherever you want. If you choose that path, I can promise you will not be left alone for long. Even though the Controllers will know you aren't on our side, they won't give up their search for you. I don't say this as a threat, but as fact. I want you to be prepared to live on the run. With your abilities, you will probably have a higher chance to evade them, but I don't know how much."

Daith's heartbeat rose again, this time in anxiety.

"I'm sorry if your life seems pre-determined. I wish more than anything you could have a clean slate. But you are involved because of who you are. At least now you have options and—friends—who can help."

"I... I think I understand."

Trey pushed back his chair and stood. "Please, take your time and think, really think this over, but I'd like your decision in two days."

"I'll let you know."

A slow, thin smile spread across his face after Daith left the room.

Trey absentmindedly cleared away the items on his desk. He recalled the conversation and couldn't find anything out of place. His trap had been set perfectly and he was positive she would take the bait.

Now only the final piece remained.

A chat with his dear younger brother.

Chapter 34

DAITH'S HEAD SPUN with information. This group called the Controllers had killed her family, they'd made her lose her memories, they were still trying to get to her through her dreams—and now Trey wanted her help to stop them once and for all.

It's too much, she thought, entering her quarters. She didn't know what to do. Joining sides in a war? What if she hurt someone? What if something went wrong?

Daith sat on her bed, her knees like jelly. She wanted to cry, but no tears came.

A soft beep came from her communications panel. She let the message play.

"*Hello Miss Tocc. This is Lieutenant Commander Cenjo. This message is to inform you there is an open position available in my beginner level combat class and Commander Xiven has approved you to join. If you are still interested, we meet tonight at 1800 hours in simulation room four. Please wear comfortable clothing that provide easy movement. Cenjo out."*

Daith glanced at her time-reader and noted the class started in a standard half hour. Wanting any kind of distraction from the jumble of thoughts in her head, Daith changed and made her way to the simulation room.

Upon arrival, she found the room quite empty, with nothing except for Cenjo, ten other trainees, and a few mats on the floor.

Cenjo beamed. He gestured for Daith to join the other students.

"Trainees this is Miss Daith Tocc. She will be joining us for this evening's class."

"Ahh—zee sehteek'as lowered herzelf to our leval. She sinks she is so much better zen us." A tall, muscular, female Mesquirian muttered under her breath. Two of the other trainees snickered.

Daith tried to ignore the insult. She presented a composed front, focusing on Cenjo's words while he described their warm-up routine, but she couldn't help imagining the satisfaction she would feel if she punched the Mesquirian in the face. *I'd probably break her nose,* she thought to herself. *She'd deserve it. Where does she get off judging me? Does she think I* chose *to come aboard this ship, lose everything, and have abilities that separate me from everyone else? Does she think I enjoy having everyone stare at me like I'm some kind of abnormal creature ready at any moment to just—SNAP!*

A loud crack rang through the room followed by a shriek.

Cenjo's words died on his lips and everyone turned toward the Mesquirian woman.

"By doze!" She held her hands over her face. Blood poured through her fingers. "She broke by doze!"

Everyone stared at Daith.

"What?" Daith asked, shocked. "How could I have...?" But she couldn't finish. She knew she'd done it. She'd projected her thoughts toward the woman and these, along with her anger, had broken the Mesquirian's nose. Daith could feel the warmth in her body receding. She hadn't even noticed the buildup had started.

"I'm sorry!" Daith sputtered at the woman. "Maybe I can help?" She reached out toward her.

"Squa-touk!" the woman screamed, terrified. Daith stopped in her tracks. Though she didn't understand the language, the woman's plea for Daith to stay away rang clear.

"Class dismissed. Someone take Sequiria to medical." The students filed out.

Daith shook. "I'm sorry," she mumbled. "I didn't mean to. I don't even know why I was so angry. She just… and my talk with Trey… and I'm sorry…."

Daith sagged to the floor. Her mind swirled with a plethora of confused thoughts and feelings. They spun in front of her, a tangled web woven in blackness she couldn't unravel. Her breath came in hiccups. Tears rolled down her face. Panic engulfed her. Her throat closed up. She couldn't breathe. The world swam in pools of gray and black.

And then sharp pain across her cheek brought her back.

Cenjo had slapped her.

"Sorry!" he said. "Please come out of this!"

Daith's shaking subsided, and the abyss pulled back like an ebbing tide. "It's okay," she croaked, her throat raw. "It's okay. I'm okay." Cenjo squatted across from her, his olive-skinned face creased with concern.

She gulped in several breaths of air. Her pulse slowed. "I'm sorry if I scared you."

Cenjo laughed, sounding relieved. "Scared me? I've never seen someone's face gray out so fast. You all right now?"

"I think so."

"What happened?"

Daith thought about it. "I don't know if I really know. I felt like I was—losing myself. Into nothing." She shuddered. "It was terrifying."

"Did you really break Sequiria's nose using your mind?" Cenjo asked, tentatively.

"I think I did. I didn't even really focus on the thought. I was angry and wanted to hit her and—and it just happened."

Cenjo whistled. "So you can really do what everyone's been talking about?"

Daith wrapped her arms around her knees. "I don't know. What have they been talking about?"

"They say you can read minds and move things by thought. I didn't really know what to believe myself until this. Even after the first time I met you."

"When I followed you from the mess hall?"

Cenjo's forehead crinkled before realization hit him. "Of course. The memory loss."

"You mean to say you've met me before?"

"Yes. About nine years ago."

Daith's eyes sparkled with eagerness. "Really? How did we meet? What was I like? Did you meet any of my family?"

He shook his head. "Nothing like that. I commanded a rescue mission to find you and bring you to safety."

"What happened?"

"You really don't remember, do you?"

"No. I don't," she said, her words tinged with a bite. "And I can't tell you how maddening that is."

"Well," Cenjo continued, "we'd gotten to your location and were bringing you back to our ship when the Controllers ambushed us. Do you remember them?"

"No. But Trey told me about them, and the war."

"Not much happened after," Cenjo went on with a shrug. "We were outnumbered and outgunned. They killed two of my men and seriously injured a third. We had to surrender."

Daith paused. "You don't like the Controllers, do you?"

"They weren't too bad at first," he said. "I think they were scared of something they didn't understand. But later, they did some pretty low and cutthroat things in the name of freedom and justice."

"What else did you think of me?"

"Can't you read my mind?" he asked, teasingly.

Daith blushed, recalling her attempt to infiltrate his thoughts and emotions in the mess hall. "I'd rather you just tell me."

He cocked his head to the side. "You really are something else, Miss Tocc."

"Please, call me Daith."

"Daith it is. You might as well cut mine short too and call me Cenjo. 'Lieutenant Commander' is quite a mouthful at times."

"Deal." She paused. "And, thank you."

"For what?"

"For giving me answers. There aren't a lot of crewmembers willing to talk to me. You treat me like someone normal—like everyone else."

Cenjo laughed. "You'll come to find no one is normal, Daith. You happen to be not normal in ways some don't know how to deal with. Their problem, not yours."

"I wish I could dismiss their reactions that easily."

Cenjo stood and offered his hand. He pulled her up with such force she bounced on the balls of her feet. "It's always easy in theory. Real life is a different story."

"I'm starting to understand all too well." Daith paused. "Thanks again for everything."

He patted her on the shoulder. “Don’t mention it. Have a good night and pleasant dreams.”

Daith watched Cenjo leave the room, thinking about the pill she’d have to take so no one could invade her mind while she slept. “I wish.”

Chapter 35

DRU SAT ACROSS from his brother, his foot tapping nervously on the carpeted floor. He had no idea what to expect. Daith hadn't talked to him since their session earlier in the day and she'd seemed upset with him for not giving her the answers she so desperately wanted. But what could he do? Trey held the power about what to tell her, not him.

But when Trey spoke about what his conversation with Daith had entailed, Dru's surety wavered.

"So now you've told her the Controllers are responsible for her family's death and her memory loss?" Dru asked.

"Yes."

Dru's eyebrows furrowed. "And you mentioned Jacin Jaxx as the leader of the Aleet Army, but not her father?"

Trey leaned back, grimacing when the chair squeaked. "If she knew that fact, she would be in the same spot as before we erased her memories. This is the only way to give her the chance to live freely, away from her family's history."

Dru's stomach squirmed. "She might have been happy. You said yourself she was at an academy for gifted students. Maybe enough time had passed since her father's death and she'd moved on?"

Trey tossed a datapad at Dru, anger in the gesture. The pad showed Daith's records from Fior Accelerated Academy. "She never once used her abilities. She simply plodded along through her classes, barely passing each year, never pushing herself to graduate. She hid herself in that place—safe from the galaxy, from her power." Trey's face softened. "Who could blame her? Do you think eight years is long enough for everyone to forget about Jaxx? Or eight decades? She was probably terrified to use her abilities. Could you imagine her life? Frightened every day she might make a mistake, which could expose her for who she really is?"

Trey pointed at the datapad. "We can give her the chance to explore her gifts without this fear. I've been salvaging what's left of Jaxx's army after the attack on our main base. This whole crew, what's left, would do anything to protect Daith. They are the only ones she can rely on."

"I guess. It's just..." Dru churned through all the lies and secrets he kept. He felt conflicted. How could she trust him when he wasn't telling the truth? "I hate having to lie to her."

"I don't like lying either. But it's the only way to give her this chance at a new life. You understand, right?"

"Yes, but—"

"There can be no 'buts'," Trey interrupted. "You have to be sure about this. You have to know what you tell her is right. You can't waver in your thoughts."

"Why not?"

"Isn't it obvious? You are working on her empathic and telepathic abilities. You are allowing her access to your mind. How long before she can sense when you lie? She's already tried to probe my thoughts and feelings."

Dru gaped. "What?"

"At our dinner. I could feel her trying to connect with my mind."

"She hasn't told me she can do that." Dru thought back to their last session when she had to locate him in the room and how Daith had seemed shaken. Had she felt his emotions and didn't want to tell him? Why would she keep that ability from him?

"She will be able to sense the truth from us, eventually, but when that happens, she will also know our intent. She will see everything we've done was to help her. Until then, she's too powerful and too fragile to be left on her own.

"And there is one more thing," Trey added.

"What?"

"I've asked Daith if she'd like to join my crew. Permanently."

Dru hadn't expected that. "Why?"

"I think she could be happy here. Of course, I'd like you to stay on and continue to work with her, but I didn't want to speak for you. If you are interested, I would extend your contract."

Dru paused, considering. "What did she say?"

"She had to think about it."

Dru realized he had some thinking of his own to do. "You really want me to stay?"

Trey's gaze flitted downward. "I know we've been estranged, but I feel these past weeks have proven how well we can work together. I respect how much you've accomplished with Daith in such a short period of time. You really are gifted at what you do."

Dru beamed inside. He'd never heard praise like that from his brother.

And yet—

Something still bothered him. He thought about how the crew reacted toward Daith—nervous, jumpy. But then he realized he felt the tension all the time, too, whether Daith was there or not. The whole ship hummed with it.

"Trey, is something else going on?"

Trey raised his head and blinked. "What do you mean?"

"There is a tension on this ship regardless of Daith's presence. I know something else is happening."

Trey's jaw twitched, but his stare remained locked with Dru's. There was a long pause before he spoke. "You're right. We are on a mission. If you decide to stay, then it must be to help. And Dru, brother, I need your help."

"Help with what?"

"You know what happened on Sintaur. You know the lives taken, the families ripped apart. You know what we lost. And then Jaxx changed everything."

"I know, Trey, but after Jaxx died—"

"Yes. After he died, the old government came back full force and took over. Old hatreds rose and war broke out again. But I believe we can reestablish peace."

"How?"

Trey hesitated. "I can't give you all the details, yet, but if you decide to stay on, help Daith, help us, we can do some real good."

"You want her to control them like her father did?" Dru guessed.

"No. I want her to get a feel for what's going on so we can gain an edge on their thoughts and plans."

"What if she decides not to help you?"

"Then we will fight for what we believe in without her."

"You mean start your own war?" Dru was shocked. "You can't."

"The stars I can't!" Trey cursed. "We lived through what those innocents are going through right now. How can you stand by and not want to do something, to stop that injustice? I'd like to try a peaceful method if I can, with Daith's help, but if she isn't ready, then I will do what I have to do. I can't turn my back on our own people.

"I want to do this without a fight. And I want you to be there. We can give our fellow citizens on Sintaur a second chance, like we are giving Daith, like we are achieving as brothers."

"What if I can't?" Dru asked slowly.

"Then you are paid after your work is completed and free to go. No different from when you started. I only want you in this if you are in all the way."

Dru's head spun. "I don't know."

"Your contract ends in two days. You can wait until then to decide."

Dru stood. "The idea is noble, but I don't know if I can be a part of it. You were always the fighter, Trey."

Trey circled around the desk to his brother. "This is the chance for you to fight with me. I know you have the strength in you. Think about it."

* * *

As Dru headed toward his quarters, his mind swirled with mixed thoughts.

He found he wanted to talk to Daith. How much his friendship had grown with her surprised him. She calmed him. And he couldn't deny the pull of energy between them.

He realized he wanted to stay more for her than for his brother, and not all because of their work. Dru felt linked to Daith. There was a mental and emotional bond. He wanted to continue the connection. Even though he felt more for her than he should, he couldn't help being drawn to her, wanting to open up to her, too.

But if Daith was keeping things from him, could he depend on her?

Or, since he was lying, could she depend on him?

No. How can she? And how can I, as her doctor, and her friend, keep doing this to her?

Once in his quarters, Dru asked the ship's computer to locate Daith. Whatever the consequences with his brother, he would tell her the truth about everything. Her past. Her present. And what might happen in her future. She deserved that much.

The computer told him she was in simulation room 4. He sent a message to her quarters.

"Daith, it's Dru. I know my brother has asked you to stay aboard and help him with his mission. He asked me to do the same." He paused. "I don't know what you will decide to do—stars, I don't know what I'd do either—but if you want someone to talk to, I want you to know you can come to me. I know things have been strained between us because of all the secrecy, but I wanted to let you know the secrecy is over. I'll tell you everything. You've become important to me. Whatever you decide about Trey's proposal, if you want to continue working on your abilities, whether you stay or not, I'd like to be a part of it. Goodnight, Daith. I will see you in the morning."

He felt lighter, freer, more content now he'd made his decision.

For the first time in a long time, Dru fell asleep without thinking about anything at all.

* * *

Daith headed to her quarters after she'd left the simulation room. Between hurting her classmate and her emotional breakdown, exhaustion enveloped her.

She didn't want to make any decisions. She didn't want to think.

She only wanted to sleep.

Daith had just curled up under the covers when her communications panel beeped, letting her know she had a message.

"No," she whined. "I don't care what the stupid message is. I want to go to sleep."

To her annoyance, the panel beeped again.

"Computer, please quiet the panel," she begged, burying her head under the blanket.

"Message indicator is now on silent mode," the computer responded.

"Oh, thank the stars."

"Unable to comply. Please restate the query."

Daith forcefully pushed the covers off her face. "I'm not talking to you!" she snapped. She heard a crack and then the smell of smoke drifted through the room. The communications panel sparked and smoldered. The message indicator beeped repeatedly while the friendly female computer voice told her there was a fire in her unit and she had sixty standard seconds before automatic emergency procedures initiated.

Groaning at the pain in her head, she cursed for having lost control of her abilities again. Daith told the computer the fire had been extinguished and she waved away the smoke.

Even though broken, the message indicator continued to beep, and the computer couldn't turn it off. Daith pressed the button to let the message play. The voice, Dru's, came through garbled due to the smoldering equipment.

"*Daith, it's Dru. I know my brother has asked you to stay aboard and help him with his mission. He asked me to do the same.*" A crackle. "*I don't know what you will decide to do*"—garbled words— *"but if you want someone to talk to, I want you to know you can come to me. I know things have been strained between us because of all the secrecy, but I wanted to let you know—"* This part was extremely distorted and Daith couldn't understand anything until *"—you've become important to me. Whatever you decide about Trey's proposal, if you want to continue working on your abilities, whether you stay or not, I'd like to be a part of it. Goodnight, Daith. I will see you in the morning."*

Daith lay back down. She thought about Dru's message and felt a smile blossom. He was important to her, too. She remembered the night they went out to dinner and he'd told her embarrassing stories to make her laugh. She thought about how patient he'd been during their sessions and how hard some of those tests were for him to do. He encompassed the only friend she could remember.

Whatever she did decide to do, she knew she wanted Dru with her.

Chapter 36

DRU WATCHED DAITH enter the simulation room, her eyes tired, her posture slumped. Pinpricks of sweat popped across his brow.

"Good morning."

"If you say so." Daith cracked her neck. "I can barely stay awake."

"Do you want to come back later? I have a pretty heavy set of tests lined up and I don't want you to overexert yourself."

Daith yawned. "No, I'm fine. Just tired. Yesterday was—long."

"I bet." Dru wondered if she'd listened to his message. He ran his fingers through his hair, slyly wiping the sweat from his hairline. "I heard what happened in your combat training class last night."

Daith scrunched up her face. "News spreads quickly, doesn't it?"

Dru grinned. "It's a small crew. So it's true you broke Sequiria's nose without actually hitting her?"

"Yeah. But I didn't really mean to. It somehow, sort of—happened. I was upset and then *crack*!"

"From what I've heard about her, she probably deserved it."

Daith raised an eyebrow.

"Her name has come up in conversation—and never under pleasant circumstances. What worries me is your abilities weren't under your control. And someone got hurt."

Daith rubbed her forehead. "I really don't need a lecture."

"I'm not trying to lecture you. I'm concerned. Your abilities are powerful—capable of extraordinary harm. If you can't learn to control them, they will control you. You *have* to remain focused all the time."

"And that was not a lecture—how?"

Dru spread his hands in front of him. "Sorry. I'm worried."

"I know you are," Daith said with a sigh. "I am, too. Plus I blew out my communications panel last night. It wouldn't stop beeping and then—poof! Smoke and sparks everywhere."

Had she not heard his message? A stray thought pushed the notion from his mind. "Wait, you broke your communications panel?"

"Yes. Why?"

"It means you caused damage to something inanimate. You weren't able to manipulate inanimate things before, remember? With the rope and the metal bar...."

"What's interesting about that?"

"Let's do today's tests first. It might give me a better understanding about what happened."

Daith replied with a shrug.

"The first test will be opposite from the test you did to reconstruct inanimate objects. This time you'll attempt to deconstruct them." Dru gestured to the objects lying on the floor—

pieces of glass, large rocks, and furniture.

* * *

With something to focus on, Daith became more alert and awake. She became swept up in the tests and after two standard hours, the room looked like a disaster zone. Shattered pieces of rock and wood littered the floor.

Except the piece of glass.

She'd spent over an hour working on it, but she couldn't find anything to hold on to. With the rock, she'd traced its cracks with her mind, wedged a build-up of energy in between them, and released the energy, causing a satisfying burst of fragments. Daith let her angry emotions loose on the pieces of furniture as she split apart the wooden fibers, with great cracking and snapping noises.

But the glass...wouldn't...break.

She tried everything she could think of—twisting, turning, bending, shaking, energy blows—but nothing worked. There weren't any cracks for her to get into or any fibers to grasp.

Exasperated, she blew a sweaty piece of hair from her forehead. "I give up. I can't do it!"

"Maybe you're thinking about this the wrong way."

"What do you mean?" Daith asked.

"Think about it. Glass is a liquid, right? It's not going to have properties like wood or stone. There won't be any splinters or cracks. So how would you destroy a liquid?

"I would..."Daith grinned and turned her attention back to the glass. Focusing once more, she channeled her energy into heat and pushed the buildup against the pane. To her delight, a bubble formed inside, puffing outwards. With a burst, liquid glass ran down its side. The fluid boiled, changing into steam.

Daith let out a yelp of delight and threw her arms around Dru in a hug. He laughed and swept her up off her feet, his arms tightening briefly before he let her go. "Very clever."

Daith smiled, her cheeks flushed from their embrace. She swallowed down the rush of excitement she'd felt in his touch. "Thanks."

"Okay. Now for the hard part." Dru's eyes twinkled. He handed her a small metal box.

"What's this?" Daith asked.

"This is a bomb."

"What do you mean 'a bomb'?"

"It's an explosive device and it's set to detonate in ten standard minutes."

Daith scoffed. "Very funny."

"Who's laughing?"

"What do you expect me to do with it?"

"I expect you to disarm it," he said, nonchalantly.

"What do I know about disarming a bomb?"

"Nothing, I presume."

Daith scrunched her eyebrows. "Well then, what am I supposed to do?"

"Go inside with your mind, determine its inner structure, and take apart the necessary components without a detonation."

"What happens if I can't?"

"It will explode."

"What?" Daith exclaimed, trying to hand the box back. "I thought this was a simulation."

"You know you can't work with simulations because they aren't real. I picked this up from the armory department, with special permission of course, and unless you want to explain to Trey and his crew why you blew a hole in their simulation room, I suggest you get to work."

Daith's mouth hung open in disbelief. "You're serious."

"Yes. And you have seven and a half minutes left."

"You're insane. I can't do this!"

"You can." Dru placed his hand on her arm and squeezed. A warmth spread from his fingertips having nothing to do with her own energy heat. "I'll be outside monitoring your progress."

"If you have so much faith in me, why do you need to leave?"

"Don't want you to be distracted," he called over his shoulder.

Daith stared at the box. Panic threatened to engulf her. Her pulse quickened. A strange feeling swept over her. The edges of her sight went hazy and gray. Her vision narrowed. The box appeared to come closer at an alarming rate. She knew at some point she would crash into it, but it kept growing in size. Heat rose in her body as she moved past the outside layer and into the box.

The inside of the circular device consisted of one moving part connected to three wires, each a trigger designed to perform a different task: one started the countdown, one stopped the countdown, and one was a trick wire which, if cut, would speed up the counter.

But which was which?

Daith traced the power flow inside each wire to determine its purpose. She found the one to stop the timer and focused the heat inside her to burn through the wire. The wire smoldered and broke in half. The timer stopped at seven minutes and two seconds.

Relief flowed through her. The box began to shrink. Her vision cleared and she opened and closed her eyes several times, blinking away the haziness.

"Um—Dru?" she called out.

The door opened and Dru stuck his head in. "You're wasting time, you know."

"I did it."

"What do you mean? I just left." Dru took the box from her, examining it.

"I know, but I stopped it."

Dru gawked.

"I'm serious. See for yourself. The timer has stopped."

Dru carefully unscrewed the top. The counter remained frozen and one of the wires had been severed. "This is incredible," he mused. "How did you do this?"

Daith explained about the haziness, how she felt mentally pulled into the box, burned through the wire, and came back.

"Amazing, Daith," he said. "It took you very little time to solve the problem. I've never seen such an instantaneous reaction in all my studies be—Oh, no!"

Dru bolted across the room to the communications panel. He frantically pressed a button and the computer chimed on. "Medical emergency to simulation room one!"

"Acknowledged." The voice on the other end said.

"Dru," Daith asked, frightened, "what's...?" The room swam. Pain shrieked inside her head.

"Dru!" she screamed. She clamped her hands over her ears to stop the horrific noise. He ran toward her, telling her something she couldn't hear.

And then, as abruptly, the pain ceased.

"Daith. Can you hear me?" Dru's voice sounded far away.

Daith nodded. She pulled her hands from her ears. They were covered in blood.

"What...?" The room wavered again. Lights popped in front of her eyes.

Dru caught her before she hit the ground. "Hang on. You're going to be okay."

* * *

Daith remembered Dru holding her...
and then a young cadet, Dr. Ludd's replacement...
She shook her head.
She stumbled through the corridors.
Dru's energy flowed through her, healing her.
She tasted something bitter. She lay down.
—it felt so good to lie down—
and darkness enveloped her.

Chapter 37

DAITH WOKE TO pitch blackness.

"Computer, lights," she murmured. The room lit up and Daith squinted in the brightness. She wasn't in her room. "Hello?" She threw back the warm covers on the unfamiliar bed and tried to stand, but her legs buckled. She sunk, unhurt, into the deep blue carpet. Why wouldn't her legs support her?

"Hello?" she called out again, louder. She had a momentary flashback to her first day on board and panicked that once again she wouldn't be answered. Before she could call out a third time, the door opened to reveal Dru—hair disheveled, eyes bleary, shirt and pants wrinkled.

"Are you okay?" Dru crossed the room, rubbing the sleep from his face.

"Yeah. I fell off the bed. My legs are tingling."

Dru helped her up. "It's probably a side-effect from the sedative. No different than if they'd fallen asleep."

"Sedative? Why was I given a sedative? And where am I?"

"You're in my quarters."

"What happened?" she asked as she rubbed her legs.

"After you fixed the bomb in the simulation room, blood started to trickle from your ear. I called for medical help. When I came back, you were screaming and holding your head. And then you stopped. I feared..." Dru trailed off, the corners of his gray eyes wrinkled with concern. "I brought you here. The doctor gave you a clotting agent and a sedative, but she didn't know what else to do for you. Doctor Ludd's notes on how to treat you are missing."

"What do you think happened to me?"

"I'm not really sure."

"I've never felt anything that loud before. How long was I out?"

"About sixteen standard hours. Although you could use more."

"Sixteen..." Daith stared at the time-reader in disbelief. "What about you? What have you been doing?"

Dru's face contorted with shame. "Mostly going over your charts—trying to understand what happened. And I don't."

Daith put her hand on his arm. "There's no way you could have known."

Dru shrugged off the sympathy. "It's my job to know. Or at least to have an idea. But what I'm dealing with here..." Dru looked at her, his gaze hard. "This is out of my league. I promised you wouldn't be harmed. Our sessions have been exciting and wonderful, but all I've done is hurt you. Your pain gets worse every test." Dru's eyes clouded with sorrow.

Daith wanted to reassure him—she had consented to this, too. She put her hand on his arm again and this time he didn't shake off her touch. She let her energy flow into him freely and she watched his eyes close with a sigh.

"Have you gotten any sleep?" she asked, stifling a yawn.

"A couple of standard hours, I guess."

Daith nodded at the floor. "The carpet's pretty comfortable. I wouldn't mind the company."

A weak smile spread across Dru's face. The grin fell away. "I could've killed you."

Daith turned his face toward hers. "But you didn't. You were there to help me. If I'd been learning on my own, I may not have made it."

Dru nodded, less angry. "I'm—I'm sorry, Daith."

She brushed a few stray strands of hair from his forehead, smoothing his worried brow. "Like you said before, we are in this together."

Dru lay down on the floor. Daith slithered under the sheet on the bed after handing Dru the extra pillow and told the computer to dim the lights seventy-five percent.

"Daith?"

"Yeah?"

"Have you made a decision about what Trey asked? We reach Sintaur's system tomorrow."

Daith thought for a moment. "All I've wanted was to know who I am. I thought going home might give me the answers I needed. But because of my abilities, I'll be hunted for the rest of my life. Even if I go back home, or whatever pile of ashes used to be my home, how could I be sure I'd be safe?

"If I stay here, I can help stop those responsible for my family's deaths. Except—I don't know if I can do it alone. Trey asked a lot from me and I think I could help, but I'm really scared. What if I can't do the things he needs? My abilities aren't exactly stable." Daith turned and caught Dru staring at her. "What?"

"I don't know this for sure—and I'll probably have to review some of your results—but I think your emotions are tied directly to the physical toll on your body."

"What do you mean?"

"Think about it," Dru said, propping himself up on his elbow. "The times you suffered physical pain, how did you feel?"

Daith thought back. "Angry, I think. I mostly remember headaches."

Dru nodded. "And the nosebleeds?"

"The same, I think—wait, no, that's not true. The time I thought you were dead, I felt scared. Or with the bomb, there was a lot of pressure and I felt panicked."

"And the times you didn't have pain? For example, when we worked with the telepathy datapads in the oceanic simulation or when you had to find me among the simulated crowd?"

"I was calm. I wasn't nervous about those tests because there wasn't really anything at stake."

"Exactly."

Daith's voice rose in excitement. "Do you think that's the solution? Control my emotions and I won't have physical pain?"

"I don't know if you won't have any, but focusing your emotions seems like a logical path. Although, diverse states do seem to give your abilities different power."

"True. I did more damage when I was angry and worked faster when I was scared." Daith returned her gaze toward the ceiling. "Do you think I should help Trey?"

"I think..." he paused. "I think it needs to be your decision. Trey's mission is noble, but also aggressive. Your life may be more difficult without Trey's protection, but I know one thing for sure—you don't have to do it alone. And if you want my help, I will be there with you."

Daith didn't have to try to sense what Dru felt. His emotions flowed open and clear. He was connected to her, and in the same way, she was connected to him.

"I want to try," she said. "I think I could help if I knew you were with me." Daith hung her hand over the side of the bed and found Dru's. He squeezed gently, energy surging freely between them.

The two of them drifted off to sleep, fingers interlaced.

Chapter 38

DAITH AWOKE TO a spicy aroma. She inhaled deeply and smiled. Opening her eyes, she saw Dru sitting cross-legged on the floor, eating from one hand, and staring at a datapad in the other.

"Hey," she said.

Dru put down the datapad. "I didn't wake you, did I?"

"No, but your food did. It smells delicious."

Dru broke off a piece of his meal, a warm pastry with a sticky top, and handed her the portion. The spicy smell intensified when she brought it to her mouth to taste. The dough melted in her mouth.

It was delicious.

Before she realized, she'd finished, but her stomach wasn't satisfied. A loud growl confirmed her continued hunger.

"Excuse me," she said, a hand on her belly.

Dru waved her words away. "You slept nearly twenty standard hours. I'm not surprised you're hungry." Dru licked his fingertips and motioned toward the communications panel. "Go ahead and order something. It's pretty early in the morning. I have a few things to attend to so I won't be back for a few standard hours. But when I return, if it's okay with you, I'd like to finish the conversation we started last night." He paused. "There are some things I want to tell you before we continue with our work."

"Sure." Daith shivered.

Concern crossed Dru's face. "Are you okay?"

"Yeah. Just—nervous. It's strange to have made a choice about where my life is headed. I feel like I've been blind and letting everyone else lead me, and now I'm making decisions, even though I still can't see everything."

Dru slipped on his shoes and stood. "Trust me, Daith. No one can see everything. You may have a few more blind spots than most, but you're doing what everyone does: listening to yourself and then making your own decisions based on what you do know and what your instincts tell you." He paused at the door and smiled. "And remember, you've got me."

* * *

Trey watched Dru leave his quarters. He flicked off the monitor in front of him with disgust. He had watched everything that had happened between Dru and Daith the previous night. He had seen their simulation room session, had seen the medical staff arrive, and had seen Dru bring Daith to his own quarters. He knew Daith had slept there with him.

And had Trey received a call?

Had the medical staff informed him of a problem with Daith?

Had Dru taken the time to send Trey a report about her progress?

No.

No.

NO!

Readying his final plans for the next two days, Trey really wished things hadn't progressed the way they had. His brother wouldn't have the stomach to go through with Trey's plan. Eventually Dru would tell Daith the truth and double-cross him. Even after everything Trey sacrificed.

Dru thought he was *so* clever, that he had everything figured out.

He had a surprise coming.

Trey sat behind his desk, his face a mask of composure. He picked up a datapad and pretended to read, holding the prop completely still—an actor waiting for his cue to begin.

And what a show it would be.

Chapter 39

THE *HORIZON* PULSED with tension. Crew members trotted through the corridors, their attention focused solely on their destinations.

Trey has definitely put together a hard-working team, Dru thought as he made his way from his quarters to his brother's office. Dru opened his empathic abilities to his surroundings. Everyone felt edgy, but confident. He'd found accessing his empathic skills easier since he'd met Daith. Being around her made him feel comfortable—willing to open up again. And he couldn't wait to see her again, to tell the truth and be fully open.

He just had to convince Trey the truth was best for everyone.

Dru flipped around the datapad with his final report on Daith. He felt proud of her for wanting to help his brother, but also uneasy. He wished Trey had told him more about his plan for Daith so he could have narrowed his tests. But he also understood why his brother hadn't told him. If Dru had decided not to work with the

Aleet Army, he shouldn't have had knowledge of their plans.

And can I blame him? He went through more than I did during the war. He sacrificed so much....

Dru paused in the middle of the thought. Trey had done so much: he'd taken over the house when their mother had been killed; he'd fought in the war when he was sixteen, he had worked to pay for Dru's schooling, and he'd joined up with a group to help fight injustice on other planets.

Dru rang the door chimes.

Trey is a hero.

"Ah, Dru," Trey said once the doors opened. "You have the report for me?"

Dru handed Trey the datapad and took a seat.

Trey ran through the report. "She has progressed and can work with inorganic materials. Good. And this note about a connection between her emotions and her abilities—interesting."

"Yes. There is less of a physical toll on her body if she is calm and in control of her emotions. Anger causes headaches while fear and panic induce nosebleeds and earbleeds."

"But her emotions also affect her abilities in a positive way?" Trey asked.

"When she's angry, her abilities are more powerful, like she uses her anger as a channel for her energy output. When she's afraid or under pressure, she is quicker and more precise. I think if I worked with her more, we could use her emotions to focus her energy."

"Sounds like a long-term project."

"It would probably take months, maybe even years to develop that kind of control."

Trey raised his eyebrows. "Does that mean you've opted to stay?"

Dru exhaled slowly. "Yes."

Trey's eyes brightened. "Which means Daith has, too. Excellent. Things are progressing smoother than I could've hoped."

Dru cleared his throat. He wanted to talk about the lying, but he thought he should ease his way into it. "Speaking of progress, I'm wondering exactly what the plan is. If I'm going to guide her, I'll need to know what you need her to do."

"Of course. I know you need answers, but I hoped you could fill in some blanks for me first."

"What do you have questions about?"

"Daith, of course."

"What do you want to know? Everything is in my report."

Trey's smile turned mischievous. "Not everything."

"Like what?"

"I need to know more about the two of you."

Dru's cheeks warmed. "The two of us? What do you mean?"

"Relax, brother. I'm not asking for intimate details. I know you two slept together last night, but I'm much more interested in—"

Dru sat up so quickly he teetered on his chair. "Wait, what?"

"She slept in your quarters last night," Trey said nonchalantly.

"How did you know?"

"The ship's computer told me."

"Why would you ask—?"

Trey tilted his head. "Did you think after Doctor Ludd's betrayal I would let her out of my sight? She's my responsibility, you know. What if something had happened to her during the night? The ship's computer sends me a report every two standard hours on her whereabouts and vitals. After your problems yesterday in the simulation room, which no one bothered to mention to me," Trey's jaw twitched, "the computer told me she was in your quarters."

Dru felt unsettled, but once again his brother had a point. Dru had never thought about checking up on her when she slept or during her time away from her sessions. What kind of doctor was he to not know her status while she worked on such dangerous abilities?

Trey continued, tapping his fingers on the desk. "But never mind that. Like I said, I'm not interested in your personal life. I'm curious what your relationship is with her, professionally. Do you think she depends on you? Would she feel better if you were present during a crisis situation? We will be up against some major obstacles and I want to make sure if she isn't prepared, she can count on your support."

"I think," he said, "Daith has come to trust me. If a difficult situation arose, I believe she would rely on me to help her through it. Truth is, I don't know if she could handle it on her own right now."

"Wonderful." Trey's breath quickened. He grabbed a datapad and started filtering through files. "If she's dependent on you, this will make things all the sweeter."

Something felt wrong. Dru noticed what lacked—he couldn't sense his brother's emotions.

At all.

There was nothing but a black hole of missing energy where his brother sat.

Trey's words came quick and clipped and he spoke as if he'd forgotten about Dru's presence. "Yes, and if anger is the key, that'll propel her all the more. Exarth will love the demonstration."

The words sank in slowly. "Trey, did you just say Exarth?"

Trey snapped his head up, his face a rigid mask.

Dru pointed his finger toward his brother. "What demonstration? And you have Exarth involved in this? She's a monster!"

"Perhaps. But she has the power I need."

Dru stood, incensed. "You can't be working with Exarth. She'll betray you. She'll kill you!"

"Exarth is a player in the game. She's necessary, but not important. I have the situation under control." Trey scoffed. "I knew you wouldn't understand."

Dru gripped the back of his chair. "This is madness. What have you gotten yourself into? What have you gotten Daith into?" Dru let go of the chair. "Daith. She needs to know the truth. She needs to know—"

Dru heard a crackly hiss. Knocked off his feet, his body flew across the room. Slamming into the door, he slid to the floor before he even realized what had happened. He glanced down. A huge scorch mark surrounded a gaping hole in his abdomen. Shock melted to searing pain.

Trey spoke, eyes glowing.

"After all I've done, this is how you repay me? We could've been great together, but you are weak, like Jacin. You don't have the courage to make a vision come true, to sacrifice anything that needs to be sacrificed. Daith will help me, and because of your precious connection with her, your death will seal her fate with me...."

Trey's words faded. Dru's breath slowed. The pain faded, too. Trey's face grew hazy. Dru felt like he was sinking into a strange dream.

A smile spread across his lips. He imagined laughing with Daith and

—he sucked in a breath—

squeezing her hand.

—the breath didn't leave his lungs—

Softness in the air

—the light bled away—

and he felt happy.

This is my second chance.

Blackness, darker than any sleep, enveloped him.

Chapter 40

HIS BROTHER WAS DEAD.

Just like that.

A chill ran through Trey's body.

He'd actually killed his brother.

Trey glanced at the electro-stun volt weapon in his shaking hand. "I don't know why they made these things illegal. They're really quite handy." Returning to his desk, he placed the weapon in the holster lodged beneath the top drawer. He felt Dru's lifeless gaze upon him.

Trey glared at the corpse.

"This is your fault, you know?" he said to the body. "We could have restored all we'd lost, all they'd taken away from us. You didn't see what they did to our mother. You don't know what they did to me...." Trey fought back the urge to vomit as the terrible memory came flooding back. "For that reason alone they all deserve to die. Since Jacin Jaxx didn't have the strength to follow through, then it is up to someone who does." Trey pressed the communications panel on the wall and called two cadets to his office.

"Remove this body," he told the cadets. "Incinerate the remains in the engines. Tell no one or you will suffer the same fate. Clear?"

The two cadets left the room with Dru's remains. After they had gone, Trey turned the recirculation vent on high to clear some of the burnt-flesh fumes from the room. He thought about how to tell Daith about Dru's death. She would never believe Dru had left without saying goodbye, and he couldn't tell her someone else had killed him.

Or could he?

His door chimes rang. Dread filled him as he imagined Daith right outside his door. He hesitated, fanning the air around him toward the vent, before calling for whoever to enter. Relief flooded over him at Lieutenant Koye's entrance.

"Yes?" Trey questioned.

"Commander, Kircla is waiting to speak to you." Koye motioned to Trey's vidlink on his desk. "No one else is aware of the connection."

"Thank you, Lieutenant. Please inform me when we have reached the Fracc system."

"Yes, Commander."

"And Lieutenant, detach Doctor Xiven's ship from the spaceport. Set the craft for a course to, oh, anywhere, and send it on its way. My brother will not need it anymore. Dismissed."

There was a slight raise to Koye's eyebrow, but he nodded curtly in agreement.

Now alone, Trey gathered his thoughts. He had to secure this last detail—the witness who'd seen Daith's abduction had to be eliminated. Taking a seat behind his desk, Trey opened up his vidlink communicator.

"Kircla," he said, tipping his head toward the viewscreen. "I see you received my communiqué. Do you have any interest in the job?"

A two and a half meter tall, sea-green skinned member of the Orcla species sat on the other end of the connection. Elaborately braided lengths of deep blue hair were pinned up in swirled patterns. Her expression captured detached impatience, and yet she still managed to emote authority. "I accept. Please transfer half the payment now. I will collect the other half when I have disposed of the witness." She paused, calculating. "This will not take long."

"Very good." Trey tapped the screen. "Your payment has been sent. I look forward to speaking with you again when this matter is settled."

Kircla bowed her head and the screen went blank.

Trey sat back in his chair and felt the tension melt from his tight shoulder muscles. Dru's death had come sooner than he'd expected, but the timing with the witness' death might be an advantage.

If Trey could spin one last lie...

* * *

After Dru left, Daith ate breakfast and thought about her decision to help Trey. She still felt nervous, but knowing she wouldn't have to deal with her abilities alone soothed her.

She stored her dirty tray in the chute and walked through the connecting door into Dru's office. She weaved through the piles of datapads on the floor, smiling while she thought of him, and opened the main door to head back to her own quarters.

As the door slid open, she nearly bumped into someone standing right outside.

A sharp pain stabbed inside her head.

Daith screamed.

She collapsed to the floor, unaware of Cenjo's presence. An image passed in front of her—a gaping hole in her abdomen, her skin curdled and black. The pain seared through her, like her insides were on fire.

The image faded. Daith realized she'd fallen to the floor. Cenjo held her shivering body, covered in vomit.

"Daith! Are you all right?"

Her nose dripped blood through her sobs. "I can't—the pain—the PAIN…."

"It's okay," he told her, hefting her to her feet. He leaned her against him. She felt comfort, but no energy connection. She craved the safety she experienced from Dru. "I've got you. We're going to see the doctor. You'll be fine."

Once they arrived, the medical cadet, Milastow, shuffled Daith into a secluded area. The young woman spoke kindly, but Daith missed Dr. Ludd's easy demeanor.

She'd asked Cenjo to send a message to Dru's room. Where was he?

Trey came into the room shortly after she'd arrived and took her hand. "Lieutenant Commander Cenjo told me you were here. How are you?" he asked, worry-lines etched in his forehead.

"I'm okay," she told him. "The pain is gone. The vision is gone. But I still feel unsteady."

Trey ordered everyone out of the room, even the doctor. "What happened?" he asked.

Daith's lip trembled, her emotions threatening to spill out. She didn't want to go back to the image.

"While leaving Dru's office I felt a sharp pain in my head. The vision felt completely real, like I could actually see and feel it."

"What did you see?"

Daith closed her eyes as her hands convulsively covered her

belly. "I think I was shot. Or, whoever I saw had been shot. Or burned." She closed her eyes tighter. "In the stomach. And I think—I think I died. Or they died."

"Did you see the shooter?"

Daith thought back. She bit her lip to staunch the pain that tried to re-emerge.

"No. I could only see my own body."

Trey had not visibly relaxed, but Daith felt his mood change. She opened her eyes as he stood abruptly.

"I need to check something," he said quickly. "You should stay here until I get back."

"Can you let Dru know I'm here?" If she could be near him, she knew she'd feel better.

He paused. "Dru isn't on the ship right now. But, don't worry. I'm sure he's fine."

It took a moment for Daith to realize what Trey meant. He needed to find out if Dru had been the one she'd seen in her vision.

If Dru was dead.

Chapter 41

NIGHTMARES TORMENTED DAITH.

She'd been given a sedative, but the doctor had not given her a dream-deflector pill.

So the nightmares came.

The wound in her stomach. Fire searing her skin. Her life bleeding away as her breath slowed.

And she couldn't scream.

Daith awoke several standard hours after Trey had left to check on Dru. The room surrounded her with darkness. The only sounds were the soft beeps from medical equipment monitoring her vitals. Cenjo, a figure in the shadows, slept in the chair next to her bed. He appeared to have fallen asleep watching her, his head propped on his hand, his neck tilted at an awkward angle.

"Cenjo?"

Cenjo stirred. "Daith? You're up. Computer, lights at twenty percent."

"Have you heard anything about Dru?" Daith asked.

"Commander Xiven came in a while ago. He told me..." Cenjo hesitated. "He told me they found Dru's body in a hotel room on a nearby planet; a burn wound in his abdomen. He's dead."

He's dead.

The words echoed inside her mind. She knew she'd heard them, but shock struck her like a blow to the chest and she couldn't process them.

"I'm so sorry, Daith." Cenjo told her. Pity radiated off him. Daith's head pounded. She couldn't shut his feelings out. They screamed at her, clawing inside her skull.

"I can't..." Daith pressed her fingertips to her forehead. "You need to leave. I'm sorry—it's just, I-I can't..."

"What is it?"

Concern drenched over her like a wave of syrup. "It's the way you feel. Stop feeling. I can't handle it. Please, Cenjo, just go."

After Cenjo left and Daith's sensations returned to normal, she rose and dressed. Worried she'd have to deal with the doctor, she tiptoed from her room, but Milastow slept at her desk, snoring loudly. Daith crept past and made her way down the dimly lit corridors, silent and cold.

Daith passed a couple crew members who looked at her oddly, but said nothing. While she traveled, she tried not to think about Dru, but how could she not? Dru had been the one thing she could depend on and now...

Daith stumbled and leaned on the wall for support. The numbness of shock threatened at any moment to falter and spill over into anger and grief.

I have to control myself. I have to focus.

Dru said you wouldn't have to do this alone, but he's gone. You are alone now.

Daith stopped outside Trey's office. She wanted to rush inside and demand to find Dru's murderer. She wanted to scream at Trey for allowing Dru to leave the ship. She wanted to sink into the floor and sob until she died.

But instead, she rang the chimes.

* * *

Trey paced. In a few standard hours he would change history. In a few hours, he would take the first step to reestablish peace.

And implement a plan that would kill thousands.

Trey stopped at this thought and a knot formed in his stomach, like chilled metal. Everything so far had gone according to his preparations, with a few minor setbacks, but even those tangents weren't enough to ruin his mission.

Still. Killing those who interfered with his plan didn't mean the same as taking innocent lives.

Trey kept telling himself they would die for the greater good. He knew he, unlike Jaxx, would not make the mistake of standing in the spotlight, but would oversee things from behind the scenes. All the lives to be sacrificed would be worth it.

Sacrifice the few to save the many.

While Trey waited for the report telling him they'd reached the Fracc system, he heard his door chimes ring.

"Daith?" he asked when the door slid open. "It's the middle of the night. What are you doing out of the medical wing?"

The smile on her face seemed forced. "I couldn't sleep."

"I assume Cenjo told you what happened," Trey said slowly. "I'm so very sorry. Dru mentioned the two of you—cared for each other." Trey did his best not to grit his teeth while he said those words. He forced himself instead to concentrate on maintaining the mental barrier to keep her from sensing his emotions.

Daith blinked, the smile faded, but didn't seem to register what Trey had said. A few moments of silence passed.

"Who is responsible?" she asked. The words came out monotone, clipped and robotic.

Trey hesitated. "I think you should return to the medical wing, Daith. It's obvious you aren't well."

Daith blinked, slowly. " *Who.*"

Trey ignored the hair creeping up on the back of his neck. He could feel her probing his mind, but in a hap-hazard way. She wasn't really searching for the truth.

She wanted someone to blame.

"He is a member of the Controllers," Trey said. "He was with you when we came to rescue you. A Controller spy. We believe he fed information to the Controllers about you and your family's whereabouts.

"I'd asked Dru to meet with him," Trey continued. "Claiming he'd defected, he would only talk to an impartial party. There was no way I could have known—"

"Where is this spy?"

"He's dead."

Daith frowned. "Dead?"

"I'm afraid so." Trey prayed Kircla would send him her report soon so he could offer proof. "Shot and killed by authorities when he fled the scene."

A myriad of emotions danced across her eyes. Trey watched her absorb and sort through what she'd heard.

Finally, she spoke. "The Controllers did this."

"Yes." He held his breath at what she might say.

The green in her eyes dulled. "I've made my choice. I'm going to help you against the Controllers."

Trey smiled. "Thank you, Daith."

Chapter 42

TREY DISCONNECTED THE vidlink call. A full day had passed since Daith told him she wanted to join his cause. Once she'd accepted, Trey's brain and body jumped into overdrive. He tightened security and planted evidence needed to show how Dru died, should Daith ever choose to investigate. Then he finally made the one call he'd been the most excited, and afraid, to make.

To Exarth.

Most didn't think she was real—a ghost you told children about at night to make them behave. A fiend from the shadows who would devour you and your family whole.

But Trey knew she existed. Powerful and influential in the Eomix galaxy, but still real. Trey needed her, her vast amount of resources, and her show of force for his plan to succeed.

With Daith in tow as a weapon, Trey knew he could get Exarth to join his cause.

And he'd been right. Once he'd sent the reports on Daith's

abilities and progress, Exarth had accepted his terms. No turning back.

For the first time in several standard weeks, Trey left his desk, went back into his room, and lay down on his bed to sleep—the first time in a long time he hadn't fallen asleep amongst datapads and maintenance reports....

Twenty-six year old Trey Xiven, captain of the *Enforcer*, second-in-command of the Aleet Army, the man directly in charge of keeping everything running smoothly, calmly, and without any problems, felt like an idiot.

Trey marched up to Jacin's door. He reached the room, pressed the button to ring the chimes, and then impatiently stepped through the door.

The room, dimly lit, smelled of stale air and rotten food. A figure, covered in shadows, sat on the couch, barely stirring at the abrupt entrance.

"By all means, Captain," the figure on the couch said with a skeletal grin, "come in."

Trey waited a few moments for his eyes to adjust to the lowered lights. He resisted the urge to turn them up to their brightest setting. His words, however, came freely.

"Don't start with me," Trey said. "I'm not in the mood."

"I can tell. What seems to be the problem?"

Trey forced himself to unclench his fists. "It's nothing, Commander."

"It must be bad if you couldn't wait three seconds for me to tell you to come in."

Trey swallowed, hard. He tired of the smug words from this man's mouth lately. But technically, Jacin Jaxx was still in charge, still the commander of the Aleet Army, even if Trey did all the work.

"It's nothing that won't be remedied soon, Commander."

The thin figure shifted. "If you aren't here to chat, why are you here?"

Trey sat. The small amount of light in the room danced across the older man's face revealing sunken eyes and pale features.

"It's about your sessions with the new doctors." Trey couldn't even say their names. Anger welled up inside him at the thought of Riel and his brother together.

"What about them?"

Trey's anger shifted toward Jacin. "Don't play games. You know what I'm talking about. Your lack of cooperation, your refusal to submit to tests, and your overall disrespect for them."

"Protective of your brother?"

The words struck Trey like a punch to his chest. "How did you know he's my brother?"

The corners of Jacin's mouth rose in the shape of a smile. Although the lips moved, there was no accompanying happiness.

"How do I know anything? It's not hard to tell. Your energies are similar and radiate off both of you."

This was the first time he knew Jacin had used his abilities on him. He wondered if there had been other times when Jacin had probed his mind—maybe even changed his thoughts?

"The female doctor, Riel, is quite gifted," Jacin continued. "But your brother—he really has a spark to him. He could become quite a powerful empath, if he would let himself. Pity he carries so much self-doubt. Perhaps someday he will meet someone he trusts enough to let himself be truly open to his surroundings."

Trey's jaw set. "If these two are so good, then why don't you let them help you? It's obvious something is wrong. You barely eat, hardly sleep, and from the smell of things, probably haven't bathed recently either."

Jacin's eyes glimmered for a moment before they dulled again. "What's the point?"

"What do you mean 'what's the point?' You're allowing yourself to waste away and to be honest, I can't keep you going anymore."

"Nobody asked you to."

"If I didn't, you would sink farther into the abyss. How are you supposed to help others when you can't even take care of yourself?"

Jacin snorted. "Help others? When is the last time I helped anyone?"

"Well, three months ago you stopped that war—"

"And how many lives were lost when rioters and protestors stormed the streets after I 'helped'?" Jacin interrupted. "How many of those protestors were then murdered by my army?"

"We have to sacrifice the few to save the many, Commander," Trey recited.

Color came back to Jacin's cheeks. "And what constitutes the few? Ten? A hundred? A million to save a billion? Would you sacrifice yourself? Your family?"

"To help create peace? Yes."

Jacin let out a wispy laugh. "Don't you see? Every time we try to do something right, something else goes wrong. We can't fix things, no one can."

"Then what's the point of doing anything?"

Jacin sat back into the couch. "If I knew the answer, I wouldn't be in the mess I'm in today."

Trey stood. "I don't believe you. I can't believe you. What about the thousands like me you saved? You can't tell me all our lives weren't worth it."

"Worth what? You wanted me to punish everyone who did anything that hurt you. Why are you more important than they are?"

"Because they are WRONG," Trey shouted while he paced. "They don't deserve to live after everything they've done. You think because you've 'fixed' those who are in control then everyone is better. What about the ones who chose to follow orders from their government? Why weren't they punished or changed? They were just as wrong."

"Says you."

Trey whipped around and glared at the man on the couch. "I am so sick of the condescending garbage coming from your mouth. You spew rhetoric that has nothing to do with justice. Those who are wrong should be made to face the consequences."

"And what gives me the right to dole out punishment? I'm not judge and jury."

"No." Trey spat the word at him. "But you seem to have no problem being the executioner when it suits your own needs."

Jacin's lips lost their smirk and thinned. "You are teetering dangerously on the edge of insubordination, Captain. Don't forget who is in charge here."

Trey let out a burst of laughter.

"In charge? Let's think for a moment, shall we? Who is in charge?" Trey knew he shouldn't speak, but the words had a life of their own. "Most, and I mean those who see you on the news or hear about you from their friends, would say you are in charge. You are the Commander and have the power, the gifts, and the ability to turn someone's brain into a pile of mush if you want.

"But what happens when the spotlights turn off and the doors close? Who's in charge then? The half-dead, power-hungry, sorry-for-himself, pitiful thing that sits before me? Or me, who at every bad turn has covered up your indiscretions, changed tactics, and kept plans in progress no matter the cost?"

Trey's emotions poured out through his words. "For five years

I've been captain of this ship and for two of those years I've run this entire operation. I make your appointments, I negotiate your contracts, I cover up your indiscretions, and I instruct the different units of our army where to go, what to do, and how to do it. Our soldiers turn to me for the final call. I have disregarded your instructions and the soldiers have followed me. I have plotted missions without your knowledge and the soldiers have followed me. They follow me because without the power, the fear, or the fanfare, I am their leader. I don't need special abilities or gifts. I still get everything done because ultimately, I am in charge."

Trey stormed toward the door. "You will meet with Riel and Dru this afternoon. You will cooperate with them and you will get better."

Jacin watched the door close behind Trey. The light diminished, leaving him once again wrapped in shadows. He pulled his feet out from underneath him and stood, heading for the washroom. He thought about having to leave his quarters in a few standard hours to see the doctors again and let out a sigh of exhaustion at the thought. He knew they were talented at what they did, but they couldn't help him.

No one could.

As he dragged his feet grudgingly along the floor, Jacin wondered: When no one can help you, what else is there left to do?

Trey awoke, ill at ease. His pillow was soft, his bed comfortable, and yet his skin crawled.

He had not expected to see the moment before Jacin decided to take his own life. He'd seen Jacin's actual suicide so many times in his previous nightmares he'd forgotten about the argument right before.

Trey believed he'd had control back then—that Jacin had become his puppet so Trey could save those who needed saving. But his belief hadn't been true, had it? Because Jacin had been right. When he died and those powers vanished, everything fell apart. No one cared what Trey had done. No one listened to him when he tried to rally those he'd fought so desperately to save.

And now here he was, trying to control the same power, this time through Daith.

But this time it's different, he thought. *This time Daith won't use her powers until I say she can. I'll have absolute control over her. And with Exarth's fleet on my side, no one will be able to challenge me.*

Trey slid uneasily back into sleep, dark like the emptiness of space.

But as blackness pulled him under, Trey wondered if he really had any control at all.

Chapter 43

DAITH SAT IN the observatory, staring straight up, out of the ship into the diamond-studded blackness of space. She thought about how much had been stolen from her. Her family murdered, her memories taken, even her chance at finding out about her past with Dru's help—before he was...

Daith shuddered, the motion rippling through her whole body. Tears caused blurring of the white dots of light above her. She rubbed her hands against each other, aware she'd never feel his energy flow into hers again.

I never even got the chance to see what could have been between us. To ever know if what I felt might have gone on to be something else, something more.

Daith wiped away the moisture from her cheeks, but her movements couldn't keep up with the flow of pain falling from her eyes. To have been so close to something real, something true, and have the possibility snatched away in a single moment.

Gone forever.

Daith's hands became fists and she struck away the tears. It wasn't fair. They took from her the one individual who could have helped her get her life back, shown her about her amazing gifts, and helped her to use them.

And they killed him.

Anger welled up. The heat turned to flame inside her. Her power fed on her rage, building in intensity until she couldn't hold back any longer.

A blood-curdling scream issued forth from her lips, her jaw slack, her neck tendons bulging. She screamed her pain, her fear, her loneliness toward the clear ceiling. Energy rushed out of her, filling the room, straining against the walls.

The ceiling burst outward toward the cosmos.

Air rushed all around her. She couldn't breathe. She couldn't see. The vacuum of space opened to her—no boundaries between herself and the void.

Instinct took over. Instinct to survive. She molded the fiery energy around her, like a cocoon of protection. Furniture knocked against her shield. Vacuum sucked against her body. But she was safe.

Alarms howled. Emergency force fields went up in place of the missing ceiling. Oxygen filled the room. She brought down her protective coating and gasped for breath.

She hadn't moved. She should have been blown straight into space, but she hadn't moved. She'd willed herself to stay.

Daith sat in silence for a few moments. The alarms had ceased. She'd fought against the force of the universe itself—and she'd won.

Who she used to be didn't matter. She had this moment, now, to decide what to do. Her future didn't lie with a dead family, a lost home, and a broken heart. All that mattered were her abilities and what she could do with them.

Trey entered the observatory, followed by Cenjo and a few other soldiers to see what had happened, to survey the scene. They came to a dead halt at her sitting in the middle of the empty room, completely fine.

"Don't worry, Trey," she said through a smile that didn't reach her eyes. "The Controllers are going to pay."

Thank you so much for reading ILLUSION!

Here's a sneak peek into the next book, **IDENTITY**!
Available Now!

IDENTITY

The sequel to *Illusion*

Daith ignored the chimes to her quarters, along with the tendril of fear climbing her spine. She adjusted her posture, feet tucked underneath her butt, back straight.

A darkened datapad lay in her hand—its smooth surface reflected the lights above her, set into her room's ceiling. They shone bright white, illuminating the grey walls, metallic bed, and deep red carpet. Daith's dark hair lay over her pale shoulders, highlighted by the harsh lights. Recirculated air hissed quietly through the vents.

Irritated, Daith pushed her hair behind her, her focus broken for a moment.

She closed her eyes and concentrated, letting her power fill her. Heat throbbed inside her gut, crawling through her insides like a flame climbing a tree. The fire filled her arms and trickled down into her fingers. She directed the energy into the datapad, searching for the pathways that would lead her to the information stored on the device without having to turn it on.

The datapad's surface bubbled and melted, its insides crackling. With a growl, she twisted the device and the plastic piece grew gooey under her fingertips, stretching apart.

A drop of blood slid from her nose, trickling over her lips. It hung for a moment on the edge of her chin before it dripped to the floor.

The chimes rang again. Daith's forehead creased.

"What?" she snapped at the interruption. Eyes now open, she hastily brushed the blood from her face. She moved her knee to cover the spot on the floor as her visitor entered.

"Daith?"

"Yes, Trey?" she asked, looking up at him from the floor.

Trey cleared his throat, his dark blue eyes narrowed, searching. "How are you?" He stood tall and straight, his uniform pressed, his short, brown hair cropped and neat.

Daith tossed the destroyed datapad towards a pile on the floor in front of him before reclosing her eyes. Clattering filled the quiet room as the datapad bounced off of the others, all half-melted in the same fashion. "I'm fine." She heard him shuffle his feet as he moved toward the datapads. She could picture his perfectly polished shoes, a contrast to the worn carpeting.

"This looks promising, but Daith—"

"I know," she interrupted. "We only have two standard weeks left. I'm working on it."

Trey muttered something she couldn't understand before she

heard the door slide closed.

Daith expelled a breath in the now empty room.

She knew Trey expected her abilities to have progressed. During several sessions with her previous doctor, Dru, she discovered she had unique mental and emotional powers, but without him to guide her, she didn't know how to learn anything new.

And her attempts to do more came at a price. Her headaches, nose and ear bleeds, and irritability had increased since she started working on her own four standard days ago.

Since Dru's death.

A tickle of sadness touched her throat, but anger swiftly took over. Emotional motivation should enhance her abilities. She learned that anger made her more powerful and fear more precise. But no matter how she pushed herself, she couldn't do any more than what she already learned with Dru—heal herself, destroy inanimate objects, and sense basic emotions and thoughts from others.

If she planned to help Trey stop the Controllers—those who killed her family and murdered Dru—she had to be able to do more. Who knew what they might be up against, what type of fight the Controllers would bring? She needed to be ready for whatever they threw at her.

And the clock seemed to tick faster and faster.

Daith palmed the wet rag next to her and rubbed at the spot on the carpet—the cloth already spotted red from her previous work during the day. She picked up the next datapad.

The tendril of fear crept once more.

About the Author

Christa Yelich-Koth is an award-winning author (2016 Novel of Excellence for Science Fiction for ILLUSION from Author's Circle Awards) of the Amazon Bestselling novels, ILLUSION and IDENTITY. Her third book in the *Eomix Galaxy Novel* collection is COILED VENGEANCE.

Christa has also moved into the world of detective fiction with her international bestselling novel, SPIDER'S TRUTH, the first in the *Detective Trann series.*

Looking for something Young Adult? Try the YA fantasy *Land of Iyah* trilogy, starting with book 1: THE JADE CASTLE.

Aside from her novels, Christa has also authored a graphic novel, HOLLOW, and 6-issue follow-up comic book series HOLLOW'S PRISM from Green-Eyed Unicorn Comics. (with illustrator Conrad Teves.)

Originally from Milwaukee, WI, Christa was exposed to many different things through her education, including an elementary Spanish immersion program, a vocal/opera program in high school, and her eventual B.S. in Biology. Her love of entomology and marine biology helped while writing her science fiction/ fantasy aliens/creatures.

As for why she writes, Christa had this to say: "I write because I have a story that needs to come out. I write because I can't NOT write. I write because I love creating something that pulls me out of my own world and lets me for a little while get lost inside someone or someplace else. And I write because I HAVE to know how the story ends."

You can find more about Christa and her other books at:
www.ChristaYelichKoth.com

Look for other books by Christa Yelich-Koth

www.ChristaYelichKoth.com

Eomix Galaxy Novels
(Sci-fi/fantasy)

ILLUSION (Book 1 of 2)
IDENTITY (Book 2 of 2)
COILED VENGEANCE

The Detective Trann series

SPIDER'S TRUTH
SPIDER'S RING
SPIDER'S QUEEN

The Land of Iyah trilogy
(YA fantasy)

THE JADE CASTLE
THE JADE ARCH
THE JADE THRONE

Graphic Novels
(Sci-fi)

HOLLOW

Comic Books
(Sci-fi)

HOLLOW'S PRSIM SERIES
(6 issues total)
Issue #1: *Aftermath*
Issue #2: *Reunion*
Issue #3: *Alliance*
Issue #4: *Trigger*
Issue #5: *Revelations*
Issue #6: *Fusion*

Lightning Source UK Ltd.
Milton Keynes UK
UKHW042304150223
417099UK00006B/39